NEVER SAY DIE

MATTHEW HATTERSLEY

VINCI BOOKS

Vinci Books

vinci-books.com

Published by Vinci Books Ltd in 2025

1

Printed and bound in Great Britain by Clays Ltd, Elcograf S.p.A.

Chapter One

It was ten minutes after seven in the morning and another beautiful day in the land of the free. Standing in the window of the Marriott's luxurious Mercantile Suite, he could see down onto the sparkling blue of the Clark Fork River, snaking all the way through the town on its way to Lake Pend Oreille up in the North. He'd read somewhere that Missoula was Montana's second largest city and what many considered to be the cultural epicentre. What that said about the rest of Montana he wasn't entirely sure, but that didn't matter one jot to him. Culture was overrated. People thought they wanted art and culture and all that sissy stuff, but such things were dumb ideals, sold to the masses by those woke pricks in the media.

He knew better. He knew what people really wanted, what they craved above all else. Respite. From their jobs, their friends, but most of all from their tedious little lives. No matter that for fifty weeks of the year their existence was one of monotonous misery, give people two weeks away in a luxurious resort, where they could kid themselves they'd made it, that they too were part of the one percent, and it kept them from swallowing a bullet for another year.

That was his gift to the world. The opportunity for people to feel like winners in this bizarre and rambunctious rollercoaster ride called life.

Letting out a throaty snicker, he screwed the freshly cut end of an Arturo Fuente Opus between his moist lips.

Winners, indeed.

He liked winners. He'd been one all his life and that wasn't going to change just because a few meagre obstacles had been placed in his path. He dropped his hand into the pocket of the complimentary robe and pulled out his gold S.T. Dupont lighter. Flicking it alight, he eyed the reflection in the window, watching as the orange glow flared then quivered. He raised the flame to the end of his cigar and puffed a large plume of flavourful smoke into the room.

There was a knock on the door. He turned, moving his entire upper body as he did, calling out, "Come."

The knocking continued.

He tried again. "Enter."

Nothing.

"For Christ's sake." He rested his cigar on the jade ashtray that sat on the coffee table and marched across the room. As he passed the dresser, he grabbed up his beaver and chinchilla fur Diamante Stetson and placed it on his head, adjusting the brim as he got to the door. Ready, he grabbed the handle and yanked it open.

"I said, come in." The small woman with dark hair standing in the doorway let out a shrill yelp. But he was used to that. At six foot seven inches, he was an imposing figure even without the wide-brimmed hat. She adjusted herself, struggling under the weight of a large tray, on top of which sat a silver dome and a jug of black coffee. The cutlery shivered and tinkled against the side of the tray as she addressed him.

"Please. Your breakfast."

She spoke with a strong accent and he did nothing to hide his disdain as he beckoned her into the room.

"Put it down there," he ordered. "No, not there. There. On the coffee table by the window."

She did as instructed, standing upright as he came over to her. "You have everything you need?"

"Wait there." He leaned over and lifted the dome, hissing through his teeth as he saw the food underneath. "I knew that dumb bastard on the front desk wasn't listening. I specifically asked for my eggs sunny side up."

The maid shifted onto her back foot, eyes alert and unblinking. Like a deer in the headlights. She was cute enough, for a Spic, but the nervous energy coming off her only served to exacerbate his annoyance.

"I can change... if you want..."

"No. Leave it," he told her, picking up the Arturo Fuente and biting down on it. "That will be all."

"Thank you, sir." She bowed her head, but hesitated. Most likely she was waiting for him to slip her a note of some denomination.

"That will be all," he told her. Twice now. If he had to say it a third time she'd wish she'd never been born. "Leave me alone."

This time she got the message, scurrying over to the door and backing out into the corridor.

"Fucking peasant," he muttered to himself.

Alone once more, he returned to the window, stretching his arms wide as he took in the new day. They might have named it the land of the free and the home of the brave, but on days like this, when he could actually smell success in the air, it sure felt more like the land of winners and the home of the wealthy.

He flinched as a vibration sent a shudder down his flank. His mobile phone in the pocket of his robe. He pursed the cigar between his lips and lowered himself onto the plush green velvet couch next to the coffee table. Once settled, he pulled out the phone and swiped it to connect.

"This better be good news," he growled into the receiver. He leaned into the couch, inhaling a mouthful of earthy smoke and rolling his head back to stare at the ceiling. "Go on then, son. Give it to me."

The line crackled. "He didn't go for it."

"Fucking idiot." He gave the words as much venom and bile as needed, exorcising his anger. He gave it a beat, and when he spoke again his tone was neutral. "What did he say?"

"Stupid son of a bitch said he didn't trust you or me one little bit and wanted no part of what we were offering."

"He said those exact words?"

"He did."

"Well, that's his prerogative."

"His prerogative? Are you kidding me?"

"Hey now, calm it down there, son."

An important aspect of business, which he'd learned over the years, was that when you let stress or anger rule your decisions, you usually made bad ones. Instead, he arched his back, stretching it out, tried to remain composed.

"There's no point in getting heated," he said. "Not yet."

"Yeah? You said this would be plain sailing. Said there was no way we'd have problems. But if he won't—"

"I said calm it down, damn it." He barked the words out, then paused, rolling the cigar between his thumb and index finger, waiting whilst his heavy breathing subsided.

"But what are we going to do?"

"When situations happen such as this we simply have to change tack. Improvise, adapt and overcome. You should know that." He shoved the cigar between his lips, letting it bob up and down as he spoke. "Don't worry. I've got it under control."

"Really?"

"Sure. Now I'm going to finish my cigar, eat some eggs, and I'll be in touch shortly."

"But I need to be kept—"

He hung up and flung the phone on the couch beside him.

Goddamn fool.

He'd meant every word just now, but these new developments did complicate matters. He shoved his fist in the palm of his other hand, cracking his knuckles as he considered his next move. Things could get problematic from here on in, but that was all par for the course. He'd not encountered a single obstacle yet that could stop him. If you had enough money, enough sway, nothing stood in your way. Capitalism at its finest. God bless the US of A.

He reached for his phone and swiped up, scrolling through his extensive contact list until he reached the bottom and hit call.

Wade picked up on the third ring. "I was wondering if I'd hear from you today."

"It's not good news."

"Oh?"

"Well, depends on how one looks at it, I guess." He leaned forward and got to his feet. "It's time for you to be put into play. You got everything you need?"

"Of course."

"Good. Get the next flight over here. Great Falls or

Glacier Park are the nearest airports, whichever is the quickest. Ring me once you're in town and we'll get together."

"No problem. I'll be in touch."

He hung up and grinned at the ghostly reflection of himself in the window. Yes siree, there was no problem he couldn't fix. Nothing that would get in his way for long.

So what if that foolish prick didn't go for his offer? It was his dumb loss. All it meant was they'd have to initiate plan B. He placed the cigar between his lips and grinned.

And there was always a plan B.

Chapter Two

The jukebox opposite the bar held a particularly crappy selection of songs. It was also ancient, but not ancient enough to be one of those cool retro types, the ones with coloured neon tubing and a quivering lever that selected actual wax discs and placed them nervously onto a rotating spindle. This one was an eighties wooden box affair, wall-mounted and with a stack of scratched CDs waiting patiently in the main cavity. A bright strip-light shone down from the top of the box, illuminating the small rectangles of yellowing card, each one containing a song title and corresponding number, which flipped over to reveal another underneath if you pressed the button on the right-hand side of the unit.

Acid Vanilla chewed on the inside of her cheek while she perused the titles, the gloomy bar fading away as she pondered her choices. Most of the songs on offer were what you might call old classics. Really that just meant they were the most obvious and overly played options from the likes of Elvis, Kenny Rogers and John Denver. Old classics for this part of the world, at least. Although from what she'd seen briefly of this sleepy town, she wouldn't be surprised if some of these tracks were considered cutting edge.

A few more flips and *Jumpin' Jack Flash* by the Stones revealed itself. She dropped a quarter into the slot down the side and jabbed in the corresponding number-code on the tacky keypad. As the opening guitar riff chimed through the dingy room, she spun around on the heel of her old Dr Marten boots and returned to the bar where a drink was waiting for her. Two drinks, in fact. A club soda and a small beer. Neither of these was her usual order (that would have been something much stronger, of the whisky or bourbon variety), but after being kicked around physically and emotionally for the last two years she was trying to keep a lid on her more destructive habits.

Trying to.

She lifted herself onto the bar stool, using the edge of the counter to steady herself as she reached for the beer. The bar was devoid of windows and the air thick with stale liquor and sweat, but she could still smell the inviting malty aroma coming off the drink. Of course, the actual healthy option would be for her to not drink any form of alcohol whatsoever, and be outside strolling in the crisp Montana air instead of sitting here in a stuffy bar. She'd been in the Land of the Shining Mountains for less than a day and yet she was already slumped over a beer in a dark room with only her thoughts for company. Some habits were hard to break.

She swigged back most of the beer in one go and closed her eyes, letting the music swell in her head. Maybe the Stones soundtracking her first drink since she'd arrived here wasn't such a bad omen. She'd never been a huge fan, but had always appreciated Keith Richards' punk swagger, and his recent declaration that giving up drinking meant he now stuck to beer and wine only instead of liquor. Not a bad way to do it. A sly smile spread across her face as voices from the past echoed in her consciousness.

Come now, sweetie. You aren't a bloody nun.

Baby steps and all that.

"Can I get you another?"

The question snapped her back into the present, wiping away the spiralling flashback her mind was setting up for her. She looked into the face of the barman. "Excuse me?"

"Oh, you're from England? Nice."

"Nice?" She rolled her eyes. But to be fair to the guy, he'd been pleasant enough when she'd first walked in. Not the sort of grunting meathead she'd expected to find working behind a bar here in Blackfell Ridge. He was good-looking, in an obvious, not-her-type kind of way. Tall, broad shoulders, clean hair. Yet as he leaned over the counter now, she noticed he held a certain rugged charm. It was there in his stubble and crooked grin. In the glimmer of mischief shining behind his eyes.

He was also either too dumb to pick up on her cattiness or was choosing to ignore it.

"Whereabout in England are you from?"

"London."

"Awesome. I've never been. But I'd love to visit."

"Oh. Are you one of those Americans who's never left the confines of their own country?"

His grin widened as he rested his forearms on the counter. "Actually, I've been all over the world. Been to the UK, just not London. Not the centre, at least, and not as a civilian."

"Oh, I see. Military?"

He nodded, but without the usual smugness you get

from military men – the ones you meet in bars anyway, who seem to think telling a woman they've served means she'll immediately want to rip their shirt off and straddle them.

"Yep. U.S. Army," he said, as his grin faded. "Three tours of duty as combat deployment, then a good few years with Special Forces, before… Well, it's in the past. Seems like an age ago now. I even made colonel, but not anymore. Now I'm a plain old civilian. Still feels weird to say that."

"Civilian?" Acid rolled the word around in her head. She wasn't overly familiar with the US military, but she'd have sworn colonels kept their titles after finishing service. "Well, that makes two of us," she added, raising her glass.

"Pardon me?"

"Both civilians," she said, before realising the implication. "I mean, I always was, obviously. But now you are too."

Jesus.

She finished off the last mouthful of beer and slid the glass towards him. "I think I will have another."

"Coming up."

He scooped up the glass and filled it from the tap. As he did, he watched her with one eye shut, like he was sussing her out and wanted her to know that's what he was doing. "We don't get many ladies in here. Not ones that look like you anyway."

"Hey, I'm no lady."

"Sorry – we don't get many women in here that look like you. Hell, I almost said chicks. Good job, huh?" The way he said it, he was joking, trying to get a rise out of her.

"It's a very good job," she replied. "And what do I look like, pray tell?" She didn't take her eyes off him, and he didn't flinch.

"Ah, you know what you look like," he said, with a

shrug. "Kinda scary-looking, but hot as hell. And like you might rip a fella's balls off if he told you that." He slid the fresh beer in front of her and she caught it.

"You're rather brave if that's the case."

"Or stupid. I'm Jareth, by the way. Jareth Hicks."

"Jareth Hicks? That's quite a name. But not colonel anymore?"

"No, ma'am. Not anymore."

She narrowed her eyes. "So, Mr Globetrotter, I take it you're not from around here. How long have you been in town?"

"Not long. In fact this is only my second shift. I blew into Blackfell Ridge end of last week. I've been travelling around the northern states. Both Dakotas before this."

"I see. Running away from something?"

He laughed. "Maybe. Ever since I left the army I've felt out of place everywhere I go. I'm hoping the time away will help me work out what to do with the rest of my life."

Acid scoffed silently to herself. Out of place everywhere. The guy might as well have been speaking for her.

"Have you come up with anything?" she asked, twisting a strand of her hair around her finger as she leaned in. "To do with the rest of your life, I mean."

He stuck out his bottom lip. "Not yet. Seeing what shows up. Hey, you never told me your name."

Here it was. The question she knew was coming, but the one she was unsure how to answer. She opened her mouth, hoping the correct response would somehow appear without her having to engage with the words. As it was, before she uttered anything, a figure loomed out from her blind spot and made a good attempt at barging her off her stool.

"Hey, watch it, dickhead," she yelled, grabbing the side

of the counter to right herself. "There is someone sitting here, you know?"

She smelled the guy's pungent body odour even before she'd twisted around to look at him. When she did, she saw he had long greasy hair tied back in a rubber band, and was big in width but not height. He also had no neck to speak of and, with his small head and large body, he reminded Acid of a tortoise. On his top half he wore a once-black t-shirt with a faded skull across the chest, and a grotesque milky-white belly protruded over his jeans. The outfit was topped off with a denim jacket and a leather vest. She scanned the chest pockets, seeing the emblems and badges sewn there, savvy enough to know it was a biker's cut. A red circle with the letters SC inside of it and an angry-looking cat's head peered back at her. The biker stepped back, swaying as much as he was sneering.

"The fuck you say to me – bitch?"

Keeping her focus as tight as her fists, Acid straightened herself. A million chaotic thoughts crashed through her mind as she looked him up and down. He didn't look to be carrying. Not a gun, at least.

"I said…"

No. She'd promised herself. She glanced at Jareth, who had been watching the exchange.

"Hey, buddy," he said, placing one hand flat on the counter and raising the other in a show of placation. "Let's all calm it down, okay? Play nice."

"Play nice?" The squat biker glared at him. "Who the hell do you think you're talking to, fucking pussy? You stay out of this."

"Excuse me, what the hell do you think is going on here?" Acid asked, shifting around on the stool to face him. "There is no *this* to stay out of. You barged into me, remember? Now, I get it, you're drunk, having a good time, whatever. All you need to do is apologise and we'll leave it there. No harm done." She caught Jareth's eye and smiled. "Everyone's happy."

The comment received a raised eyebrow from her new friend behind the bar, but a less positive response from the drunk biker. Acid saw the look of indignation curling his lip, saw his shoulders tighten as he clenched his fists. He wasn't going to apologise. He wasn't going to play nice.

"Dumb fucking bitch. I'll—"

Before he could finish she jumped off her seat, wrapped his ponytail around her hand and yanked his head back. The snap movement caught the guy by surprise and, coupled with the looseness caused by the beer and whatever else he'd been ingesting, he offered little resistance as she leapt up, hair still in her fist, and smashed his face into the bar top. His nose made a delicious crunching sound as blood and spittle burst out over the polished wood. As she let go of him he slumped back and she followed with a swift knee to the groin, which seemed to knock not only the air out of him, but also his reason, lifeforce, and ability to make noise. He dropped to his knee and clutched at his crotch, blood gushing down his face.

"Turtle? What the hell's going on?"

Shit.

A second biker rushed out from the backroom, holding a pool cue in his hand. He was over to them in a few strides, as Jareth leapt over the bar and took up a position beside her. The biker glared at them both.

"What did you do to Turtle?"

So she wasn't the only one who'd made the observation about the man's appearance. "He was being obnoxious," she replied.

"What did he do?" This new guy wasn't as big or as mean-looking as his friend – and he wasn't as drunk or as stupid either. As he eyed the tall, muscular barman standing beside her, all anger dissipated from his voice. "He left the game to get us some more drinks."

He moved around the front of his friend and put his hand on his shoulder. The bleeding from the biker's nose had ceased somewhat, but a low, pained growl emanated from deep inside of him. It sounded to Acid like he was engaged in taking a rather problematic shit.

"I take it this is your buddy?" Jareth asked, grabbing a handful of napkins off the bar and handing them over.

"He's my buddy and my brother. And you wouldn't have messed with him, not if you knew who we were." Begrudgingly he accepted the napkins and held them to his friend's nose. "Come on, Turtle. Let's get you up." Struggling to get his head under his friend's arm, he about managed it before hauling the big man to his feet.

"Here, let me help," Jareth said, stepping forward.

"We can manage," came the snarled reply, the guy shrugging Jareth away.

"He started it," Acid called after them, as they staggered back into the depths of the pool room. "Tell him to be more careful who he barges into in future."

Neither of the bikers turned around, but she saw the thinner guy lean into Turtle and whisper something in his ear. As he looked back over his shoulder, she saw only malice in his eyes. She saw, too, the patches on the back of their cuts and the words Streetwalkin' Cheetahs Motorcycle Club, Blackfell Ridge Order.

Once they'd disappeared into the backroom, she leaned into the barman. "Sorry about that. Is it going to cause you problems?"

"Nothing I can't handle. But you'd better be careful. From everything I've heard about the Cheetahs, they're bad news."

Acid turned and looked at him. "You did see what happened, didn't you?"

"Oh, I saw all right. I'm not saying you can't handle yourself. But that dude was out of his head and off guard." He moved down the length of the bar and ducked under a hatch before reappearing around the other side. "If I were you I'd lie low for a few days, or get gone. You don't want his club coming at you."

"I see," she said. "You think I got lucky."

"I don't think anything. All I'm saying is, be careful. The Cheetahs think this is their town. A lot of the townsfolk think the same."

"I've dealt with worse. Much worse. Drunk or not." She stretched her neck to one side and then the other.

"Have it your way. You want a refill?"

"Huh?"

He lifted an empty glass from behind the bar, the other having been smashed in the melee. "Another beer?"

Acid paused. Absolutely she wanted one. But she was also done talking, and the two things seemed mutually exclusive right now.

"No. Thank you." She grabbed her leather jacket from off the stool and slipped it on.

"I guess I'll see you around," Jareth said. "Unless you... No, forget it."

"Go on. Say it."

He shrugged. "I don't know. Seems to me we're in a similar boat. New in town, don't know anyone. And I was kind of enjoying talking with you. How about I buy you dinner tomorrow night?"

"No. I don't think so. Sorry." She moved towards the door, walking backwards as she spoke. "Like you said, it's probably a good idea I move on. Plenty of America to see."

"Sure, I get it. Well maybe I'll see you before you go." He sounded nonchalant, but his face betrayed him and she paused once more at the door.

Damn it.

Gazing at his rugged features and defiant expression, the way his crooked grin formed a dimple in one cheek, she could easily have said yes.

Shit.

Would it be so bad to meet up? A few drinks. A laugh. Maybe more.

She thought hard about it, but the answer had to be no. She'd come to this sleepy town specifically to get some peace and quiet. Admittedly her zen-like qualities might need some work, considering what had transpired. But she was adamant. No more mess. No more chaos. From now on she would keep her head down and her mind clear. As was the plan. That meant no more drinking in dive bars, no more getting herself into ridiculous fights. She'd come away specifically for rest and recuperation, in the hope that nourishing fresh air might blow away the cobwebs in her soul and the demons in her head. And that also meant no distractions. Of any kind.

She met Jareth's gaze.

No.

Time to go.

"Thanks for being cool about... everything," she called back, gesturing with her hand at the broken glass, the blood on the counter.

"All in a day's work."

"Don't I know it."

She tucked her hair behind her ears. Turning around she pushed the door open, and let it swing shut behind her.

———

OUTSIDE, the air had a chill to it. But despite the late hour, it was still good quality air. One of the reasons Acid had settled on Blackfell Ridge for her break (rather than, say, Mauritius or a similar tropical paradise) was that the old mining community at the foothills of Glacier National Park couldn't get more outdoorsy if it tried. In the middle of nowhere, with a tiny population and not much in the way of entertainment, the idea was that the enforced boredom would mean she worked out some of her issues without distractions (that word again) whilst walking in the luscious forests. Of which there were plenty. Indeed, everywhere she looked, in any direction, she saw rocky mountains, tall trees and winding rivers. She hadn't put a time limit on how long she'd spend here, but it would be long enough for it to count. Anything was better than the alternative. She'd grown weary of being caught up in her stressful thinking, second-guessing herself at every turn. This was her time. A way to reflect and recharge. After that, who knew?

She took a right outside the bar and headed down the side of the building, back to the authentic wooden cabin several streets away that was her accommodation. As she walked, the fresh mountain air revived her, and when she got to the end of the road she paused and sucked back a deep lungful of almost pure oxygen. Yes. She was feeling good. Maybe the best she'd felt in a long while. That little altercation back in the bar was only a blip. And it was bound to happen. She'd spent the last two decades living on her wits, avoiding detection and death at every turn, so when she saw a threat she acted instinctively. It was who she was, but she was fine with that. She was journeying into a new world and finally making peace with the baggage she carried with her. If anything, that Turtle guy got off lightly. Once, she'd have followed the knee to the balls with a bottle over his head and the broken shards jammed into his throat. Once. Not anymore. She was a civilian now. And civilians didn't go around killing people.

"Hey, bitch."

The words stopped her dead in her tracks. Turning around she was greeted with the sight of Turtle standing a few feet away. In the light thrown out from the back door of the bar, she saw he was holding a pool cue gripped in both hands. His nose was broken and he'd done little to wipe the blood from his face, but the drunken stupor he'd been lost in a few minutes earlier had now dissipated, replaced with anger and lusty energy.

He raised what should have been his chin. "I'll fucking kill you."

Acid's fists were already tight. Her knuckles ached with readiness, but in her head she heard the voice. The one she'd been hearing a lot lately. The voice of reason, you might call it. It was a bloody pest.

"Listen, mate," she told him, holding her hands up, palms out. "Things got heated in there, but I don't want any trouble. Why don't we both call it a night? Go on home."

She didn't wait for his reply. She turned on her heels and sauntered off towards her cabin, pleased with herself for the restraint shown. That was, until she looked up into the leering face of the second biker.

"Ah, shit."

In the moonlight she saw the glint of metal in his hand. And as he stepped forward her concerns were confirmed. A hunting knife. A bloody great big one at that. He pointed the blade towards her. "You don't come into our town, rough up my brother and get to walk away," he told her. "I think it's time Turtle and me show you how we do things around here."

She shot a look over her shoulder, seeing Turtle grinding the pool cue between his fists, like an eager Italian waiter with a pepper grinder. He snorted back a disgusting amount of blood snot and spat it out on the ground in front of her, fixing her dead in the eyes.

"Time to pay. Bitch."

Chapter Three

Acid Vanilla had struggled with her mental health for a large part of her life. When she was younger, she'd put the intense, prickly energy that soared through her veins – and had her acting stupid or dangerous – down to teenage angst. Hormones. But as she'd got older and these actions became more dangerous and more frequent, she'd wondered if something else was at play. She was not like other girls. Not even the ones in Crest Hill, the home for 'psychologically dangerous girls' where she found herself after 'the incident' (she found it helped to distance herself from what had happened if she called it that). Of course, she'd never regret what she did – Oscar Duke was a shit of the highest order and she'd happily kill him again – yet that one act sparked a chain of events and led her to become… well, Acid Vanilla. And until recently she'd struggled with whether that was a good thing or not.

It was at Crest Hill where they put a name to her condition, and her therapist, Jacqueline, helped her hone those intense rushes of manic energy in a way that became useful to her. Valuable, even. Once she'd gotten out of that awful place, finding herself under the wing of Beowulf Caesar, she'd started to think of her Cyclothymia (a rare form of bipolar, they told her) as something of a superpower. With the highs came a keen increase in both her senses and creativity. Her thinking and perception often expanded to the point she saw events before they happened. She could spend days needing little or no sleep, took big risks that often paid off. All topped off with an overriding sense of invincibility. None of these facets would be immensely useful if she was working in an office, say, or behind a checkout, but as an international assassin they were the perfect attributes.

Of course, you had the downsides as well. The big risks didn't always pay off and her feelings of invincibility were only that – feelings. They often led her to act impulsively and make silly mistakes, not to mention she rarely looked after her wellbeing. She found herself sleeping with the wrong people, making extravagant payments for items of furniture and clothing she neither wanted nor needed. These dark aspects of her condition kept her on her toes, but over time she'd learnt to harness them to useful effect. The depression, though, not so much. The dark manatee of doubt and dismay, which lay heavy on her shoulders, could take away all her thoughts and numb her for weeks. She saw it as a manatee because it was the first creature that came to mind when Jacqueline recommended visualising her conflicting moods as different animals. The idea was simple. By outwardly personifying these troubling elements of her psychology, she wouldn't identify with them so much. Alice Vandella wasn't depressed so much as the manatee was in town. That sort of thing. The manatee's counterpart, the flipside to her depression, the manic creative part of Acid which helped her become one of the deadliest assassins in the world (and had kept her alive for the last two decades) she named 'the bats'.

And it was these bats that were now screeching across her consciousness, sending waves of white heat energy up her spine as she stared into Turtle's mean piggy eyes.

"Time to pay. Bitch."

The words were a threat, but they were also a battle cry, designed to strike fear into his opponent. Except they gave him away. He might have had a pool cue gripped in his fists, he might even be ready to kill, but a part of him was afraid and trying to make himself look scarier than he was. Killers kill, they don't talk about it. Buoyed with this knowledge and the tooth-grinding manic energy burning at the base of her skull, she sprang towards him. The movement caught him off guard, and as he awkwardly swung the cue at her head she grabbed it with one hand. Keeping a tight hold she spun around, the force prising it from his grip as she smashed her elbow into his already bust-up face. He staggered back and she steadied her footing, leaping out of the way of his buddy who had lunged at her with the hunting knife. As he moved past, she clubbed him around the back of the head with the heavy end of the cue, knocking a loud grunt out of his windpipe. He stumbled forward and she brought the cue over her shoulder, swinging it like a baseball bat into his stomach. She felt the vibration shudder through her torso on impact as he crumpled to the ground like a broken squeezebox.

She turned back to Turtle. He was sitting on the ground with his head back, holding the bridge of his nose. Defeated. She straightened her spine and let her shoulders drop, drawing back a few deep breaths as she did. She was more out of shape than she'd realised. But that was another reason why she had travelled north to the mountains. Exercise and fresh air. Just what the doctor ordered, and other cliches. As far removed from her old life as possible. Which was why she was doubly pissed these losers had jumped her. It seemed trouble still had a way of finding her wherever she went.

"As I said," she gasped, pointing a crimson nail into Turtle's face. "Let's call it a night, shall we?"

He glared down his zig-zag nose at her. "Oh yeah. I'd say. Good night. Bitch."

"Listen, pinhead," she said. "I don't like——"

She stopped short as something like a large train slammed into the side of her head and knocked the entire world off its axis. She staggered to one side, her legs giving way as the pain in her cheek mushroomed into her sinuses and brain. Swinging wildly with the cue, she found nothing but air, and the momentum sent her spinning off into the cosmos before gravity grabbed hold of her and pulled her back to the earth face first. She landed with a thud, a heavy weight pressing down on her stomach.

"Dumb bitch. How do you like this?"

Turtle's buddy was on top of her. She wriggled to get free, but he pressed his knees onto the tops of her arms, pinning her down. Hands clutched around her throat, thumbs on her windpipe, squeezing hard. She gnashed her teeth. Bucked her hips. But despite his wiry frame and weaselly demeanour he held on, squeezed tighter. The bats screamed. Acid grunted, tensing every muscle and sinew in her neck to try and stay conscious. The pain in her head had gone, numbed by a heady mix of manic energy and fight-or-flight juice.

Above her the biker snarled and spat, pressing his

weight down on her. She felt her lifeforce fading. Another second and she'd be unconscious. Another second and…

She rolled over in the dirt as the weight left her, gasping into the darkness and hauling deep breaths into her taut lungs. Her hands felt at her neck, at her windpipe. It felt sore and bruised but she didn't think it was damaged. Where had he gone? Was he stepping back for a final blow? Retrieving his blade?

She flipped over, scrambling forward in the dirt to put distance between them.

"Hey. It's okay."

"Huh?"

She looked back to see Jareth standing beside the fallen biker.

"He's out cold," he said, opening out his fist and shaking his hand like it was on fire. "Guess I got the bastard with a lucky punch. You okay?"

"Yes. I'm fine," she said, ignoring his offered hand and getting to her feet. "I could have handled them."

He held up his palm. "Oh, I don't doubt it."

Acid brushed herself down. "Yeah, well. I suppose you were some help."

She was being prickly, she couldn't help it. She'd never played well with others. But for once her cantankerous manner elicited a chuckle and a wag of the finger from the barman.

"You know, I got it wrong about you."

"Oh yes?"

He tilted his head to one side and grinned. "I said you looked scary-looking, right? Well, I take it back. You're just plain scary."

"I see." She frowned and stuck out her bottom lip. "But wasn't there a second part to your description?"

"Don't think so."

"Right. I must have been hearing things."

"Must have." Jareth looked around him, at the bruised and bloody bikers, then back at her, his eyes twinkling in the moonlight. "If I didn't know better, I'd say we were flirting. Is that weird?"

Acid's turn to shrug. "I don't know. If we were flirting – which we aren't – I'd say that was a normal response. Stressful situations like this often breed other heightened emotions."

"Is that so? Well, you certainly can handle yourself. You sure you haven't got some kind of military background?"

A snorting scoff tried to escape her but she managed to pull it back in time, covering it with a cough. "Erm… not entirely. But something along those lines."

He looked at her. His eyebrow twitched. "A woman of mystery, huh? Just my—"

"Hold that thought," she told him, pressing her hand onto his chest. Stepping around him, she picked up the broken pool cue and strode over to where Turtle was now sitting upright.

"Screw you," he muttered, as she approached. "You'll get what's coming to you soon enough, don't worry. Fucking bitch."

"Is that so?"

A million invisible bats screeched in her head.

Do it.

Kill him.

She raised the cue to shouts of protest from the barman, but his words were muffled as if coming down an old telephone wire. The bat chorus grew more intense. Nothing else existed but her and this pathetic waste of flesh at her feet. She tightened her grip around the thin end of the cue, ready to strike, ready to wrap the makeshift club around Turtle's pugnacious face. But before she could act, a high-pitched screech sent her focus spiralling. For a second she thought it was the bats, but as the noise shrilled through the air for a second time it snapped her awareness back to reality. She saw Turtle was now bathed in white light.

"Hold it right there," a man's voice called.

Acid turned and was immediately dazzled by the high beams of a vehicle. Lowering the pool cue, she lifted her other arm to shield her eyes and saw the outline of a figure standing behind the open driver's door of a police patrol car. She also saw the service revolver aimed at her.

"Drop the weapon," the officer called over. "And put your hands up."

Acid hesitated, but did as she was told as the cop crab-walked around the side of the car door with his gun raised. He was about her height (five-six when she wasn't slouching so much) but had the sort of body that would make a sack of potatoes appealing in comparison. What was most remarkable, however, was the expression of utter glee that played across his chubby features as he peered past her.

"Well, shit. Two of the Cheetahs all beat up. You been causing trouble, boys? I reckon Chief Hunger might like to see you."

He stepped forward, but as he did Acid heard movement behind her. Turning, she saw Turtle and his buddy scrambling to their feet, falling over each other as they ran off in the opposite direction.

"Goddamn— Get back here, you punks." The cop pushed past her, shooting into the night sky. "Stop or I'll blow your fucking heads off."

When neither of the men stopped he lowered his weapon and fired off two rounds. But it was no use. There was already too much distance between them. He fired once more, out of frustration rather than an actual attempt at taking the men down.

Acid glanced over at Jareth, who had positioned himself a way back. Their eyes met and they exchanged a look before Acid turned to the cop. He was still poised in firing position, chewing on his bottom lip like it was a piece of prime tenderloin.

"You should have taken them down as soon as they moved," she told him.

The cop lowered the gun, nostrils flaring as he looked her up and down. "And who the hell asked you?"

"I think we'd best get going," Jareth said, coming over and holding his arm in the space between her and the cop, fixing her dead in the eye. "Don't you think?"

Before she could answer he turned his attention to the panting cop. "Thank you. If you hadn't come along when you did I don't know what would have happened. Those fellas seemed awful mean."

This Jareth guy was a charming bastard, she'd give him that, but the cop wasn't biting.

"Seriously, who the hell asked you?" he asked her again. "And why the hell are you still holding that thing? You plan on using it?"

Acid looked at the broken pool cue in her hand. "Oh no, I…"

She dropped it on the ground. But it was too late.

"Don't move." The cop stepped one leg back and raised his gun at her. "Hands in the air."

Acid raised her hands, resisting the urge to ask how she was supposed to do this whilst not moving. The cop marched over and grabbed her by the wrist, yanking her arm down with some force and pulling it behind her back.

"Let's see how chatty you are back at the station."

"Oh come on, officer, I was—"

"Shut it. I mean it. I'll string you up myself if you don't shut that Limey mouth of yours."

He holstered his pistol and reached for her right arm, bringing it down and tugging it back to meet her other. With him standing behind her, breathing heavily on her neck, the urge to headbutt him was overwhelming. But she fought against it, succumbing to the situation as the cold steel of cuffs pinched at her wrists. He clicked them tight before rasping in her ear. "Not so funny now, are ya, Morticia?"

Morticia Adams.

She'd had it before and it was usually places like this. Small towns with small-town mentalities. Where a woman with dark hair, who wore a fair amount of kohl around her eyes and who dressed predominantly in black, was seen as some kind of witch. Still, Morticia Adams was quite the fox. There were worse people to be compared to, Acid mused, as the cop hustled her over to his patrol car and slammed her face first onto the hood.

"Dumb bitch."

"Hey, come on now, man," she heard Jareth yell. "No need to be so damn rough."

"Oh yeah? You want a night in the cells too, Brad Pitt?"

Despite the cold metal of the hood pressing against her already bruised face, Acid couldn't help but scoff at the comparison. Jareth was a decent-looking guy, but that was where the similarities stopped. But then, she supposed, any man with a full complement of DNA looked like a movie star alongside the redneck cop.

"We don't want any trouble," Jareth added. But the damage was already done.

"Too late for that," the cop told him. "Sounds to me like you both want to spend the night in jail. Come here."

He left Acid bent over the patrol car and marched over to where Jareth was throwing his arms out to the sides.

"You're arresting me. Seriously?"

"You bet I am." The cop grabbed him by the arm and bent it behind his back before leading him over to the car.

"Officer, please. I've got a bar to run. You know Al, right? I'm his new hire. Come on now."

But any protests fell on deaf ears as he was frog-marched over to the waiting patrol car. Considering the rugged barman could have easily tossed the stout cop over his head, Acid was disappointed that he submitted so readily. But it was probably for the best.

What was the saying?

When you're in a hole, stop digging.

She flinched as Jareth's head was slammed down on the hood a few inches from hers. The cop held him there for a moment before lifting his hand away. And as he did, Jareth opened his eyes to meet her gaze.

"You all right?" he whispered.

"Oh, sure. Never better." She blew a piece of hair from out of her mouth and twisted her head so she could watch the cop. He had his weapon drawn once more and held it on them as he leaned in through the driver's window to grab the radio. As he called it in, she turned her attention back to the barman.

"Sorry about this," she said. "My fault. I do have a nasty habit of getting myself and others into shitty situations."

The manic bat energy was already dissipating and in its place she found herself feeling foolish. This shouldn't have happened. She'd come here for peace and quiet. For rest and recuperation. Yet she'd been here less than twenty-four hours and had already been in a bar fight with two bikers and gotten herself arrested. As she closed her eyes, she heard her friend Spook's disappointed voice echoing in her head.

"Don't worry about it," Jareth replied. "It was a quiet night, anyway."

She opened her eyes and smiled. "Thank you."

"Hey," he said. "I just realised. You never told me your name."

Even in the cool night air, even with her cheeks bruised and raw, she felt a prickle of heat cross her face.

"My name's Alice," she told him. "Alice Vandella."

Chapter Four

There were two holding cells at Blackfell Ridge police station, but luckily (or unluckily for the newly arrested outsiders) they were both lying empty. Jareth Hicks had hoped the holding cells would be teeming with local rogues and scoundrels, full enough that the cops would have no choice but to put him in with his bizarre and engaging new friend. But it wasn't to be.

After the arresting officer (who turned out to be a state trooper, name of Crawford) had processed him, Jareth was offered the much heralded *one phone call*. This he used to call Al, the owner of the bar, who, not to any surprise, didn't take kindly to the news. After having his eardrums rattled for going on five minutes, Jareth hung up, and a different officer (this one more fresh-faced, but displaying the same low levels of refinement as Trooper Crawford) escorted him into the back portion of the tiny police station where they presented him with two grey metal doors, one closed, one hanging open. Beyond the open doorway he saw a small box room, rendered floor to ceiling in thick terracotta paint and containing a low metal bench he presumed doubled as a bed. Standard holding cell get-up. As were the brushed metal sink and toilet unit, revealed to him as the young cop shoved him into the room.

"Sleep well," the kid muttered, before backing away and slamming the door shut.

As the lock clicked behind him, Jareth stepped into the centre of the twelve-by-twelve room and weighed up his options. Of which there was really only one. Grin and bear it. Wait it out until morning. Even a crotchety local trooper like Crawford would be hard-pushed to get *breach of the peace* to stick. He could, perhaps, claim they assaulted him if he wanted to teach them a lesson, but neither he nor his young counterpart seemed the kind of folk who were keen on report writing. Jareth's guess was they'd leave them overnight to stew before releasing them in the morning without charge. It could be worse. Could be a whole lot better as well, but maybe this was a sign. The gods of fate telling him it was time to move on. Along with his belt and boot laces, the duty officer had also confiscated his watch, but he still had the clock in his head, which told him it was around midnight. He stretched his arms over his head and yawned. Best he could do was try to get a few hours' sleep.

He settled down on the bench and laid his head on the cold, hard steel.

A few hours' sleep?

Hmm. Maybe not.

He closed his eyes regardless.

"Man, what a dumbass."

"Jareth?" a voice whispered through from the next room.

"Hey," he replied. "That you, Rolling Stones?"

"Excuse me?"

"You put the Stones on in the bar earlier. I meant to say at the time, good choice." He placed his hands behind his head. It wasn't any more comfortable.

"Best of a poor selection," came the response.

"Fair enough. Not a fan then?"

She didn't answer.

He grinned at the ceiling. "Last I recall you were telling me about your non-military background."

"Was I?"

"Just before you took a swing at No-Neck."

She was silent again, prompting Jareth to raise himself up onto his elbows.

"Sorry, I wasn't prying. If you can't talk about it, I understand."

"Yeah, it's… complicated."

He blew out a breath. "Hell, I know all about complicated."

He glanced around the room, contemplating the heavy metal door, the tiny window not big enough to fit his head through but with steel bars across it regardless. Yet, despite the grim decor and the fact he was a big man locked in a cramped space, it didn't feel overly oppressive. He'd stayed in worse places over the years. And it sure was a lot different to the only other jail cell he'd ever spent time in. That one was made entirely of chrome and rubber and had no windows or furniture whatsoever. With no sense of order, and kept awake by a high-pitched buzzer that went off every hour, he'd lost all sense of himself. After a few days his internal clock was so shot to pieces he didn't know night from day, up from down, right from wrong.

But that was exactly how they got you. How they made you pliable.

After a week of those conditions, with no human

contact and little food, you were ready to admit to stuff you hadn't done, sign whatever they wanted you to sign, just to get out of there. He gave the US military the best years of his life and they treated him like he was fucking Al-Qaeda. Those happy-go-lucky bastards at the good old Central Intelligence Agency.

"Do you think they'll charge us?"

The voice from next door snapped him out of his funk.

He lay back down. "Nah, I doubt it. Crawford's a lazy bastard. You embarrassed him and he wanted to make sure you knew he had the upper hand. But let's play it cool from now on, okay?"

He thought he heard a snort of derision, and her tone when she spoke confirmed it. "Thank you. I'll try."

"Just do it, all right? You don't have to kiss the guy's ass, but don't antagonise him anymore."

"Yes, yes."

He shook his head, laughing silently to himself. "You're a real piece of work, you know that?"

"It's what everyone tells me."

"I don't doubt. So what is your story, Alice?"

More silence, but this time he sensed discomfort on the other side of the wall. Twenty-plus years in the military, most of those spent overseas in hostile environments with hostile locals, you quickly learn the importance of reading non-verbal signals. Every tic and twitch in a person's face, every huff and sigh, every pause and hesitation, they all told a story. You learned to pick up on those nuances fast, or you died.

"Sorry," he said again. "I shouldn't pry."

"No. It's not that," she muttered. "Well… it is, but it's more than that, too." She was speaking fast, her voice tight and breathy. "Alice. That is my name, but I don't use it much. If that makes sense. I prefer Acid. Acid Vanilla."

"*Acid Vanilla?* What's that, some kind of nickname?"

"Yeah. Something along those lines."

"Acid Vanilla." He rolled the words around on his tongue. "I like it. Sounds cool. Makes me think of one of those guys from Warhol's factory. Candy Darling. Holly Woodlawn. Hey, wasn't there a Cherry Vanilla?"

The caustic silence melted away in the next cell and he heard her chuckle. "Yes. There was," she said. "You know your stuff. Impressive. For a military man."

Jareth raised his head as he heard shouting coming through from the front of the police station. Two men. Arguing. But it was hard to make out what they were saying. He listened for a moment longer before turning his attention back to his neighbour.

"Right. For a military man." He repeated her words back to her. "You know, that's a shame. You didn't strike me as someone who'd fall prey to such lazy stereotyping."

Another laugh. "You're right. I apologise. So you're into the old New York scene, too?"

"Not so much. But I was in a band in my youth. Called ourselves You Rebel Scum. We thought it was a cool name."

It was his turn to laugh. He hadn't thought about his band days in such a long while, but they were good times. Before he screwed it all up and was forced down the path he'd been on for the last quarter century.

"Were you any good?"

"We thought so. Did some all right gigs. It was the nineties, so it was full-on grunge. Long hair, plaid shirts, angry lyrics. I was obsessed with Nirvana and Black Flag and the Pixies. All the usual subjects."

Next door Acid sighed. "It passed me by, all that scene. I

had other shit to worry about. But my mum had an extensive music collection, so I listened to all her old stuff. Bowie,
Sabbath, Johnny Thunders, Ramones, Television, most of
the New York punk stuff. She lived in New York briefly,
before moving to the UK. Worst decision she ever made."

"Oh?"

"It's a long story."

The way she said it, there was a big fat period at the end
of that sentence. Meaning, don't ask.

"Did you know those guys from earlier?" she asked.

He sat all the way up and leaned his head against the
wall in the same way he imagined she was doing on the
other side. "Nah. Like I said, I've only been in town a week
or so. I've not had much to do with the old Streetwalkin'
Cheetahs, but the townsfolk seem to have a healthy respect
for them, bordering on fear. Al, my boss – ex-boss now – he
told me the local law enforcement have had a hard time
with them over the years. Which has meant real unrest at
times, especially for such a sleepy little place as Blackfell
Ridge. Not the idyllic getaway I was hoping for. Which is
why I'm planning on moving on, the next chance I get. You
know the mayor has gone missing?"

"What's that?"

"Yep. One of the guys at the bar was telling me before
you walked in. Apparently he's only two months into his
first term. Guy called Douglas Donovan. Two days ago they
found his car up on Crow Mountain, but he's nowhere to be
seen. They've had choppers and search parties out looking
for him. No sign."

"Right, yeah. I saw the choppers."

"Word around town is the Cheetahs have something to
do with it. Only rumours, of course, but it makes sense.
Donovan's big policy was to crack down on crime in the

area. Zero tolerance. Which obviously won't go down well with the Cheetahs if they're as bad as everyone makes them out to be. I've heard talk about drugs, guns, whores. The usual shit."

"Do you think they killed him?"

"Maybe. But he only went missing two days ago. He might turn up."

More shouts drifted under the door. Louder this time. Angrier, too. Then footsteps – they moved along the corridor outside the cells, turned a corner and faded away.

"It might be a good idea we both move on after this," she told him. "I came here looking for a quiet break, as well. Not a load of bloody unrest."

"Is that so? I'd say you might want to rethink how you conduct yourself…"

"Yes, yes. I know."

Jareth raised his head, listening lest she continue. But she didn't.

"Sure is a shame, though."

"Is it?"

"I don't know. Maybe. You got someone? You got people?"

"Have I got *people*?"

He straightened his back, ready to explain himself (or change the subject) when he heard a key turn in the lock. The metal door shuddered open to reveal the young officer from earlier, who jutted his weak chin at Jareth.

"You. Time to go."

Jareth frowned. "We've only been here a few hours. What time is it?"

"A little after five. Almost dawn."

"Damn," Jareth replied, getting to his feet. "Time sure flies when you're having fun."

The young cop ushered him out of the room, led him down the corridor and back through to the front desk. There they were met by Crawford, who was showing great interest in the checked lino under his feet. Beside him stood an older cop, one that was wizened and wiry and in stark contrast to Crawford who was portly and porcine. He regarded Jareth with a cruel sneer and too-close-together eyes.

"Colonel Jareth Hicks?" he asked.

Jareth shrugged. "Once."

"Speak up, boy."

He drew himself up to his full height. "Yes, sir. That's me."

The man nodded dismissively. With his downturned lips wet with moisture, he resembled a pissed trout.

"Yes, well, Crawford here was probably a little hasty throwing you in the cells tonight."

"Is that so? And you are?"

The man stepped towards him and lifted his chin high, as though trying to gain a few inches. The result was the top of his head still only reached Jareth's top lip.

"I am Blackfell Ridge's Chief of Police. That's who I am, boy. The name's Aldous Hunger III."

"Aldous Hunger?"

"Aldous Hunger *the third*."

"Well – Chief – I appreciate the apology. And I guess there's no harm done. Is my friend also being released?"

As if on cue, he heard shuffling behind him and turned to see Acid Vanilla (the name still excited him, for some reason), the crutch of her arm gripped by the young officer. When they got close, she shook the guy's hand away.

"You good?" Jareth asked.

She rolled her eyes at him. A tiredness had descended

on her since they last saw each other, but he was struck now – beneath the stark lights of the police station – with the realisation that her eyes were different colours. One brown. One blue. He thought briefly about mentioning it but stopped himself. Women like Acid hated cheap compliments, and over the years she'd have heard every comment and joke there was regarding those exotic eyes. Never go for the obvious. That was Jareth's motto. Plus, he never wanted to be one of those guys who masked their insecurities and lack of personality with cheesy lines and bad jokes. Getting a forced laugh wasn't worth a dime.

"Are we being released?" Acid asked, glancing around the side of him.

"So they tell me."

Jareth turned back to see Crawford leaning over the front desk, filling out a form attached to a blue clipboard. His tongue licked at his thin lips as he wrote, concentrating hard. Once done, he stepped back and surveyed his handiwork with one eye shut.

"Here you go," Hunger said, picking up the clipboard. "If you wouldn't mind signing this release form, we can get you on your way." He shoved the clipboard towards him, stabbing a crooked finger at the form.

Jareth perused the piece of paper for a moment before scrawling his signature at the bottom and handing it back. Hunger peeled the sheet over the top of the clipboard and stepped around him to address Acid.

"And you, miss. Sign here."

They both watched as she took the pen and signed. As she handed the clipboard back to Hunger, she looked up at Jareth and frowned.

"That's it, we're free?"

Hunger chuckled humourlessly. "I think we can put last

night's shenanigans down to a misunderstanding. No need for lots of unnecessary fuss or paperwork." He glared at Crawford as he said this last bit.

"Here you go," Crawford mumbled, as he swaggered over and handed Jareth and Acid zip-sealed plastic bags containing their belongings. He didn't look them in the eyes. "I don't want to see either of you around here again, understood?"

Jareth looked at Hunger to see if he'd heard. He had, but was nodding in agreement.

"You heard the man. Blackfell Ridge is a fine town, full of good, honest people, in the main. And I don't take kindly to being woken in the middle of the night to deal with the likes of you." He pointed his finger at Jareth, waving it between him and Acid as he went on. "I suggest from now on you both keep your heads down and stay clear of those damn Cheetahs. In fact, better still, clear out of here as soon as you get the chance. This a working town. Nothing here for visitors or tourists."

The way he said *tourists,* it was like the word tasted rotten in his mouth.

"You can't order us to leave," Acid said, prompting Jareth to turn and shoot her a wide-eyed stare.

Please… don't start.

"You're a feisty one, ain't ya?" Hunger jeered, prompting Jareth to grind his teeth together.

Please… don't rile her.

He watched without breathing as Acid chewed on the side of her lip, but she didn't respond.

"Listen, missy," the chief continued. "I'm not ordering you to do anything. I'm suggesting that you might be happier elsewhere. Hell, you've got the Great Falls a few hours' drive south, and Helena-Lewis and Clark National

Forest another couple after that. Beautiful places, them both."

Acid and Jareth exchanged glances. "Thanks," Jareth told him. "We'll bear that in mind."

"Good to hear," Hunger said, with a grin so false it bordered on grotesque. "I guess we'll be seeing you now. Stay honest. Stay safe." He stepped over to the front door of the station and beckoned them forward. "Now let's get you gone, and I can go back to bed for a few more hours."

Still reeling from the sudden about-face, Jareth followed him over to the door. "I appreciate you not charging us," he said, as he waited for Acid to join him. "You're a good man."

"That I am, Colonel. I'll be seeing you." He practically shoved them out into the dusky morning and shut the door behind them.

Jareth stepped down onto the sidewalk and stretched. "Could have been a lot worse," he said, yawning as he spoke. He looked down to see Acid Vanilla staring up at him with a face like a rainy Sunday.

"*You're a good man*," she mocked. "Jesus Christ."

He laughed. "It pays to be humble in situations such as that. I've dealt with men like Aldous Hunger—"

"*The third.*"

"—Aldous Hunger III all my adult life. Mainly they're full of ego and bullshit. You've just got to tickle their balls a little and they play nice."

Acid stuck out her bottom lip and blew her thick bangs from her eyes. "Well, it certainly was a fun night. I'll see you around, soldier boy."

With that, she turned and marched back towards the edge of town. Jareth watched her go, telling himself to leave well alone.

Right up to the point where he hurried after her.

"Wait," he called out. "What will you do now?"

"Now?" she asked, spinning around and gesturing with open arms at the orange skies above. "Not much to do, is there? I'm going back to my cabin, get some sleep."

"Right, yeah, sure. And I don't suppose you've changed your mind about dinner later? There's a decent enough diner across town."

She smiled. But it was that thin-lipped, pitying kind of smile. The sort of smile women reserved for men they weren't interested in.

"I don't think so," she said, wrinkling her nose. "Sorry. It was nice to meet you though." She turned to face him fully and tilted her head to one side. "What will you do next? You're not going to listen to Aldous Hungry the Turd, are you?"

"No. The hell with that." Without thinking he tilted his head the same way, mirroring her. He immediately wished he hadn't, as a smirk spread across her lips. "I'm paid until the end of next week where I'm staying, but after that I'll probably move on."

"So soon?"

He shifted his jeans up a way. "I used my one phone call on the owner of the bar, Al. He wasn't too happy I'd left the place unattended, so now I'm without a job. It's fine. I might hire some kit and head along the river, do a little fishing."

Acid stuffed her hands in the pockets of her leather jacket. "Sounds like hell, but each to their own." She fixed him in the eye and for a moment the space between them bristled with anticipation.

Jareth looked down with a grin. "I get it. Loud and

clear. Although you never answered my question back there."

"What was that?"

"About having people. Who'd you use your phone call on?"

She stopped, her perfectly arched eyebrows butting together over the top of her nose, as though the question had her stumped. "I didn't ring anyone," she said, speaking as if to herself. "Maybe I should have. Didn't think."

Jareth studied her expression as she fought with the concept. In the early morning light, she looked wired and unkempt. But that was understandable. He probably looked the same.

"I do have people," she said, hitting him with a hard stare. "But not the way you mean."

"I see. Well, they're probably worried about you."

She twisted her mouth to one side and dropped her shoulders, and in that moment all the spikiness faded from her demeanour. Instead, she reminded Jareth of a naughty kid.

"She'll be fast asleep right now," she said. "And when she finds out I got arrested, any concern will quickly turn to exasperation. But I'd better get back. I'll see you around."

Before he could respond, she spun around and swaggered off in the opposite direction, leaving him standing alone in the middle of the deserted street.

"Yeah," he said to himself. "I'll see you around, Acid Vanilla."

Chapter Five

On the other side of town, Spook Horowitz was absolutely not asleep. In fact, she was currently wearing out the hearth rug in the small wooden cabin she and Acid were renting for the month. She'd been doing this since 4.21 a.m., when she'd woken to use the bathroom and discovered Acid's bed empty. With no way of contacting her errant friend, and no actual knowledge of where she'd been the previous evening expect for a curt utterance that she was 'going for a walk', her anger and fears were growing by the minute.

Worried didn't cut it.

Try apoplectic.

Try overcome with seething fury.

Not that she was surprised, of course. This is what Acid Vanilla was like. She did what she wanted when she wanted, with never a second thought for those who might care about her wellbeing. After everything that had happened these last two years. And all the promises she'd made after getting back from Iran; that she'd calm down, curb her drinking, try to fit into the role of an upstanding civilian. Spook had been under no illusion that it was going to be hard for her, of course. After spending the best part of two decades killing people for money, living out of a suitcase and with a thousand different aliases and personalities, the simple life was never going to be plain sailing. Yet what else could she do? Every bridge had been burnt. Spook just wished Acid would accept that.

It wasn't like she hadn't been wanting out of that life anyway. Even before she met Spook and their worlds were intertwined in the most terrifying and crazy way, Acid had been wrestling with many aspects of her life and career. It was the main reason Spook was still alive, truth be told. If Acid hadn't had been in the middle of an existential crisis when they first met, she'd have killed her right there in Paris.

Back in the cabin, she went through into her room and sat on the edge of the bed. "Damn it, Acid," she whispered out of the window. "Where the hell are you?"

She was glad, of course, that her friend had completed her revenge mission in one piece (just about) and left that evil world behind. But the fact remained, ever since Acid had parted company with Beowulf Caesar and Annihilation Pest Control she'd been struggling. Spook had experienced her mood swings first-hand and it had not been pleasant. At best, Acid was single-minded and uncompromising. At worst, she lost herself in a gloomy abyss of self-doubt and downright nastiness. Spook had hoped (stupidly, she realised now) that life might have grown more stable once Acid's old crew were all dead. Yet here she was again, staring at the door in the middle of the night, startling at every sound, worried sick.

She picked the soft pillow up off the bed and hugged it to her chest.

Why was she still putting herself through this?

The problem was, of course, she cared for Acid. She understood her, even if the infuriating woman didn't always understand herself. Despite her own protestations to the contrary, Acid had a good heart beating behind her frosty exterior. She could wear all the leather jackets and black clothing she wanted, Spook had seen who she was. And she wasn't going to let her forget that.

"Acid? That you?"

A noise outside startled her. She sat upright, listening intently for the sound of a key in the door so she could breathe again, but it never came. The noise was probably a raccoon or some other critter going through the garbage out back.

Come on, Spook. Get a grip.

If Acid Vanilla was still a cold, calculating killer, Spook might be less worried (she'd also not have come on vacation with her, but that was another matter), yet they both knew she was no longer the person she had been, physically or mentally. Even back when they'd first met she was becoming sloppy in her work, making silly mistakes. Spook now understood this was an outer symptom of what was going on inside her troubled mind, but recently had wondered, too, whether Acid knew her star was on the descent and this was one reason she'd wanted out of the killing business. Spook would never have suggested this to Acid, of course. She might no longer fit into the role of highly skilled and calculating killer, but she was still tough as nails, and scary as hell when she wanted to be.

Spook rocked on the bed, pressing her mouth and nose into the pillow and steaming her glasses up as she breathed into the fabric. "She'll be all right," she whispered. "She can look after herself."

Outside the window the sun was now making itself known over the top of the mountains, the sky a glorious watercolour of gold and fuchsia. She'd give her another half hour, then she'd get dressed and go out looking for her.

The thought was fresh in her mind, the resolve boosting her mood, when a moment later she heard another noise, this time louder than before. Like footsteps. She tilted her head to one side as the wooden planks on the porch creaked and groaned.

"Hey, that you?"

She placed the pillow down and moved across the room, stopping as she reached the doorway and leaning against the frame with arms folded. It was the way she wanted Acid to see her when she eased open the front door, ready to sneak back to her room without being seen.

"Hello?" she called out, as the creaking noise continued but the door didn't open.

What was she doing out there? And if it wasn't Acid, then who the hell was creeping about on the porch? A wolf? Some big mountain man readying himself to break down the door and rape her to death…?

Spook tiptoed over to the stone fireplace and grabbed up the metal poker before returning to the front door. As she placed her ear against the painted wood, she could hear a dog barking and, off in the distance, the sound of a motorcycle revving its engine. Feeling braver with the addition of familiar daytime sounds, she reached for the key hanging from the hook next to the door. Clutching the poker tight, she inserted the key into the lock and turned it. Then, before her imagination got the better of her, she grabbed the handle and yanked it open.

"Hello? Hello?" she called out, jerking her head through

the open doorway and casting her gaze left and right. "Who's there?"

But the area was clear on both sides. Nothing but rows of benign pine trees cha-cha-cha-ing in the morning breeze on one side, and another cabin similar to theirs on the other. Satisfied there was no one about to attack her, she lowered the poker. As she did, she looked down and saw muddy paw prints on the edge of the porch.

"O-kay."

Feeling silly and pathetic, but no stranger to either of those feelings, she locked the door and went back into her room. The idea of going back to bed crossed her mind, but she was wide awake. She sighed. May as well get dressed and go look for her errant friend.

———

TWENTY MINUTES later Spook was standing on the main street of Blackfell Ridge. Regardless of the hour – a few minutes after six, if the old clock in the cabin was correct – the town was already awake and making good use of the day. Delivery trucks trundled down the wide streets, piled high with crates of fruit and vegetables and other groceries. Men and women sauntered past, walking their dogs or heading to work on foot.

After a brief tour of the town on arrival, Spook already had some idea of where everything was. If she followed the main strip over to the west, she'd find the most modern and developed area of the town, comprised of a couple of decent diners and a town square complete with a selection of official-looking buildings: a police station, a courthouse. Conversely, the road down to the east rapidly turned to dust and dirt, and then forest and mountains. But there were also a couple of dive bars at that end of town, which Spook knew would have been the biggest draw, considering the sort of mood Acid had been in yesterday.

She pulled her hair back into a high ponytail, rolling the hair-tie off her wrist and around the base, doubling and tripling it over. Ready for some serious searching, she headed east, but had walked only a minute or two down the road when she heard a distressed shout. She stopped, placing the sounds as coming from the next street, the one that intersected this one and which was obscured by a wooden two-story building on the corner.

Staying alert, moving with caution the way Acid always told her, she edged around the side of the building. Identical low-rise houses flanked the street, each one surrounded by bushy fir trees. About a hundred metres down, and standing in the middle of the quiet street, a young woman was arguing noisily with an older man.

Spook waited on the corner, watching the exchange from the cover of the building. The woman looked to be around her age (or rather, she was in her mid-twenties, the age Spook still thought of herself in her head instead of her actual age of twenty-nine) and was of similar build – short and slight and with little in the way of womanly curves. Her hair, too, was similar. Thick and black and cut into bangs. But as Spook crept closer, she saw that the straight-as-a-die, shoulder-length hairstyle framed elegant Hispanic features, rather than her own half-Malaysian countenance. She also saw those same features were distorted in an angry scowl, the woman's full lips flicking with spittle as she screamed at the man. It was a bold move, Spook realised, dressed as he was in a freshly ironed police uniform.

"Do something, please. He's all I have."

The cop held his hands up as she yelled in his face, tears running down her cheeks.

"He's all I have."

He's all I have.

She kept saying it, her voice trembling with emotion. She pushed the cop away and set off marching down the street. Spook tensed, her mind racing. Should she chase after? Make sure she was okay? Stalled by her indecision, though, the cop turned and caught sight of her.

"What the hell are you doing?" he shouted.

"Sorry. Wrong way."

She put her head down and scurried in the opposite direction to the one the woman had taken, not stopping until she disappeared from view around the side of the building. The cop kept on yelling after her but he didn't follow. Once she'd put enough distance between them, she slowed her pace and stopped outside a grocery store.

Do something.

He's all I have.

She heard the woman's cries in her head. Poor thing, she sure was upset. Angry, too. It struck Spook as strange that the police officer hardly reacted to the woman's aggression.

She stopped in her tracks and turned around. Then turned back again, doing a full three-sixty on the spot and feeling self-conscious and angry with herself all at once. *Damn it.* She should have gone after her. She turned back once more and returned to her lookout spot of earlier, straining her neck to see around the side of the building. But the woman was long gone. As was the police officer.

"Ah, man."

Nothing she could do now, but if she saw her again she'd approach her. Ask her if she needed help. Despite all the shit she'd endured the last few years, Spook's primary drivers were still empathy and compassion. Being this way was often to her detriment, but she'd rather put herself out there for others than be cynical and uncaring like...

Acid?

There she was. Swaggering down the street in her usual ramshackle way, like she didn't have a care in the world. She saw Spook at the same time and raised her hand.

"Jesus," Spook muttered, taking in her friend's appearance.

Acid's dark hair was greasy and matted, and her smoky eye make-up had been smudged around so much she looked like an angry panda. A hungover one, too, if the bloodshot eyes and cracked lips were any indication. Her black jeans were grey with dust and her battered leather jacket hung off one shoulder.

As she neared, she hit Spook with a beaming smile and a wink. "Morning, darling," she said, putting on a voice like she was the Queen of England. "How are you?"

"How am I? Worried," Spook replied, folding her arms. "Wondering where the hell you were."

Acid didn't stop as she got up to her. "Well, here I am," she said, sauntering past.

"This is not fair," Spook turned and called. She waited enough time to give Acid the chance to stop and explain herself but, when she didn't, she ran after her. "Hey. I'm talking to you."

As she got alongside her, Acid stopped. "I went out for a few drinks and one thing led to another. Okay? But I'm fine. No harm done."

"*One thing led to another.* What the hell does that mean?"

But she'd set off walking again. "I need some sleep," she called back. "We can talk about it later."

Spook seethed in silence as Acid strode away, swaying as she went and rolling her head around her shoulders as if she were some pathetic junkie rock star. Spook knew it was all part of her shtick – masking her emotions by playing it cool – but it still pissed her off. She wondered briefly if it might be best to respect Acid's wishes, leave her to sleep it off. She could walk into town, get some breakfast, browse the shops. But as she watched her friend zig-zagging up the street, she realised her anger was too overbearing.

We can talk about it later.

"Hell, no," Spook called. "We can talk about it now."

Chapter Six

Acid wrestled with her key in the front door of the cabin. "Come on, stupid bloody lock."

She struggled some more, about to give up and see if her boot might have better luck, when Spook appeared alongside her.

"Need a hand?" she asked dryly and, without waiting for a reply, leaned over and made easy work of releasing the lock.

Out the corner of her eye, Acid clocked Spook's supercilious expression, the arched eyebrow "I think my key is twisted or something," she told her, pushing past the open door and striding into the cabin.

"So that's it?" Spook asked, following behind. "No apology at all?"

Acid sighed but didn't turn around. "What do I have to apologise for?"

"I thought this was supposed to be a relaxing break. For both of us. And what the hell are those marks on your neck? Bruises?"

"It's nothing. A little run in with some crazy bikers. I'm fine." Acid turned to see Spook's face screwed in a scowl, her round cheeks flushed with what could be exertion, or ire. Probably both.

She lowered her head, hair dropping over her glasses. "You're not being fair, Alice."

"Life isn't fair, Spook." She moved behind the counter belonging to the small kitchen on the far side of the room and picked up the kettle. Sleep was obviously not on the cards, so she'd go for the next best option. Coffee. "Why aren't I being fair?"

Spook held her arms out wide and made a coughing noise. "Hmm, let's think," she said, stepping up to the counter. "Not telling me where you're going. Staying out all night. Then, when I'm out looking for you in case you're in a ditch somewhere, walking away from me as if I'm the one with the problem. Come on, Alice, we talked about this. No more destructive behaviour. It doesn't do anyone any good. Least of all you."

There it was again. Her old name.

She gripped the kettle handle tight, resisting the urge to smash it off the side of the countertop. "About that," she said, fighting to stay in control of herself. "I'm not sure I'm feeling the whole Alice Vandella thing."

Spook's eyes widened. "Excuse me?"

"We tried it. And I am grateful. For everything you did and—"

"Great, thanks. Because it took me the best part of two months and cost over six thousand euros to retrieve some of your old records. But you exist again, Alice. You're a real person with a past. All right, not your real past, but on your ID cards, on your passport, on any system that matters, you're… you. You're Alice Vandella."

Acid turned to the sink and filled the kettle with cold water, keeping her back to Spook as she spoke. "But that's not who I am. Not anymore. Yes, I still need a decent alias and that's as good as any – and I appreciate how hard it was finding anything about me online – but day-to-day, with you, with other people, I want to be Acid."

"But don't you think that means you've still one foot in your old life? How can you live a normal existence when you're still calling yourself Acid Vanilla?"

The barman's face flashed across Acid's mind. The crooked half-smile. The way his eyes crinkled at the corners. "I'll tell people it's a nickname. Anyway, there are weirder names, *Spook Horowitz*." She turned off the tap and closed her eyes. "Sorry, that wasn't called for."

Behind her, Spook scoffed. "Wow, you can actually tell when you've overstepped the mark, then? Good to know."

Acid placed the kettle on its base and flicked it on. "Can we start again? I'm sorry if you were worried. But I'm fine. I promise."

"Where were you?"

"I only went out for one drink – maybe two. My nerves were snappy and I needed to unwind. You know how I get, and the jet lag doesn't help."

"Fair enough. And…?"

She sighed, her eyes roaming around the room, taking in the wood-burning stove in the corner, the two-seater sofa with the patchwork blanket draped over the back – looking anywhere but at Spook. "I sort of got into a fight." She narrowed her eyes as her gaze fell on her long-suffering friend, who raised her head and nodded at the neck bruises, doing her best impression of a dissatisfied parent.

"That all?"

"I sort of got arrested, too." She rolled her shoulders

back and straightened to her full height. "But don't worry. It's all sorted."

"Is it all sorted? Well, that's great news, *Acid*."

"I see. Back to this, is it?"

Spook shook her head, but Acid noticed her anger was fading, replaced by something much worse. Disappointment. "It was symbolic. That's how I saw it," she said. "Becoming Alice again was you moving away from your old life. Putting the past behind you. Changing your name and your ways."

"But we can't change who we are, Spook. And I'm a bad person. I might not be the person I once was, but that's because I'm older and more fucked up. You want to save me, I get that, and I appreciate it, I do, but I've done too much horrible shit to be saved." She held her hands up, palms facing outwards. "I'm not depressed about it anymore. I'm not struggling with what I've done. I'm accepting it. But there's a difference between acceptance and completely moving past something to become someone else. I am who I am."

"And who is that?"

She offered her hand, accompanied by a manic grin. "Acid Vanilla, pleased to meet you."

Spook looked away. "Fine. Be like that. I thought you wanted to use your skills and experience to help people, that's all. That's what you told me."

"I do help people."

"Who? Who do you help?"

Acid pulled her hand back. "Do you know what? Screw this. I'm going for a walk."

Leaving Spook spluttering in her wake she stormed into her bedroom and, slamming the door behind her, moved over to the nightstand where she had her iPod connected to a Bluetooth speaker. She clicked on shuffle, pleased when the rousing opening bars of Black Sabbath's *Never Say Die* filled the room.

It was a good sentiment.

Apt, she thought.

She took off her jacket and flung it on the chair, before hauling her suitcase onto the bed and flipping it open. She pulled out fresh underwear, a clean pair of black skinny-fit jeans, a grey t-shirt and a black hooded top. Leaving Geezer Butler's bass notes worrying the small speaker, she grabbed her towel off the back of the door and made a beeline for the shower. Her plan now was to rid herself of the smells and stains from last night and then take a walk up Crow Mountain. Experience some of this fresh air everyone was always banging on about.

———

SPOOK WAS SITTING on the couch sipping from a mug of coffee when Acid slipped out of her room thirty minutes later. With freshly washed hair and in clean clothes, she felt like a different person. But although she'd let her friend down – again – she was not yet ready to apologise. She'd go for a walk, let them both cool off, then when she got back she'd sit Spook down and tell her she was sorry. She'd even tell her she was ready to move forward with her agency idea if it wiped that sour expression from her face.

Bloody hell.

That damned agency.

The one Spook had been harping on about at every available opportunity since they'd met. The big idea was for the two of them to set up as consultants, vigilantes for hire, to help people who the authorities couldn't or wouldn't help. Despite remaining dubious about the idea, Acid had been contemplating the notion more consciously of late, not least as they needed money coming in from somewhere, and fast. She'd worked out she had about three months before her Cayman Islands bank account (where she'd placed her ill-gotten gains over the years) was emptied of all savings. What would she do then? Live on the streets? Get an office job?

Neither of those options were any less appealing than the other one, but now was not the time to raise the topic. She needed to clear her head. She grabbed her jacket, along with the backpack she'd bought especially for the occasion, and headed out of the room. Spook was still sitting on the couch, but said nothing as she loaded the bag with a couple of bottles of water and a handful of snack bars. At the front door, she stopped.

"I'm going to take a walk up the mountain," she said, looking back. "When I get back why don't we go get some food, have a proper chat. Sound good?"

She'd been attempting a breezy and affable tone (as breezy and affable as she ever got), but Spook didn't turn around as she replied. "Fine. Be careful, yeah?"

The thorny energy coming off her was palpable. Acid paused, her hand on the door handle.

How the hell had they got here?

Neither Acid nor Spook had been under any illusion regarding how different they were from one another. Spook was kind where Acid was sarcastic, friendly where she was impassive, level-headed where she was... What was the word? Chaotic? Anarchic? Fucked up? But irrespective of their differences they had become friends. Initially, at least. It was certainly true Spook had been an excellent ally these last two years, her hacking and coding skills having come in handy on more than one occasion. And despite all the disjointed thoughts flying around in her head, Acid was glad to have her around. Even if that meant having to think about someone other than herself for the first time in her adult life.

But maybe it was time to admit it. They were too different. And perhaps it would be best for both of them to part ways, accept their friendship wasn't a genuine one but more a symbiotic exchange, borne from a situation that no longer existed.

Acid rolled her head around her shoulders, still gripping the door handle.

Come on. One last try.

She was a civilian now, after all. Civilians had friends. They had people.

She grinned. "Come on, sweetie. I'm always careful. You know that."

It was supposed to be a joke, but neither of them laughed. Acid gave it another couple of seconds, then she pulled the door open and slipped out.

Chapter Seven

The bright morning sun was perched directly on top of the highest peak of the nearby mountain as Acid stepped out onto the street and stretched her arms wide. Crow Mountain, the guidebooks called it, and it was easy to see why. A long jagged rock hung out over the highest point, resembling a bird's hooked beak.

"All right, you bastard," Acid said, addressing the mountain and slipping her arms into the straps of the backpack. "Let's be having you."

Summoning a renewed enthusiasm, she set off, enjoying the crisp air on her face as she strode past the scene of last night's troubles and out to where the asphalt stopped and dense woodland began. And as she climbed high into the mountains, she was amazed at how good the fresh air made her feel (it appeared all those 'healthy lifestyle' bores had been correct after all), but it was the stillness and quiet she most appreciated. She had grown up in Dagenham in East London and, except for her imposed stint at Crest Hill, had lived or worked in big cities all her life. Indeed, she couldn't remember a time when she'd experienced such serenity, such calm. It was almost oppressive, so unfamiliar was it to her sensibilities. But glorious, too.

As she continued up the winding track, with enormous fir trees and impressive redwoods on either side, she felt her neck and shoulder muscles relax and a heavy burden leave her soul. Why was it she only realised she'd been stressed after the event? For most of the last twenty years, she'd existed on a heightened plane of awareness. It was how she had to be to survive. But survive she had. She'd been shot, stabbed, blown up, and broken almost every bone in her body at one time or another. After everything she'd been through, it was laughable to think she could live a normal life. Normal in the way other people talked about normal, anyway. Not her bizarre, bloodstained version.

She pressed on through a dense stretch of forestland, where the trees were so tall and leafy it was as though night had fallen. It took her at least twenty minutes to negotiate the landscape of tall wiry grass and sharp sinewy branches that reached out for her as she passed by. Once on the other side of it, she discovered the track was now non-existent and the rocky terrain more brutal and unforgiving. But that was a good thing.

If the birds nesting in the trees above had any awareness of human nature they might have assumed Acid wasn't enjoying herself, given the heavy scowl creasing her forehead and the way she huffed and puffed with each difficult step. But this challenging environment, with its sense of adventure, was how Spook had sold her the idea of coming to Montana in the first place. Acid's hope was that being out in the wild (the true wild, not the lame version you got back in England) would be the perfect way to reset her system. The way Spook had put it – if she was having difficulty fitting into civilian life, then it might be helpful to get away from civilisation for a while. Out in the fresh air, with the piney scent of evergreen trees in her nostrils and the chirruping sounds of nature in her ears, Acid had to agree it was a good plan. Perhaps Spook understood her more than she was sometimes willing to admit.

A large rock formation jutted out across the path and she stopped to rest, closing her eyes and drawing back long, deliberate breaths. The veins in her legs throbbed with exertion, but this too felt agreeable. And as she faced the bright sun with her hands on her hips, a reflexive smile spread across her lips.

For the first time in a long time, her mind was uncluttered by chatter and chaotic thinking and she was thankful of that fact. Over the last few months she'd noticed an unpleasant sensation in the pit of her stomach, accompanied by a niggling voice in her head. It told her she'd been lucky not to have been killed these last two years, that she was no longer an elite killing machine, able to spot an enemy at a hundred paces and deal with them without breaking a sweat. And it told her that, sooner or later, her luck was going to run out.

Still, as she gazed out over the tops of the trees and sucked back another deep breath, it was hard not to feel grateful to be here. To be anywhere at all. She reflected on the late morning sun, shining off the dew that still clung to the leaves at this cooler altitude, and on the ospreys hovering overhead. A wave of serenity washed over her. What others might have called peace of mind.

It was a strange feeling.

But welcome.

Acid might not yet have stepped fully into the light field of a new life, but for the first time since she was a kid she was thinking of the future, with a desire to better herself. That had to mean something.

Her bliss was short-lived, however, as a loud noise cut through the peaceful scene, scaring the ospreys away and sending a flock of smaller birds scattering out from the cover of the trees. Acid spun around, while the familiar chatter of a million bats screeched across her nervous system. Something was off. She felt it in her bones, too.

Gripping the straps of her backpack, she edged around the side of the rock face and into the trees. This part of the mountain was more level than the first stage, but in places the incline was steep and treacherous. A hundred meters up in front of her the area was clear of trees, but from her current position she couldn't see over the edge of the landscape. As she listened, she heard the roar and splutter of an engine. And voices that echoed off the rocks before being swallowed by the forest. They were distinct enough, however; she could place them as male voices. Two men. Maybe more.

She scanned the immediate vicinity, searching for clues as to what was going on. Reason and logic told her to leave immediately, to head back down the mountain or take another path. There was most likely an innocent explanation for their presence – local men on a hunting expedition, for instance – but there were other possibilities too. In Acid's experience, if a situation could go awry then it often did, and it was best to prepare oneself for these eventualities rather than be caught out. Trouble still had a nasty way of finding her.

The engine noise stopped and she wondered if whoever it was had moved on. But then the voices came again. Gruffer now. Louder too. Gripping her backpack straps tight she pressed on, moving over to the far edge of the incline which would allow her to approach from a wide arc. Because despite reason and logic telling her to run as fast as possible in the opposite direction, a deeper and more integral element of her psyche needed to know what was going on. It was this same part of her that also said she was invincible and strong and without equal. The same part of her that had been sitting firmly in the driving seat on every mission she'd been involved with.

Sticking to the trees, using the trunks and branches to haul herself through the dense vegetation, she made her way up to where the terrain levelled off. Here she saw a worn dirt track that spiralled around the mountain and disappeared on the other side. Moving under the cover of a thick row of fir trees, she peered through the branches. Three motorcycles – Harley Davidsons – were parked in a line around fifty metres in front of her, and next to them a dusty Dodge pickup, positioned with the cab facing her and obscuring her view of what was on the flatbed.

A short way down the track and up to the right, four men were gathered in a semi-circle. Despite them facing the opposite direction, she recognised two of them. Her dancing partners from the bar, Turtle and his weasel friend. The other two she didn't know, but the Streetwalkin' Cheetahs insignia on their backs gave them away. Weasel Boy and another were hacking at the ground with a spade and pickaxe, watched on by Turtle and an older guy who towered over the other three.

From her location, Acid couldn't make out the size or shape of the hole being dug. Yet from the way they were standing, and the angle of their tools, she estimated it to be around seven by two by three. The perfect size for a shallow grave.

She narrowed her eyes.

What are you up to, boys?

Then,

Shit.

Instinct had her darting back into the trees as the tall biker turned and pointed directly at her. Branches scratched at her cheeks and neck as bursts of adrenaline roused her senses. But the man wasn't pointing at her, he was pointing at the truck.

The bats nibbled at Acid's nervous system as the squat-necked Turtle and his colleagues swaggered over to the pickup. The voice in her head was telling her to leave this well alone, to forget about it, to head back down the mountain. It would have been the sensible option. The safer one too. But when had either of those concepts ever counted for anything in Acid's world?

With stealth and caution, she weaved through the close network of trees, moving further up the side of the mountain to where she'd have a better view of whatever was in the truck. Here the terrain became more uneven and she grabbed onto the thin tree trunks, pulling herself up and steadying herself as she went, wary of stepping on a rogue twig and the noise giving her away. Down in the clearing the rear panel of the truck had been lowered and two of the bikers were dragging something out of the back. From her new vantage point she saw it was a large human-shaped bundle, wrapped in green tarpaulin. She hauled herself around the side of a pine tree, eager for a better view. But as she did, the earth gave way and her right foot buckled beneath her.

"Oh, sh—"

She bit her tongue, tensing every muscle in her body and screwing her face to stop from yelling. Frozen in this position, she performed a swift internal body scan, praying to whichever gods were looking out for her she hadn't broken her ankle. Moving with caution, she lifted her foot and rotated the joint. It didn't feel broken, but her jeans were ripped and covered in streaks of dirt and bright green moss. As she held her leg out in the sunlight spearing through the trees, she saw the thin layer of skin covering her calf had been scraped away. It burnt like an absolute bitch, but that would diminish soon enough. She was okay.

For now.

But a second later she heard rustling and a terrible squawking sound a few feet away. As she turned, a large bird burst forth from the undergrowth. With another squawk, wings beating loudly against the surrounding branches, it shot into the sky above, screeching some more as it flew away.

Or that could have been the bats.

"Hey. You."

Acid looked down to see the bikers staring at her, their faces distorted in confusion and anger.

"Shit."

Launching herself off the nearest tree, she skidded down the mountain, zig-zagging away from the men as branches and rocks tried to slow her path. On the last part of the slope she scrambled to her feet and set off at pace along the level shelf. A rudimentary track had been cut into the mountain but it wasn't clear where it led. She was preparing to take her chances when the distinct sonic crack of gunfire permeated the still mountain air.

"Stop right there," one of the Cheetahs shouted.

Acid glanced back over her shoulder but wasn't waiting around to see what he had to say. Crossing the track she dived for the cover of the trees as another shot rang out. The first one had been a warning, up in the air, but this second one whizzed through the trees a short distance to her right. Too close. Before he had a chance to rectify his aim, she leapt for the cover of the steep mountainside, skidding on her heels and butt and using her hands and elbows to steady herself. Below her the trees were dense and unforgiving, but beyond these she knew the terrain levelled out towards the foot of the mountain. Her hope was to make it clear before the bikers rode down the main path and cut her off. Behind her she heard the bass-throb of engines revving and more gruff yells.

They were coming for her. And they were not happy.

As if to drive this point home, a bullet thudded into the tree trunk in front of her. That one was far too close. Still in motion, she pushed off from the ground, getting to her feet from the semi-lying position she'd been in. The downward momentum meant she almost fell forward, but after getting to grips with her own velocity she was able to cover the last few meters and dive into a bushy fir tree. She tumbled through the dense branches, screwing up her eyes against the sharp ends that scratched at her face and hands. In the confusion she heard the motorcycle engines growing quieter as the bikers set off around the far side of the mountain. They were on their way.

Scrambling through the trees something abruptly yanked her to one side. Turning, she saw her backpack was caught on a thick branch. She struggled with it before slipping her arms out of the straps and falling into the clearing below.

"Bollocks."

She landed badly and her ankle buckled under her. Gasping for air, she pushed herself off the ground, but then felt the tight grip of a hand on the top of her arm. With the screech of a million invisible bats clouding her chaotic mind, she swung her fist at the enormous presence. Her only thought was to get away. The Cheetahs couldn't have a witness to what they were doing, but she was damned if she was going out without a fight.

"Go to hell."

Running on adrenaline and manic energy, she felt nothing as her knuckles connected with something hard. Twisting around, she launched herself at her attacker, leading with an elbow.

"Hey, stop that. What the fuck?"

He shifted out of the way, leaving Acid to stagger forward while she thrashed at fresh air. With her teeth gritted in white-hot fury and fists so tight her knuckles burnt, she swung at him again.

"Alice. Acid. It's me." He stepped back, holding his hands aloft. And in that moment she saw his face.

"Jareth," she gasped. "What the hell are you doing here?"

Perhaps satisfied she wasn't going to claw his eyes out, he stepped towards her and took hold of her wrist. "Saving your ass, that's what," he replied. "Now follow me. I know a shortcut to the road."

Acid yanked her hand away. "Excuse me? I don't need saving."

Jareth raised a finger in the air. "Listen."

The air here was still and the sound of engines coming from the other side of the mountain muffled. But they were growing louder and more distinct by the second.

"I know a quick way we can get to the river," Jareth whispered. "From there we can make our way back into town whilst avoiding the roads. Come on." He looked her in the eyes. Not pleading with her. Telling her.

Acid hesitated, unsure why she trusted this man so

readily (it certainly wasn't her default response to people she'd known for less than twenty-four hours). But either way the Cheetahs were closing in and she was out of options. She gave the barman a curt nod.

"Fine," she told him, glancing back over her shoulder. "Lead the way."

Chapter Eight

Once on firm ground, Jareth hurried his equally gutsy and tetchy new friend across the dirt track and towards the old wooden fence on the far side. He vaulted it in one bound, but as he turned back to help Acid he was met with a sharp look.

"I can manage. Thanks," she said, hoisting her leg over the top.

"Sure you can."

Although the bikers were fast approaching, he couldn't help but chuckle to himself. Still as prickly despite being shot at. Who the hell was this woman?

"Are you hurt?" he asked, suspecting this too would be met with a frosty response. And a moment later, as she jumped from the fence, it was.

"Nothing I can't handle."

Below them the Askook River wound back into Blackfell Ridge and into the neighbouring towns beyond.

"This way," he told her, leading by example as he slid down the side of a small levee to where a narrow bank stretched alongside the river. It was here where he'd been sitting, with his thoughts and a fishing rod, when he'd heard the first gunshot resonate down from the mountain.

Once Acid had joined him, they lay back against the side of the levee as the sound of motorcycles drew nearer.

"What the hell did you do to piss them off this time?" he whispered.

"I wasn't doing anything," she whispered back. "I was taking a walk in the mountains for some fresh air and exercise. Last time I try that. Fat lot of good it did me. I happened upon them by accident. They were burying something up there. Or rather, some*one*."

Jareth stared out over the river, all his focus on the approaching motorcycles. From his reckoning, they were close. Very close. He braced himself, his mind cycling through the probable outcomes; what to do if they were discovered. He had a fishing rod and a box of worms. Not his weapons of choice, but if he had to use them he'd make them count. But as they waited there, he heard the bikes approach, then ride right past.

He gave it another thirty seconds. And another thirty, to be safe. Then, as the sound of the engines disappeared into the ether, he pushed himself upright and allowed his shoulders to relax.

"Okay," he said, his voice back to its usual deep timbre. "I think you're safe. For now, at least."

"Gee thanks. My hero." She stood and pulled at the cuffs of her leather jacket. "I would have been fine, you know."

"I don't doubt it."

He watched as she brushed herself down, but that heavyweight scowl remained in place, creasing her features. It was a shame. They were excellent features. Feminine but not too fine, her full lips and high cheekbones perfectly complementing her straight nose and square jawline. She was good-looking all right, and with her dark hair and complexion, very much Jareth's type. Nevertheless, he wouldn't be so dumb as to convey any of these feelings. Not now – with the both of them breathless after being chased by gun-toting bikers – but not at any other time either. Jareth had known many strong women over the years, but this one was something else. Not the type of woman you won over with lame compliments and bullshit affirmations.

Not that he was trying to win her over, of course.

Not much.

"Well, there you go getting me into trouble again," he heard himself say, his damn mouth going off before he had a chance to think. "We'll have to stop meeting like this."

She shot him a vicious look, the kind with teeth. "Were you spying on me?"

"What?"

Jareth held his ground as she turned and jabbed a crimson shellac fingernail into his chest. "Because that's not cool. At all. I ought to—"

"No. Of course I wasn't *spying* on you." He pushed his chest out. "I was here, fishing. See?" He waved his hand over the scene, at the old hickory rod resting untroubled on a metal holder; at the box of live bait, wriggling and squirming as one; at his canvas travel bag. He'd also set up a small camping stove, which had a jug of water heating on top. "I was here by the river having some 'me' time. *Trying* to mind my own business."

Acid looked him up and down. "Yeah?" she said. "And how's that working out for you?"

"Not great."

"Yes… Well… Perhaps you should try harder." Her

tone was as cutting as before, but as she turned away he saw the scowl fade and a smile part her lips. It was only for an instant and, as she turned back to him with an expression as caustic as her name, he wondered if he'd imagined it.

"Listen," she said. "I'm sorry for involving you in my shit. I'm bad news. I suggest you stay the hell away from me."

Jareth tilted his head to one side. But she wasn't joking.

"Hey, don't worry about me," he told her. "I can handle myself." His gaze drifted back to the bubbling jug of water. "You want some tea, Bad News?"

"Tea?" She said it like he'd offered her a warm jug of piss to drink.

"Fine. You don't like tea." He settled next to the stove and reached into his bag, taking out his steel canteen mug and a zip-lock bag containing five teabags. He held them up. "Just as well. I only have the one mug."

Acid smiled for real now, without trying to hide it. She sat beside him and threw her legs out in front of her. "I don't suppose you've got anything stronger in that little man-bag of yours?"

He laughed. "I wish. But no. I'm trying to keep my head in one piece for the time being. That means staying away from the hard stuff."

She pushed out her bottom lip and nodded as if she understood. Jareth placed a teabag into the mug and poured hot water on top. Leaving it to brew, he sat back, seeing her torn jeans up close. "You sure you ain't hurt?"

"I've told you, I'll live." She let her head roll back and made a sound like an angry she-wolf. "Pissing hell. I am going to have to move on now, aren't I? Can't hang around Blackfell Ridge after pissing off the Aryan brotherhood."

"Maybe you do. Maybe you don't. I don't think they're like that, though."

"How do you mean?"

"The Cheetahs aren't the nicest folk in the world, from what I hear, but they ain't white supremacists, and they don't go looking for trouble. In fact, it's in their best interests to keep a low profile. Especially now with all eyes on them regarding the mayor's disappearance."

Acid shot him a look. "They were burying a body up there," she said.

"You sure of that?"

"Not a hundred percent, but what else do you bury wrapped in tarpaulin?"

Jareth picked up his tea and blew at it before taking a sip. It wasn't ready yet and tasted like weak orangeade mixed with cat piss. He kept hold of the mug, letting the steam warm his face as he gazed out over the river.

"Sounds like you got experience in burying tarp-wrapped bodies." When she didn't answer right away, he turned to face her. "Do you?"

"Don't be ridiculous," she said. "I've watched enough movies, that's all."

Jareth raised his head. There was something about the way she answered that didn't sit right. "What is it you said you did again?"

She narrowed her eyes at him, as though trying to get a read. The same thing he was doing to her. "I didn't."

"That's right. You didn't. But it's sort of like the military. But complicated. That's what you said, right?"

"Jesus." She sat upright and reached for a bunch of reeds that were growing next to the river. She broke one off and rolled the stem between her fingers. "I'll be careful what I say around you. You're like a bloody tape recorder."

"*Tape recorder*?" He crinkled his nose. "Cool reference, sis. Really on it."

"Piss off." She was laughing but it was short-lived, and after a few seconds they fell silent. It gave Jareth time to gather his thoughts. He turned to see her sucking her cheeks in, that bright red pout aimed at the river.

"I never wanted to join the military," he said. "In fact, I used to hate authority with a passion. All types of authority."

She didn't flinch, except he noticed her eyes narrow a touch as she said, "That's right. You Rebel Scum. Kings of grunge."

"I'm not sure about that."

She cricked her neck to one side. "You still listen to all that stuff?"

The question was fair enough, but there was no energy behind it. She was going through the motions, being polite.

"Only occasionally, but I still love music. Warren Zevon, John Prine, Townes Van Zandt."

Acid stuck out her bottom lip. "Never heard of them."

"Seriously?"

She sniffed. "Should I have?"

"I'd say so. They're amazing. Great lyricists, superb storytellers. I guess that's what I'm into these days. Words."

She turned to look at him, but it wasn't the sort of look he'd been trying for. Instead, her expression was one of pity.

"Go on then, what happened?" she asked. "You joining the military, I mean, not you listening to boring old man music."

"They're not boring. At all. But anyway…" He sighed, preparing himself to tell the story he hadn't told in so long. "I grew up in a small place called Noble. It's in Cleveland County, Oklahoma. Not an awful place to grow up, but not particularly inspiring either. I found solace in music but also in weed and booze, and speed on occasion. After a gig one night, I was in town buying some shit for me and my band. I had the use of my daddy's pickup truck, so I'd opted to make the deal. Only there must have been a tip-off, because soon as I had the baggies in my hand two police cars showed up and I got arrested."

Beside him Acid sucked air through her teeth. "That is shitty luck."

"I know, right? Made a hundred times worse because my old man was local police. Captain Jacob Hicks. We already had a strained relationship after my mom died, and this tipped him over the edge. He wasn't a dirty cop as such, but he was selfish and greedy. He made sure he looked after himself, did what suited him. He couldn't stand to have his only kid in prison, so he leaned on some of his contacts and got me a deal. Enlist in the army or spend the next five years in the Joseph Harp Correctional Centre. It was an easy choice. Or so I thought. This was around ninety-nine. My idea was to get through my two tours and that'd be it, return to making music or whatever."

He'd been looking out over the river, playing the past back in his mind's eye. As he glanced at Acid, he saw her eyes were wide and eager. "So?" she said. "What happened?"

"Nine-eleven happened, that's what. That was September. By late October I was in Afghanistan. My battalion was one of the first deployed to Mazar-i Sharif after we took it back from the Taliban. That's where I got noticed. I'd impressed my superiors in training and had already proved myself to be a good soldier in combat. I was fast, savvy, skilled at combat, both armed and unarmed. I've always been a hard worker and, whilst I hated authority, the way I saw it, I had to be there, so I might as well do the work to the best of my ability. I viewed it in a Absurdist kind of way, like the Myth of Sisyphus. You know it?"

Acid pulled a face. "Camus? Quite the enigma, aren't you, soldier boy?"

"You can talk. But yeah, I guess. I read lots when I was young, before music became my outlet. *Anyway*, I got stationed in Afghanistan and began to make a name for myself as a strong tactician. People took notice. Not least a guy called Walker, who was head of the CIA's Special Activities Division. One night I woke up with a bag over my head and was taken out to the desert to a room with no windows. They told me I was being recruited for a Black Ops unit."

"Wow," Acid replied. "That's hardcore. So tell me again how you came to be slinging beers in some backwater?"

Jareth stretched out his back. "That's a longer story. And there's no happy ending."

"Oh, I see. Like that, is it? Playing games."

"No. Just a part of my life I don't like to think too much about. Maybe I'll tell you about it later."

"Later? Is there going to be a later?"

He narrowed his eyes. "I hope so. You've not told me your story yet."

"Nothing much to tell. It's a tale full of darkness and trauma and best left where it is. In the past." She turned and lowered her chin. "These days I'm all about positivity and light."

"Perhaps you should tell that to whoever does your wardrobe."

She laughed. "Don't let my steely exterior give you the wrong impression, Jareth Hicks. I'm an absolute pussycat when you get to know me."

Jareth coughed. Just about kept himself together. "I see."

"Sorry," she said, straightening her spine. " I don't enjoy talking about myself, that's all."

"Ten four. Down with that. Though you sure are a mystery, *Acid Vanilla.*"

She pursed her lips to one side, almost as if she was fighting a smirk. "You need to get over that. It's a name. A nickname."

"Fair enough."

They were looking into each other's eyes, the air between them electric. He leaned closer. She stayed put.

"You're incredibly confident, aren't you?" she said.

"Am I?"

"I'd say. Forward, if anything. It's not a problem. Given you've also a certain… I don't know… *ramshackle* charm."

"Ramshackle charm? I suppose I'll take that." He moved closer. "I've always subscribed to the old 'look them in the eyes and tell them what you want' school of social interaction. Beats messing around."

"Absolutely."

He was so close now he could smell her. A hint of perfume, of leather and body odour, topped off with the cool scent of the outside. He closed his eyes. Moved in for a kiss.

"Woah. What the fuck?"

He opened his eyes to see her scrambling to her feet.

"No. I thought—"

"Did you? Well, you got it wrong." She rubbed her hands on the front of her jeans and shook her head in anger. "Damn it, Jareth. We were talking."

"We were flirting." He sat up but didn't make to stand.

"Maybe. But come on. There's forward and there's lunging at someone."

He shook his head and looked out over the river. "Fine. I'm sorry. I misread the situation."

"Yes, you did."

She stood over him. He sensed her staring at him, but he didn't look up.

"Look, thanks for your help. But I'm going to get going. I'll see you around."

As he turned, she did too, before marching away along the riverbank towards town.

"Keep your eyes out for the Cheetahs," he shouted after her, getting a raised hand in response.

He watched her until she'd strutted around the bend and out of sight, then he grabbed a handful of worms and, like a petulant kid, chucked them into the river.

"Ah, man. Fuck."

When was he going to damn well learn? He and women weren't meant to be. He was better off alone. It was safer that way. And a lot easier.

He lay back on the grass and closed his eyes. That settled it. It was time to get out of this lousy town. Time for Jareth Hicks to pack his things and get gone. The open road was calling him once again.

Chapter Nine

The sun glimmered majestically off the ripples and swells in the slow-flowing river as Acid trudged in the direction of the town. Not that she really noticed the delightful patterns made by the sun's reflection. Or indeed anything. Her attention was focused only on her thoughts, going over the last ten minutes, cursing herself for how perfectly ridiculous she'd acted.

This was not like her.

Not like her at all.

"That cocky bastard," she muttered to herself. "I mean, *Jareth Hicks.* Jesus Christ. What sort of name is that?"

As soon as she said it, she realised. She was one to talk about silly names. But whilst the irony wasn't lost on her, it didn't foster even the suggestion of a smile. Not even a caustic huff. That's where her head was right now. She was pissed off. Angry as hell. The problem was she couldn't entirely put her finger on why.

She knew it had something to do with Jareth, but it wasn't that he'd tried to kiss her. In fact, she was achingly close to meeting his advances before she'd pulled away, remembering she'd vowed herself off men. Off sex of any kind. With anyone. Same reason she was off the booze (trying to be, at least). Because whatever happened next, wherever she went, whoever she became, she wanted to do it with zero baggage and none of the usual chaos that followed her around.

Well, shit.

That thought did foster a smile, but there was little humour or joy behind it. Mainly just grim realisation that she was fighting a losing battle. Or had already lost.

She was a few hundred meters from the town and up ahead the path alongside the river fell away, too narrow to walk along. Hoping Jareth was correct about the bikers not looking for trouble (but only half-caring either way), she climbed up the side of the levee and cast a furtive look over the area. She was at the point where the main road turned abruptly into a dirt track, but there was no one in sight. Acid climbed over the fence and headed back to town.

What a place this was. Blackfell Ridge at the foot of Crow Mountain, surrounded by green trees, wide ravines and… space. So much bloody space.

What had she been thinking?

Even with the threat of marauding biker gangs hanging over her head, this place was far too serene for someone with her sensibilities. She needed noise. She needed the bustle and thrum of a working city. If nothing else, it helped drown out the chatter in her head.

On the way to her cabin, she mentally rehearsed the conversation with Spook. Telling her she was leaving, that she'd had enough. Spook would be mightily pissed off, of course, but she'd have to live with it. Or she could stay in

Montana without her. Nothing wrong with that. It might do her good. She was nearly thirty years old, after all.

The thought brought with it a renewed acceptance and vigour, and Acid quickened her pace as she strode along the main street now fully awake with locals. She watched them as they conversed on street corners or dipped in and out of the small grocery store and post office. Because apart from a few dive bars and a diner, that seemed to be as good as it got here in Blackfell Ridge.

Yes. The decision was made and it was the right one. She'd get the next flight back to the UK and continue her renaissance somewhere more familiar, with more home comforts, away from bikers and treacherous mountains and Jareth bloody Hicks.

She sneered loudly to herself, a way to cover the smile which had been unexpectedly and annoyingly brought forth.

"Stop that. Now."

She shook her head, hoping this might disperse the thought before she articulated it to herself. That maybe… perhaps… she'd like to catch up with Jareth before she left.

No.

Wasn't going to happen. Not a chance. And that strange sensation in her stomach? It was because she hadn't eaten yet today. It sure as hell wasn't her feeling vulnerable or nervous. And so what if being around him made her feel weird? She was only looking for a distraction. Same as always. For her, sex was an outlet, a way of expending the copious amounts of wired energy she had at her disposal. She'd lost count of the times she'd woken up next to someone she shouldn't have. Men and women alike, it didn't matter to her. But people got hurt – and not always in ways they'd requested. One of those people was Spook Horowitz, soon after they'd first met, back when Acid was still running around like she had a firework up her ass and a Catherine wheel temperament. It seemed like three lifetimes ago now, but Acid suspected Spook still held a torch for her.

Ah, Spook.

She wasn't all bad, was she? And she had been a good friend over the last couple of years. The only friend Acid had. She'd go easy on her when she told her she was leaving, but she remained adamant – she *was* leaving. In the same way she'd left behind her life with Annihilation Pest Control – and her life as Alice Vandella before that – it was important to move on quickly. Without fuss. All farewells must be sudden, the future beckoned. Whether or not this future had Spook in it, Acid wasn't sure. All she knew was she needed to be at home, surrounded by her music and her clothes and her own bed. It was there – accompanied by an expensive bottle of red – where she'd best work out what to do next with her life, not five thousand miles away in a place she didn't understand. She'd spent twenty years honing her condition so it worked for her rather than against her. There was no reason she couldn't do that again. She'd focus her creativity and manic energy, her impulsive rage and bloodlust, into more constructive pursuits. Maybe she'd take up baking. Or knitting.

She was still up in her head, considering the next steps in the gentrification and settlement of Acid Vanilla, when a shrill beep from behind snapped her attention back to the present.

"You're still in town, I see?"

A car appeared alongside her, white and black, with a distinct gold badge painted on the driver's door. Aldous Hunger III – for it was he who had shouted after her – leaned his head out the open window. He was wearing a pair of mirrored aviator shades that hid most of his gaunt face.

"Hey, miss? I'm talking to you."

Acid kept on walking as the car crept alongside her. "What do you want, Chief?"

"I thought you said you were moving on."

"No. You said that." She stopped and so did the car. She peered over Hunger's scrawny frame to see his sizeable colleague, Trooper Crawford, sitting beside him. He met her gaze and bared his teeth. She gave him a nod. "Are you allowed to stop people in the street like this?"

"I'm allowed to do whatever I want," Hunger replied, waving a crooked finger at her. "I'm the law round here. Keep that in mind, miss."

Acid straightened, squinting into the noonday sun as she did. She had half a mind to tell him about what she'd seen up in the mountains, get the prick off her back and give the Cheetahs something else to worry about – but she couldn't do it. She suspected Hunger and his cronies were simply bored, eager to exercise their egos anyway they could. But she was also hard-wired to avoid interactions with law enforcement at all costs. And she was no snitch.

"Actually, officer, I'm on my way to the cabin to pack up my stuff. So, you're in luck."

Hunger peered over the top of his shades and ran his tongue across his top set of teeth. "I told you that was the right move. Good for you. By the way, you haven't seen any motorcycles at all? In the last half hour?"

The muscles across her back tensed. A part of her ready to spill. It would teach those dirty bastards a lesson. "Not sure," she said. "Don't think so. The Cheetahs causing you trouble?"

Hunger gripped the steering wheel. "They're always

causing trouble of some kind." He sniffed. It sounded like he was snorting a tub of jellyfish. "We'll keep looking. I hope I don't see you again. Miss."

He pulled the car away, waving his bony hand out the window as he went. Acid watched as the car got to the end of the street, indicated right, and disappeared around the corner.

That really did decide it. A gang of murderous bikers on her tail, a bunch of redneck cops breathing down her neck – she knew when she wasn't wanted. Time to go home. All that mattered now was breaking the news to Spook. No sweat.

"ARE YOU FUCKING KIDDING ME? I cannot believe you're doing this. Although, no, forget I said that. I totally can. Because this is you all over, isn't it? Argh." Spook turned away, feeling the rage physically in her body. "I knew you'd do this. I knew it. But no, I told myself this time it'd be different. She's changed, I said to myself. She wants to be called Alice again. She's turned a corner. Then... what? Our first night on vacation and you get arrested for a drunken brawl and now you want to go home. Well, tough. I'm not leaving."

She turned around and a shiver of fear rippled down her spine. She'd never spoken to Acid like this before. She felt giddy, but knew she was pushing her luck. After all this time, after everything they'd been through, she trusted Acid not to hurt her, but she was still erratic and unpredictable. She was still someone who'd killed well over a hundred people.

Before the dark presence staring at her could respond,

Spook grabbed up her satchel and the new red beret she'd bought for the trip and headed for the door.

"Where the hell are you going?"

"Away from you," Spook yelled, without looking back. "If you're not here when I get back, I'll assume you've gone back to London. Have a pleasant flight. *Alice.*"

She yanked open the door of the cabin and left, slamming it with as much force as she could. She'd walked all the way down the street and had turned the corner towards the centre of town before she took a proper breath.

"Infuriating... stupid..." she muttered to herself, as a sense of emptiness washed over her.

Where was she going? And if Acid really was leaving her here alone, what would she do? Spook wasn't much of a sociable creature. That's where she and her terrifying and intense counterpart were similar. But whereas Acid's hostility towards others came from trauma and hurt and spending the best part of three decades knowing she could trust no one but herself, Spook's societal unease was brought on by that typical tryptic of nuances faced by many highly intelligent but nerdy adults – mainly crushing anxiety and introversion, topped off with a big scoop of tongue-tied shyness.

So when she turned down the next street and saw the woman from earlier walking towards her, a tingling feeling returned in her chest that she recognised all too well. Yet as the woman got nearer, any nerves or concern over what to say left Spook's mind. In one of the many self-help books she'd devoured over the years, she'd read the best way to deal with nervousness was to put your attention on the other person. The idea was this got you out of your own head so you stopped overthinking absolutely everything. Spook had always felt that this was easier said than done (like most of the advice in self-help books), and if you were the sort of person who was calm enough to remember this advice under pressure, you probably didn't need it in the first place.

But not today. The poor woman's cheeks were wet with tears and she looked so despondent and downright sad that any awkwardness Spook might have been experiencing faded entirely, leaving only compassion. "Hey," Spook called out, holding her hands up. "Are you okay?"

The woman regarded Spook from under a heavy scowl. "No," she said. "I'm not." She twisted away, leading with her shoulder to get past.

"Is there anything I can do to help?" Spook tried. "I know how it feels to be where you are. Scared. Like you don't have a friend in the world."

She stopped and looked back. "You don't know how I feel," she snarled. "You know nothing about me."

"Of course," Spook replied. "But I do know that talking helps. It sounds like the biggest cliché in the world, but it's true. I'm Spook, by the way. Spook Horowitz." She held out her hand.

The woman stared at it, then back at her.

"Spook Horowitz?" She didn't smile, but there was something in her face that made Spook think she'd tempered the hurt momentarily. Her name had that effect on people.

"That's right," she said with a goofy shrug. "My parents were hippies. What ya gonna do?"

The young woman sniffed as the grim cheerlessness descended over her once more. "At least you've got parents."

Spook pushed her glasses up the bridge of her nose. "Actually, I haven't. They're both dead."

"Oh, shit. I'm sorry." She rubbed the heel of her thumb across her eyes. "I didn't mean to—"

"It's fine," Spook said, with a smile. She peered down the street, spotting a small diner on the other side. "How about we grab some coffee? And you can tell me what's going on. Or not. Whatever you want."

The woman sniffed again but returned Spook's smile. It looked like the hardest act in the world. "Thank you," she said.

The two of them crossed over the road in silence. Her initial flurry of confidence had now faded, and Spook racked her brain for something to say. It wasn't until they were settled in one of the diner's booths that she found her voice.

"Not a bad place," she offered, removing her hat and casting her gaze around the room.

It was a typical sort of place, with a counter running down one side and eight booths opposite, done out in beech and beige leather and with space for six people in each. At the front of the diner, three round tables stood in front of a large picture window displaying the name of the place, *Mel's Diner*. Spook turned back to her new acquaintance. "You been in here before?"

"My name's Cynthia," the woman said, ignoring the question. "Cynthia Donovan."

Spook sat back, smudging herself into the comfortable leather seating. "Pleased to meet you, Cynthia. I'm Spook. I mean, I already told you that, but hi. Again."

She cringed internally. Her gawkiness was never hidden for too long, but it made Cynthia smile. She looked down at her hands, clasped together over the table.

"Thank you, Spook. For stopping me. I wanted to knock your head off at first, but I did need a timeout. I've no clue where I was going or what I was about to do." She glanced at the ceiling as the smile faded. "It's been a shitty few days."

Spook pulled her mouth to one side. "Want to talk about it?"

Cynthia looked up with an expression of dread sagging her pretty features. Spook thought she was about to up and leave, before a voice caught both their attention.

"What can I get you ladies?"

The small woman standing next to their table, poised with an old-fashioned notepad and worn-down pencil, must have been pushing eighty. Not that it mattered, of course. It was just unusual. As was her bright orange hair pulled back into a high ponytail, and the heavy smears of electric blue eye shadow painted over her lids.

Spook glanced at Cynthia, offering her the chance to order first, but she was staring straight ahead.

"We'll have two coffees, please," Spook told the waitress.

"No problem," she said, writing the order on her pad. "Anything else?"

"Maybe some pie?" Spook said, looking to Cynthia for agreement – or any kind of response. Getting none, Spook took the decision for herself. "Yes, we'll have some pie. If you have it."

"Sure do. We got cherry or blueberry."

"Cherry," Spook replied. "Thank you."

She watched the old woman as she shuffled away down the side of the counter and disappeared through a pair of saloon doors that presumably led to the kitchen. When she returned her attention to Cynthia, she found her staring ahead without blinking, as if willing the tears in her eyes to stay put.

"My dad's missing," she said in a low voice. "I'm so scared."

Spook sat upright. "Oh gosh. Since when?"

"Three days now. And no one seems to know what the hell's going on. I've been to the police every day, but it feels like they're too busy to even talk to me. I don't know. I'm scared that he's... You know... Ah shit, I don't know what to think anymore." She rubbed at her eyes. "I'm sorry."

"Hey there." Spook reached out and held onto her wrist. "Don't you dare apologise. I'm so sorry, Cynthia. That's awful. Do you know where he was when he went missing. Sorry, I know that's a dumb question..."

Cynthia sniffed back her tears. "They found his car half-way up Crow Mountain. The police said it looked like he'd lost control and run it off the track. But he was nowhere to be seen. They combed the area all day, but no sign of him. Chief Hunger thinks the Cheetahs have something to do with it."

Spook squeezed her wrist. "Cheetahs? Shit. I didn't know there were cheetahs around these parts."

Cynthia closed her eyes and smiled joylessly. "No. Not those kinds of cheetahs. I mean the Streetwalkin' Cheetahs. They're the local motorcycle club. Their clubhouse is over on the edge of town."

"Was your dad mixed up with them or something?"

"No. Not at all." She opened her eyes and looked directly at Spook. "He's a good man. He was – is – the mayor of the town, after getting elected this summer. The first real mayor we've had in Blackfell Ridge for over a hundred years, now that we've reverted from a council-manager system back to a mayor-council. It's a big deal. But he's only been in position for a few months and then this happens. He was trying to crack down on crime in the area, which is why the police think the Cheetahs are involved. Says they've a lot to gain if he disappears. But I don't know."

Spook let go of her wrist and sat back as the ageing waitress appeared, carrying a tray containing two mugs of coffee and a slice of pie on a pink, fine China plate.

"Here we go." She placed the tray down on the edge of the table and lifted the plate from out of the centimetre of spilt coffee. "One piece of cherry pie and two coffees. You girls want cream?"

Cynthia shook her head, so Spook decided she'd do without. "We're good, thanks."

"No problem. You need a top up or anything, just holla."

"Thanks." Spook waited for her to leave before leaning over the table. "So, you don't think these Cheetah guys are involved?"

"I don't know what to think. I'm scared and confused and I want my dad back. He's all I've got in the world."

"You poor thing," Spook whispered. "I can only imagine what you're going through."

Cynthia pulled the mug of coffee towards her and stared into its murky depths. "The weird part is there was no reason for him to be up on the mountain." She spun the coffee mug in her hands but made little move to drink it. "I don't know. It's all so strange. Chief Hunger says they still have hope they'll find him alive, so I'm trying to keep that in mind."

As she considered the information, Spook sipped at her own coffee. It was bitter and lukewarm and rather unpleasant. Leaving it alone, she picked up the spoon lying next to the pie and scooped out a crescent. The crust was crumbly and the dark cherry filling thick.

"Would you like me to help you find him?" She asked the question, and stuffed pie in her mouth before a shiver of anxiety robbed her resolve.

Cynthia sat back. "You'd do that?"

Spook, chewing away at the sweet pie, nodded. "Uh-huh." She swallowed and picked up her mug of coffee. "I'll do what I can," she added, watching as Cynthia's expression fell from hopeful to something approaching sorrow.

"I can't ask you to do that," she said, in a voice so quiet it was almost non-existent. "Chief Hunger and Trooper Crawford told me in no uncertain terms that I was to stay away and let them do their work. Besides, if we go snooping around it could be dangerous."

Spook glanced over Cynthia's shoulder, looking for the waitress. "Don't worry about that," she told her, any feelings of anxiety making way for a flush of adrenaline. "I might look nerdy and weak, but I know danger. Hell, do I know danger."

Cynthia frowned and tilted her head to one side. "You serious?"

"Damn right I am. And if we have to delve anywhere risky, I know someone who can help us. She's pretty scary, but she's also totally badass."

"And she'll help look for my dad?"

"Sure," Spook replied, hoping Cynthia didn't catch the trace of doubt in her voice. "I'm certain of it."

The waitress appeared from the kitchen and Spook raised her hand, miming the action for the check. It was the first time she'd done so in her whole life and it made her feel kind of giddy. Who'd have thought it? She enjoyed being the dominant one for a change.

She fixed Cynthia dead in the eyes. "If your dad's out there, then we'll find him. Now, let's pay for these drinks and get out of here. We've got work to do."

Chapter Ten

Jareth stuck his arm into the wardrobe and clotheslined the six shirts he had hanging there into a pile before yanking them out, snapping the flimsy plastic coat hangers in the process. He walked his legless dance partner over to the bed and stuffed the shirts unceremoniously into his open holdall. Next, he walked over to the old bureau that faced the bed and opened each drawer, scooping out the contents as he went. Five black t-shirts, socks and pants, an extra pair of Levi's (his only concession to 'designer wear'), they all got shoved into the holdall. Finished, he sat on the bed.

"Dumb bastard."

The fact he'd woefully misread the situation with Acid was bad enough, but he'd let his guard down, talked about his past. And now it was all he could think about.

He gripped hold of his thighs above the knee, holding on for dear life as he stared through the open door into the bathroom. From this position he saw the shower cubicle, and the towel he'd used that morning screwed up in a heap on the tiled floor. In front of this, obscured slightly by the door, he saw the sink unit and the handle of his overnight bag hanging down from the shelf above. But he wasn't really seeing any of these things. Instead, Jareth's focus was on the brutal and bloody images playing out on the cursed cinema screen in his head.

He saw the derelict township as clear as if what had happened was only yesterday rather than... what? Two? No, nearer three years ago now. He saw the apartment block, already pockmarked with mortar and machine gun fire, the dark, dusty stairwell with its laser show of red fire-flies as his unit ascended up the first few flights. If he closed his eyes he could even smell the place, pungent with dirt and body odour and fear. He recalled the taste of dust in his throat, followed by the stench of burnt flesh seconds later when the chaos began. He heard the shouts of anger and confusion, the pulse and thrum of machine gun fire and then the deafening white noise as the IEDs went off.

They knew we were coming...

He shook his head in the same way he always did when he thought about that day. He'd known. He'd damn well known something wasn't right. Which was why he'd ordered his men to stand down, told Walker he wanted to wait another day before they advanced. Until more intel came their way. But that wasn't to be.

Walker's smug sonofabitch face loomed out of the swirling images in his mind. Even now, with so much space and time between them, it tightened Jareth's chest and made his jaw rigid. The expression on the CIA man's face was the same as when Jareth had tried arguing his case. His eyes full of disdain and hatred.

We need more time, sir.

"Motherfucker." Jareth looked down at his hands, not surprised to see them clenched in tight fists, the knuckles burning to match the rage and condemnation surging through him.

No.

He wasn't going to let that bastard get to him. He'd carried a heavy burden of hate and hurt for too long and was damned if he was carrying it any longer.

Making a conscious effort, he relaxed his hands, running his fingers through his hair before going through into the bathroom. There he turned on the faucet and splashed water in his face, making a rudimentary vessel with his hand and slurping up a couple of mouthfuls of the ice-cold water. It felt good in his parched throat and, as he raised his head, his reflection shot back a firm stare.

"Come on, man. Pull your head out your ass."

While he had recuperated in hospital following last year's heart attack, he'd vowed to never let anyone or anything affect him negatively again. And that meant himself as much as any outside influence. He was the pilot of his own life. The navigator, too. It was his sole responsibility to guide this plane to green and pleasant lands. Which is why getting out of Blackfell Ridge was now his best (only) option.

On paper, the quiet town in the mountains had seemed ideal, with plenty of fresh air and luscious scenery, where he could walk and fish and contemplate life. But the reality he found was a community gripped with paranoia and unrest. After his run-in with the cops and those damned bikers – not to mention his embarrassing performance with Acid – all signs pointed the same way.

Exit stage right.

Now.

While he still had some dignity.

He walked over to the nightstand and picked up his

wallet. "Balls." He was still owed a week's wage. He thought about cutting his losses and getting out of town this instant. But that idea lasted all of five seconds before he picked up his phone and opened the contacts list. The last thing he needed was to speak with Al again but he was running depressingly low on funds, and if he was moving on he needed money.

The phone was a piece of shit, bought for twenty bucks to use whilst travelling and so small and flimsy it felt like a toy in his rough hands. It also only had three numbers stored in the address book, so he located Al's details quickly and tapped *Call*.

"The hell you want?" a gruff voice answered.

"Jesus, man. You okay? You sound sick."

Al coughed, the disgusting sound of phlegm in his throat amplified down the line. "I am sick. Sick of people letting me down."

Jareth strolled over to the motel window and peeled back the curtain. "Yeah, well, I said I was sorry about that. It shouldn't have happened."

Through the window he saw two young boys in the street below, throwing a soccer ball to each other. They looked to be only around five or six years old. Tiny kids, playing in the street with not a parent in sight. What struck him the most was it didn't seem odd. But it was a different world up here in the mountains. Well… until it wasn't. One thing Jareth had learnt over the years – evil existed everywhere. Even the places you least expected it.

On the line he heard Al muttering under his breath. "What do you want, Hicks?"

Jareth straightened his back and stretched out his chest. "You still owe me two hundred bucks."

"You serious? Cheeky fuck. I had to shut up early that

night. You lost me a lot of custom and made me look bad, getting the cops out like that."

"Wasn't my fault."

The line went silent except for the wheeze of Al's breath. He could picture his ratty face and grey-toothed snarl.

"How about you give me one-seven-five and we call it quits?" Jareth added. Normally he'd never have given in so easily, but he wanted this boxed off quick.

"I'll give you one-fifty. Call into the bar. But not before seven."

Jareth lolled his head back, appealing to the yellowing ceiling tiles for mercy. "Can't you get it any…?"

Shit.

What was the point?

"Yeah, that's fine. I'll see you then."

He hung up and tossed the phone on top of his holdall. It seemed he was to be in town a few hours longer.

Whoop-de-fucking-doo.

He grabbed his jacket and the room key and headed out.

Chapter Eleven

The fine hairs on the back of Spook's neck bristled with intensity and she had a vague sense that she was about to pass out. But, regardless, she held her nerve while Acid sat on the couch in front of her and stared into the unlit fireplace.

"Why can't you do the right thing first time I ask? Why is it always such a battle with you?"

Acid snickered in that nasty sort of way teenagers did when asked to do chores, or indeed anything that didn't benefit them. But that was Acid Vanilla for you. An eternal moody teenager, driven by dark angst and self-obsession.

Most of the time Spook gave her a wide berth when she was like this. She knew what Acid had been through and gave her the benefit of the doubt as much as possible. It stood to reason, after killing her mother's attacker and being sent to a juvenile facility at an impressionable age, that she might suffer from arrested development. Being so bright and outwardly confident, it was easy to forget Acid Vanilla had a multitude of issues going on. Still, Spook had thought they'd been making ground lately in terms of her rehabilitation. She'd talked Acid into coming away on vacation, after all, and had reintroduced her idea for the Avenging Angels agency without getting it completely shot down. She had thought Acid was warming to the idea of helping people. But perhaps not.

It didn't help Spook that Cynthia was standing right next to her. Nor did it help that on the walk back to the cabin, she'd been telling her new friend all about Acid and how cool and highly skilled she was.

The person you want on your side when things go bad.

Those were Spook's exact words to Cynthia, spoken a few minutes earlier as they'd approached the cabin's front door. And now here that person was, sneering at any suggestion she might help. Not even looking their way.

"It sounds to me like this is a matter for the police, sweetie. Don't you?"

Spook bit her lip, tried to stay calm. "They're doing what they can but they're local cops, more used to dealing with traffic violations – or drunks." She gave the words some gusto, but if Acid picked up on it she didn't flinch. Spook went on. "They aren't cut out for situations like this. But you are. We are. We can help."

Acid turned to look at her. "You want me to work with the police?"

"No. I want you to help me and Cynthia find her dad."

"How, Spook? How do I do that?"

Spook swallowed. She hadn't thought that far in advance. "I don't know," she said, hoping more words would come to her. "But there's a possibility these bikers, the Streetwalkin' Cheetahs, have something to do with it. They're the ones you got into a fight with, yes?"

Acid snorted. "Those idiots? And you expect me to walk

into their clubhouse and demand they hand over the mayor. *Naughty bikers. You really shouldn't kidnap people!*" She shook her head and 'tsked' quietly to herself. "Anyway, sweetie, I've already told you, I'm leaving. I wondered whether your return meant you'd seen the error of your ways and were coming with me."

Spook chewed on her lip some more, heat rising up her throat as she felt the presence of the young woman at her side but couldn't look at her. "I told Cynthia we'd help her."

"Well, you shouldn't have done that, should you?"

"We need to help her!" She yelled the words, then stood rigid and defiant. Every bone in her body felt like it would shatter to dust in an instant, but she'd come too far, said too much.

"You help her," Acid said. "I'll see you back in London." She glared at Spook with a cruel smirk curling her lips. She was calling her bluff. Expecting her to back down.

But screw that. Wasn't going to happen.

Not this time.

"Okay. Fine," Spook replied, with as much nonchalance as she could.

It was in this moment – standing proud and with her head raised, whilst her heart pounded against her ribs and a million anxious thoughts fogged her brain – that Spook truly understood that clichéd duck metaphor. Serene on the surface of the pond, but with a flurry of unseen activity under the surface. She supposed, however, that - strong swimmers as they were - ducks would not experience this same sinking feeling. She pushed the words out before she had a chance to falter.

"I'm going to help her. On my own."

"Oh, don't be ridiculous." Acid got up off the couch

and moved across the room. In the doorway leading to her bedroom, she stopped and turned to Cynthia. "Look, kid. I'm sorry your father's gone missing, but this really is a job for the cops. Give them a few days, I'm sure they'll find him."

Cynthia nodded, but there were tears forming and it looked like she was doing all she could not to break down. "I don't know if they will. I don't know anything..."

Spook went to her and placed an arm around her shoulders. "I'm going to stay here with you. Acid's right, he will turn up. I'm sure of it. But there's no reason you have to go through this alone. Besides, my return plane ticket isn't for another four weeks. So I'm going to stay." She regarded Acid, telling her the same. "I'm staying here."

Acid rested her arm up against the doorframe and leaned her forehead into it. "Come on, Spook. You're being foolish."

"No. I'm not. I'm looking out for others. Helping people in need. Because that's what people should do. Especially those who understand all too well what it feels like to be scared and alone." She paused, realising her voice had risen substantially. "But you do what you want, Acid. Like you always do. I'll see you back in London. Come on, Cynthia. Let's get out of here."

She grabbed the still blubbering young woman by the arm and led her over to the door, moving fast before Acid hit back, or before she changed her mind. As she opened the door and the bright afternoon sun hit her in the face, she felt a rush of adrenaline shoot up her spine and a rush of fear just as strong. But she was committed. She was going to help Cynthia. And if Acid didn't like it, she could go to hell.

Chapter Twelve

Spook was out of the cabin and heading for the main street before the red mist parted enough she was able to speak, or indeed slow down. When she looked back, Cynthia was a good few paces behind, slouching along in a nervy fashion. It reminded her of how she used to be with Acid.

But not anymore.

"I'm sorry about her," she said, as Cynthia caught up with her. "I honestly thought she'd have stepped up to help."

"She seemed pissed about something. You guys had a fight?"

Spook considered the question. When were they not fighting about something? Disagreeing, at least. The problem was, Acid had a knack of always making Spook feel like she was the one in the wrong. Well, not this time.

"I knew it'd be a tough sell," she said. "And she's volatile at the best of times, but I had hoped she might have seen how important this is. But screw her. We don't need her. Like I told you already, I may not look like much but I've experienced a lot of scary shit these last few years and survived it all. It's made me strong."

Cynthia scanned her up and down. "Really?"

"Oh yeah. Try having not one but three elite assassins sent to kill you. Try getting thrown out of an airplane and land on an island full of sick billionaires eager to hunt and kill you. Try living with Acid Vanilla for two years." She laughed at that last one, but there was only shock on Cynthia's face, and the realisation of what Spook had just expressed made her belly sour.

"Are you actually serious?" Cynthia said. "But... how? Why?"

Spook scratched at her ear, scanning the street for some kind of distraction. There was nothing. "It's... umm... kind of a long story. I'll explain more later, but my point is we don't need Acid. We can find your dad. We will. Now, is there anything you can think of − anything at all − that might give us some clue as to what he was doing up on Crow Mountain?"

Cynthia's already substantial eyebrows grew heavy. She twisted her mouth to one side. "He kept a tight calendar for his business meetings, I know that. But he saved it on his computer and I don't have the password. I've been trying to get into it ever since he went missing."

At this, Spook smiled. "Oh, don't you worry about that," she said, feeling the tension Acid had induced drop away. "That is something I can most certainly help you with."

———

BACK AT CYNTHIA'S house on the other side of town, Spook hadn't told her new friend that she'd written her first code at the age of six, been a hacker since she was nine, and by thirteen had infiltrated the White House's secure network. She didn't want her thinking she was some kind of nerd. But she also couldn't hide her smug satisfaction when it took her all of twelve and a half minutes to get inside Mayor Donovan's iMac.

"I'm in," she announced, sitting back in the mayor's leather office chair as the machine chimed into life.

"As easy as that?" Cynthia called through from the kitchen where she was fixing them a drink.

"Easy for me," Spook replied, as the screen came up and a browser window automatically opened. Chrome. Not her browser of choice (like most hackers, she preferred Opera or Firefox), but it sure beat Safari. Next a welcome message appeared, seemingly from a productivity extension Cynthia's dad had installed.

Good day, Douglas Donovan.

What goals would you like to set today?

Spook clicked the message closed and opened the calendar app.

"That's amazing, Spook. I'm impressed."

Cynthia appeared at the desk with two large glasses of orange soda. She'd gotten changed and was now wearing a pair of cut-off denim shorts. On her top half she wore a strappy tank top and a pink cardigan which she pulled around herself once she'd placed the glasses on the computer desk.

"All in a day's work," Spook replied, forcing her eyes back to the screen.

She waited for Cynthia to settle herself in a chair beside her, then enlarged the calendar to full size.

He kept a tight calendar.

She wasn't joking. In silence, the two women scanned

the plethora of appointments and diary entries the mayor had made.

"When did you say he went missing?" Spook asked, reaching for the mouse and almost knocking over her glass of soda.

"Three days ago."

Focusing herself, Spook hovered the cursor over the relevant entry – Tuesday, seventh of September. She clicked it open and the two of them leaned forward to read what Douglas Donovan, the new mayor of Blackfell Ridge, had planned for that day.

Skim-reading and murmuring as she read, Spook ran down the list. "Pick up prescription… Meeting with LJ at the town hall…"

"That's Lorna James," Cynthia said. "She's on the council. She's nice. She worked on my daddy's campaign."

Spook narrowed her eyes, continued reading. "Lunch with C…"

"That's me. He couldn't make it in the end. Too busy."

"Hey, what's this?"

She sat back as Cynthia read the entry.

"Meet G. Crow M. 4 p.m."

Spook folded her arms. "You have any idea who this G person is?"

She looked at Cynthia for an answer, but the way she'd screwed her nose up answered the question.

"Do you think we should tell Chief Hunger?" Cynthia asked.

Spook removed her glasses and nipped up the edge of her t-shirt to clean the lens with the soft material. "Perhaps. It is new information."

Involving the cops would be the last thing Acid would have ever resorted to. She knew that. But what other option did they have? Any excitement Cynthia had exhibited in relation to Spook helping her had already faded away. Her entire body sagged, and the strain showed in her face.

"Are they good guys, the local cops?" Spook asked her. "I saw you before, arguing with one of them in the street."

"That was Trooper Crawford. He's a bit of prick, but I probably wasn't helping myself either. The rest of the cops around here seem fine. My dad got on well with Chief Hunger and Officer Brooke – he's the deputy, I think." She smiled weakly. "We should tell them what we've found out. It's a new lead, isn't it? That's what they say on the TV."

Spook returned the smile, dialling hers all the way up in the hope some positivity might rub off on her new friend. "That's right."

Cynthia's gaze dropped. "Thanks for helping, Spook. I don't know how I would have carried on if you hadn't found me. I was so distraught. So—"

"Hey, don't worry about it." She pushed back against the desk and got to her feet. "You ready?"

"Let me get my bag."

Spook watched her leave the room and then powered down her dad's computer. A part of her felt a little guilty – given the circumstances – that she was enjoying this new adventure. But she pushed those thoughts away. It was her anxiety talking. Besides, it wasn't as if adventure was the real reason she was doing this. She was here because she wanted to help someone in need. Because she was a decent human being, for Christ's sake. And because Acid wasn't always right. She didn't know everything. She'd made mistakes. Plenty of them. And anyway, she wasn't here.

"Ready." Cynthia appeared in the doorway.

Spook walked over and rested her hand on her shoulder. "Cool. Let's go tell the cops what we've discovered."

Chapter Thirteen

Aldous Hunger III scratched the inside of his thigh and considered the world outside his office window. A disgust that he felt in his chest twisted his face as he watched a mangy dog taking a dump against the old tree on the far side of the parking lot.

"Dirty beast."

His hand went instinctively to the handle of his piece, holstered on his hip. A Taurus Model 82 rather than the standard police-issue Beretta. He'd not had much cause to use his weapon since being transferred up to Blackfell Ridge, but he liked the fact he carried a revolver. He'd have preferred a real Smith & Wesson Model 10 – at one time the mainstay of law enforcement agencies in the United States – but this was the best he could get at short notice. And the 82 was an exact copy of the 10, so it still made him feel like an old-time sheriff from bygone times. Moving from the cut and thrust of LAPD's Vice department to this lame backwater, he had to sell it to himself somehow.

Lousy bastards.

How he missed the bustle and excitement of those mean neon streets – not to mention all the perks that came with that kind of work. It still irked Aldous what had happened. None of those righteous pricks had any kind of actual proof. But you throw enough shit, as they say. They were all younger cops, trying to make a name for themselves (trying to present themselves as chivalrous and woke to their female counterparts while they were at it). The way Aldous had seen it, he was helping everyone out. Those girls were hookers, for Christ's sake. What was another quick handjob between friends? His way they avoided a night in the slammer, or worse, and he got his rocks off and swerved a bunch of report writing. A win-win situation.

The dog finished curling out its mess and looked right at him. It had a stupid face and sad watery eyes, and Aldous had half a mind to open the window and blow the dirty mutt's brains out. It'd be more of a clean-up operation than the turd, of course, but he'd get Brooke or Earl to do it. It would certainly make him feel a whole lot better.

He turned from the window and sat behind his large rosewood desk. It didn't help matters he hadn't slept well these last few nights, but soon all the stress and worry would be over. Soon he'd be living it up like a movie star. Man, the girls he'd get with that kind of money would make those skanks from Vice look like flesh-eating zombies. The thought must have shown itself on his face, because as Brooke rapped his knuckles on the door and entered without waiting to be called (he always did that and Aldous despised him for it), he frowned in mock-surprise.

"Something tickle your fancy, Chief?"

Aldous sat upright and stuck out his chest. "I was thinking of a joke some fellow told me, is all. You wouldn't get it."

Brooke, standing to attention in front of his desk like a dumb GI Joe figurine, ignored the comment. "There's two young women out front want to see you."

"Oh?"

"One of them is Cynthia Donovan."

"I see." He pulled his lips back over his teeth. "How are we doing with the missing person case?"

Brooke frowned again, but serious now. The earnest prick. "I wanted to speak to you about that. I'm not sure we're making much ground. I think we need to put more men on it."

"More men?" Aldous spluttered out the words. "We don't have more men, son. We got me, you, Earl when he ain't got gut rot. Plus Trooper Crawford. Now be assured this case is important to me. And I am on it!"

"But Mayor Donovan's been missing going on seventy-six hours now and, it goes without saying, the first seventy-two are the most critical. It feels… I don't know… Like we're dragging our heels a little." Brooke stiffened and his Adam's apple rose and fell. He clearly wanted to say more, but he was being chickenshit about it.

Aldous sucked a piece of gristle out of his tooth. It had been bothering him all morning, and it felt like a small victory. He lowered his head and considered Brooke through wiry eyebrows. He wasn't a bad cop but, boy, was he green. He wouldn't have lasted five minutes in West Adams or Little Tokyo. In fact, Aldous had long suspected that if Brooke's old man hadn't been the chief around here (before the old coot's heart exploded and Aldous was hastily transferred into the role), his son would never have become a cop. A career as a farmer or Sunday school teacher was more up his alley.

"These girls say what they want?"

"Not really, Chief. Said they needed to speak with you."

"Fine. Show them in."

As Brooke scurried out, Aldous got to his feet. He strolled over to the window, positioning himself the way he always did, head turned away from the door, body twisted to extenuate his waist and shoulders, thumbs looped through his belt. Standing like this, he knew it made him look important. Like a cop on TV. Like a good cop should look.

He heard the door open and footsteps shuffle into the room. "Can I help you, ladies?" he asked, turning his head slowly.

Young Cynthia Donovan, wearing itty bitty short shorts and a thin cardigan top, stood in the centre of the room. The other girl he hadn't seen before. She was shorter than Cynthia and looked to be from East Asian stock, with round, thick-rimmed glasses and straight black hair. He couldn't place her age, but assumed her to be the same as Cynthia, early twenties. Although, it was always harder to tell with Orientals. He'd found that out to his cost. This girl, however, was as far removed from the young girls of Koreatown as it was possible to be. Dressed in black jeans and an oversized hoodie, she was clearly a dyke. Behind the girls, Henry Brooke Jr. hovered in the doorway like a nasty smell.

"I was hoping you might have some news about my dad," Cynthia said. Her voice was soft but went vibrato towards the end of her statement.

"Ah, Cynthia," he said, turning fully to face her and holding out his hands. "You look worn out. Have you had any sleep?"

She sniffed and shook her head.

"We're doing all we can. I promise you that." He lowered his voice, speaking as slowly as possible without tempering any of the compassion. "I've got my best men on the case and I'm personally overseeing the investigation. But right now, I'll be honest, we've hit somewhat of an impasse."

"We might have some information that could help," the second girl announced, stepping forward. "I'm Spook, by the way. Spook Horowitz."

She held her hand out to him.

"Spook Horowitz?" He shook her limp fingers, glancing over at Brooke, who shrugged. "That is quite a name you got there."

"So they tell me," she said. "And thanks for seeing us, Chief. Like I say, I think we've found something that might help."

She was forthright this one, he'd give her that.

But Spook? Really? Come on.

He held a finger up, instigating some control over the situation before she had a chance to continue. "Won't you ladies both have a seat?"

He gestured at the wooden chairs that he'd shoved against the wall yesterday afternoon (he'd needed the floor space to practice his putting game and had forgotten to place them back in front of his desk). As the girls dragged the shabby chairs over, he returned to his large black-leather chief's chair and sat. Meeting Brooke's eye, he waved him away with a flick of his wrist, before turning his attention back to the girls sitting opposite.

"You said you have information?"

"I think so. I mean… Yes. We do." Cynthia's eyes flittered between him and Spook. "No one seems to know why he was up on Crow Mountain, why our car was found up there, but we got onto his computer and saw an entry in his calendar. *Meet G at Crow Mountain.*"

"And then a time. 4 p.m.," the one called Spook added, beaming like she'd cracked the Zodiac Killer's cypher.

"I see," Aldous replied, with little emphasis on his part. "And do you have any idea who 'G' refers to?"

Cynthia looked into her lap. "No. Not at all."

It was tragic how sad she was. He didn't know the kid well, but she was always polite and good-natured when they passed each other in the town, or on that one occasion when he'd called in to see Donovan at home. It was a shame she had to go through this.

"G," he repeated, muttering it to himself over and over. "G... G... G... I don't suppose it could be...? Nah... Although..."

"What?" the two girls asked as one.

"Hmm. I'm not sure I should say." He jammed his tongue into his top molars, searching for the piece of gristle he'd forgotten was gone. When he found nothing, he grimaced and sat forward. "I don't want to worry you unnecessarily, Cynthia. Not before I have a chance to look into it myself."

"Please, Chief Hunger. I can't sleep. I can't eat. Tell me what you're thinking. I promise it won't be as bad as the hundred and one awful scenarios I've been picturing these last three days."

Aldous Hunger III grasped his hands together on the desk in front of him. He shook his head, looked away, sighed. When he turned back to Cynthia, he saw by her reaction she understood this would be just between them.

"There is a G I'm thinking of. A man called Donny Rivers."

"Donny Rivers?" Cynthia said. "I know that name. But it doesn't begin with G."

"He goes by the name Donny Guitar, or just Guitar.

He's the vice president of that there biker gang, the Street-walkin' Cheetahs."

As he said the name, the two girls snapped a look at each other. That told him they'd already been talking about the Cheetahs and their likely involvement.

"I don't think it's him," Cynthia said. "And even if it was, why would my daddy be meeting Donny Guitar half-way up Crow Mountain?"

"That's what we need to find out. And by *we*, I mean *us*. Blackfell Ridge PD." He waved a finger at the two of them. "You did good bringing this to me, you hear? But I don't want you getting any more involved. That motorcycle club is bad news, and this is a police matter."

"But what if it's not—"

"I said, leave it." He cut the Asian off dead. She was getting up his damn nose. "I mean that. Do you hear me? Both of you?" He waved his finger with more force, staring down the girls until they nodded.

"Yes."

"Yeah."

"Good. Now if you don't mind, I need to get on." He stood and gestured at the door. "Soon as I know anything, Cynthia, I'll let you know. But for the time being, try to get some rest. Like I told you, we still have faith we'll find your pop safe and well."

"Thanks."

Aldous remained standing as the Asian linked Cynthia's arm in hers (yeah, he was right about her) and led her to the door. As she opened it, Cynthia turned back, about to say something.

"We'll find him," he said before she could speak, holding up a fist in solidarity. It was an empty gesture but it seemed to help. She smiled feebly before the two girls shuffled out.

"Jesus H Christ," he muttered to himself, sinking into his chair.

"Everything all right, Chief?" Brooke appeared in the open doorway. "We got a new lead?"

"Maybe. They said Donovan was meeting someone with the initial G on the day he went missing."

Brooke scrunched up his face. "Any ideas?"

"Unfortunately, yes. I'm thinking Donny 'Guitar' Rivers."

"O-kay," Brooke said, gripping onto the back of one of the chairs. "I can see why you came to that conclusion about the initial. But why would they be meeting?"

"I'm not sure. But those dirty bastards have got motive and means in spades."

Brooke looked up. "Do you think he's dead?"

"Again. Not sure. I didn't tell Cynthia that, of course. Poor kid. You got to feel sorry for her."

Brooke blew out a silent whistle. "You going to see the Cheetahs?"

"Top of my list."

"I'll come with you."

Aldous bared his teeth. "No. You stay here. Man the fort in case of any further developments."

"But, Chief, I—"

Aldous slammed his fist down on the desk. "I said, no."

"Hell's teeth." Brooke jumped back, making Aldous rethink his approach.

"Listen, Brooke – Henry – I know you don't like me too much. But you've got me wrong, I swear. Yes, I've done things in the past that I'm not proud of. But that ain't me no more. I am an officer of the law, and it is my job to ensure the good folk of Blackfell Ridge feel safe and are kept safe. No child should have to go through what Cynthia Donovan is. But it's down to those disgusting devils on their Harley Davidsons. If they are involved in the mayor's disappearance, then I'll find out, and I'll make them pay. All of them." He slammed his fist down again, and this time Brooke stood up straight; the disdain that was written all over his face a few moments earlier, replaced now with something closer to respect.

"I appreciate you saying that, Chief. I feel exactly the same. You know, my daddy used to always say—"

"Thank you, son. That'll be all for now. I'm certain we both have work to do."

"Oh yes. Sure thing, Chief. Very good."

The stupid bastard went to salute him before turning on his overly shined boots and marching out of the room. Aldous walked to the door and shut it behind him. He listened at the glass for a few seconds as Brooke's clip-clop gait disappeared down the corridor. Then he moved back around his desk and picked up the phone. By now he knew the number from memory, and after two rings a gruff voice answered.

"Chief Hunger. I thought we weren't talking for a while."

"Yeah, well, something's come up," Aldous replied. "Could be nothing, could be something."

"Shi-it, you know I hate cryptic bullshit. Talk to me."

Aldous raised his head, eyes on the door. He saw no movement on the other side of the frosted glass, but his heart thumped heavy in his chest all the same. "Not on the phone. Let's meet up."

The line went silent and Aldous rolled his neck to one side. He'd been holding himself tight these last ten minutes.

"Usual place. Usual time," came the answer. Then the phone went dead.

Aldous replaced the receiver in its cradle and resumed his stance at the window. The old dog was nowhere to be seen, but he saw the pile of turds it had left behind.

This fucking town.

He walked over to the coat stand in the corner of the room and unhooked his bomber jacket, slipping it on as he left the office. He told Brooke and the others he was going to get some lunch, that he'd be back in an hour.

An hour.

Plenty of time for what he had to do.

Chapter Fourteen

The promise of a pleasant day faded as it drifted into late afternoon. The sun had disappeared behind a thick bank of grey clouds as Acid left the cabin, slamming the door behind her. It was a pointless gesture, Spook having flounced out four hours ago and yet to return, but it made her feel better. For one second, at least.

"Stupid, dumb kid," she mumbled to herself, as she lowered her suitcase onto the street. "Get yourself killed, see if I care."

Not that she believed that would be the case. Spook was impetuous and had enough neuroses to keep a team of shrinks busy for the rest of their lives, but she was also super-intelligent and was more experienced than most in high-pressure situations. The kid wasn't a kid anymore (never had been, in all fairness). She could handle herself.

Standing in front of the cabin, Acid scanned left and right down the street. She saw no sign of her, but she didn't expect to.

Whatever… See you back in London.

"Well, there you go," she told herself. "You finally managed it."

Her manic and chaotic nature notwithstanding, Acid was self-aware enough to know she'd been systematically pushing Spook away ever since they'd met. Like she had done with every single person she'd ever got close to. It was a pattern. A safety mechanism. There for good reason once, but now she wasn't so sure.

She set off towards the train station on the other side of town. From there she'd get a connection to a place called Lower Rattlesnake, before a seven-hour train journey took her to Bozeman Yellowstone International Airport. Her plan was to get the first available flight out of there and hoped the journey would allow her time to unwind, to relax and reflect. Of course, this trip away was supposed to do all of those things, but maybe what she really needed was the imposed solitude and air-conditioned penance only long-haul plane travel could provide. And there was always the refreshments trolley.

Up on main street Acid put her head down and quickened her step, trundling her wheeled suitcase along in her wake and making more noise than she'd have liked to have done. But even late afternoon, a time when most towns and cities were at their busiest, Blackfell Ridge was quiet and serene. At a crossroads she paused, casting her gaze down the wide empty streets, narrowing her eyes at a couple of young girls walking in the opposite direction. One of them was wearing the same stupid red hat as Spook, but as Acid watched on she realised her movements were all wrong. The strides were bouncy and confident, whereas Spook favoured a flat-footed shuffle.

That settled it then.

Spook wasn't coming. But so what. Let her play detective with her new friend for a few weeks. Acid would see her back in London. Maybe then – once properly rested and with time for them both to cool off – they'd sit down and talk about their future.

Bugger.

Wasn't that the eternal bloody question? What the hell did one do with a life spent on the right side of the law? Every single option seemed so dull, so... not her.

She was about to set off again when something caught her eye across the street. It was lying on the ground in a narrow alleyway that ran down the side of two buildings. She wouldn't have spotted it except for the bright red material standing out against the grey asphalt. With her breath frozen in her chest, she crossed the street for a closer inspection.

"Spook..."

She knelt down and picked up the scarlet beret. It was relatively clean. Acid stood and looked around.

"Spook?" she called out. "Anyone there?"

But except for a young couple walking arm and arm on the other side of the street, there was no one around.

Clutching the beret to her chest, dragging her suitcase behind her she moved further along the alley. The shadows from the buildings on either side made it hard to see, but on close inspection she saw a hint of footprints in the dust. They told her whoever had been here was moving at pace. Further along, she noticed a skid mark, as if someone had slipped over. If that was Spook, she probably lost the beret at the same time. But why was she running?

"For heaven's sake."

Acid kicked her suitcase. She couldn't go anywhere now. Not until she knew Spook was safe. She lifted the beret to her face. It smelled of apple and mango. Spook's shampoo.

"Where the hell are you, kid?"

She set off back to the cabin. She needed to drop off her cumbersome suitcase, at least, if she was to conduct a proper search of the area. As she stormed across the street, a million tiny bat wings beat against her nervous system. Screw it. Rest and relaxation, be damned. It was the twin drivers of pain and rage that were now in charge.

No rest for the wicked.

Head down, she barged through a group of people milling around outside the post office, muttering to herself as she went.

"Stupid fucking civilians…"

Her case knocked against the side of the building and spun off its wheels, but she didn't stop, dragging the damn thing behind her with the canvas front scraping against the ground. She had to find Spook. And soon. If those bastard bikers really were behind this, she'd—

"Hey. Watch where you're going."

She bounced off someone coming the other way.

"Piss off, will you? Oh." She looked up into the face of a cop. Thankfully, not one she'd dealt with previously. This one regarded her with kind eyes, full of concern.

"You okay?" he asked and smiled, causing his feeble attempt at a moustache to spread, caterpillar-like, across his top lip.

"Sorry," she mumbled. "I'm a little stressed."

She tried to manoeuvre around him, but he side-stepped in front of her. "Wait a minute. I recognise you. Weren't you in the station yesterday morning?"

Acid stopped and glared at the sky. "Yes, that's right. But it was a misunderstanding. Can I get past, please?"

"Where are you heading in such a hurry?" He stepped back and took her in. "Hey, where'd you get that? The hat?"

Acid held it up. "It belongs to my friend. I'm looking for her." She concentrated all her energy on not elbowing him in the throat.

"Strange," he said. "I know the young lady who was wearing that hat. I remember because she got me humming Raspberry Beret to myself. You know, the Prince number?"

Acid stuck her tongue up under her top lip and nodded. "Uh-huh."

"She was over at the station, talking with the chief."

"When?"

"About an hour ago," he said. "She was with Cynthia Donovan. I think the two of them are friends."

"Yes, that's right," Acid spat. "They were looking for Cynthia's father. Wanted me to help. They mentioned something about the Cheetahs. The local biker gang. Do you think she might have gone to their clubhouse? Do you know where it is?"

He stepped back and held his hands up. "Now, miss. That's police business. I'm not sure I can divulge such—"

"I need to find her." She sucked back a shuddering breath, letting her lip quiver as she did and making sure he saw it. "Please. I'm very worried indeed, Officer."

The cop smiled and gave an empathetic nod. "Deputy Brooke's the name. And I get it, you're concerned. But I can't have you barging into people. You nearly sent old Mr Tucker flying back there. Why don't you come to the station with me and we can talk some more? I'm sure your friend is fine…"

He trailed off as though he'd remembered something and it had knocked his train of thought.

"What? What is it? Do you think she's in danger?"

"No. Of course not. Neither of them are."

"But she was with Cynthia."

"I already told you that."

"Then I need to make a move," she said. "I have to find them before they do anything stupid."

"Miss. I said I want you to come to the station." His expression had turned stony.

Fucking cops.

"What? You're arresting me?"

"You're clearly distressed, and if your friend has gone missing, then it might be in conjunction with another case we're working on. That's all I can say right now. Look, I'm parked over there. It's only a two-minute drive and, once there, you can make a statement, provide some details on your friend." His moustache bowed over a genuine smile. "Don't worry, miss. I'm police. I'll look after you."

Jesus.

She'd maybe gone too far with the old damsel in distress routine. But the last thing she needed was to piss off the local PD and get thrown back in jail. Besides, her instincts told her this guy knew something.

She fluttered her eyelashes. "Thank you, Officer," she said. "I appreciate it."

———

"YOU DID WHAT? Where the hell is she?"

Acid was sitting in Deputy Henry Brooke's office, so couldn't see who was yelling, but she recognised the voice.

Wonderful.

Absolutely pissing perfect.

She sat, adjusting her poise and pout (her poison pout) ready to face him. A second later Aldous Hunger III strode into the office. Deputy Brooke followed on behind, not looking at her as the chief marched up to her chair and loomed over her.

"What a surprise. I thought you'd be half-way back to the UK about now."

Acid gestured at the suitcase by her feet. "I wish I was, believe you me. Yet, here we are."

Without taking his eyes off her, Hunger grabbed a chair from in front of the desk and spun it into position opposite her. Then he made a big show of sitting down and adjusting the cuffs on his pants. When he looked up, his face was rigid and without emotion.

"Deputy Brooke tells me you're worried about your friend. Now why is that? She a trouble-causer too?"

"No. She's good as gold. But I found her beret and I don't think she'd have left it lying in an alley like that. Something must have happened to her."

"Something?"

Acid held his gaze, her face still but her brain turning over at a million miles per second. How much did he know? How much could she tell him?

"She was here earlier, wasn't she?" She looked over at Brooke, but he wouldn't meet her eye. In fact, the question seemed to make him shrink a few inches. When she looked back at Hunger, his face had a stern quality to it she found disconcerting. But it wasn't anger, per se, more like contempt.

"She was indeed," he replied, his voice quiet. "I think your friend fancies herself as a private investigator or the like. I told her she should stay out of police business. That we'd investigate any claims ourselves."

"What claims? What do you mean?" Deputy Brooke finally raised his head to look at her and she turned to address him direct. "What does he mean, police business?"

"The chief believes the Cheetahs might be involved in the mayor's disappearance," he replied, as Hunger twisted in his chair to glare at him. "We're looking into it."

"But don't you see," Acid said, "if Spook and Cynthia believe the same, they might have gone to the Cheetahs' clubhouse."

"I told those girls, specifically, to leave well enough alone," Hunger spat, turning back to her. "And I'm telling you the same. Those are bad people and this is a police matter. Jesus H. Christ, the mayor goes missing and all of a sudden the town's overrun by goddamn vigilantes." He leaned forward, stubbing a finger into the palm of his other hand, speaking slow. "Leave it to the police. Let us do our job."

Acid sat back, feeling the hard wood of the chair against her shoulder blades and trying to ignore the screeching in her head. Her eyes fell on a metal letter opener on Brooke's desk. She could grab it and thrust it into his upper thigh before he knew what had happened. Straight into the femoral artery. Leave him to bleed out. He'd be dead in under five minutes. Condescending prick.

She remained still. "But you'll check this out? You'll talk with the Cheetahs?"

"I was on my way to do just that when you two showed up."

"Where is their clubhouse?"

Hunger made a face. "I'm not divulging that information. All you need to know is I'm on it. Okay? Now, can I get on?"

"Yes." She moved her chair back and got to her feet. "But you'll let me know as soon as you know anything? I'm staying in one of those log cabins on the other side of town. Fifth along from the road."

She looked from Hunger to Brooke, who shot her the briefest of nods. She smiled, told them both thanks, promised again she'd leave them to it and grabbed up he suitcase. Then, for the second time in as many days she was escorted out of the police station.

"Don't worry yourself," Brooke told her as they got outside. "The chief can be a little bullish, but he's a good cop. He'll find your friend. I'm sure of it."

"I hope so." She lowered her head and peered up at him through her eyelashes. "Where did you say the Cheetahs' clubhouse was?"

Brooke folded his arms. "I didn't, and you shouldn't be asking. You heard what the chief said."

"You're right. I did hear. And I'm sorry. I'm curious, that's all. Of course I won't go up there. What am I going to do, confront a gang of vicious bikers? I don't think so." She stuck out her bottom lip, moving effortlessly from damsel in distress to coquettish innocent. "If you don't want to tell me, that's fine. I'm sure I can find out easily enough."

Brooke looked over his shoulder. When he looked back, his voice was low and his eyes wide. "It's over on the edge of town, at the base of Crow Mountain. Take the road that leads down the side of the town hall and follow it to the end."

Acid smiled. He seemed an actual decent guy. For a cop. Dumb as shit and as wet as a baby's arse, but decent. "Thank you," she whispered.

"You didn't hear that from me," he told her. "And don't do anything stupid. Promise me."

"Aww, of course I won't do anything stupid." She touched his arm. "I'm actually incredibly sensible and boring. I'll see you around."

She turned, flicking her hair over her shoulder and

leaving Brooke standing in the doorway. She sensed his eyes on her all the way to the end of the block and made sure she gave her hips extra sway.

At the corner, she stopped. "Police matter, my arse," she muttered to herself, before giving Brooke a flirtatious salute and dragging her suitcase down the next street. "This is my domain."

If those miserable bikers hurt Spook in any way, she'd destroy every single last one of them. Troubled relationship or not, the prospect of losing the kid didn't bear thinking about. It was time to get back in the saddle, time for Alice Vandella to go back in her box, and for Acid Vanilla to step unabashed into the spotlight.

Spook needed her.

The game was on.

Chapter Fifteen

Acid didn't shut the door of the cabin. After making a beeline for her room, she dumped her case on the bed and headed back outside. The sun had remained hidden for the rest of the afternoon, but now night was falling. The emerald-coloured trees that climbed up the side of the mountain looked washed out in the dusk light, like a watercolour painting. The thought had crossed Acid's mind to make a detour to the local hunting shop on her way to the Cheetahs' clubhouse. To buy herself some insurance in the shape of the Ruger she'd seen displayed in the window on their first day in town. But, no. Even if the shop had been open at this late hour, this was a small community. It wouldn't take long, she suspected, for news to get back to Chief Hunger that the weird English woman had been eager to purchase a large hunting pistol. And anyway, she was still hopeful this was an error on her part. The niggling energy of the bats, coupled with the jet lag, sending her paranoid. Either way, this was to be a stealth mission. She'd approach the clubhouse in the shadows and see if any clues showed themselves. No point bursting in with guns blazing until she knew what she was dealing with.

Brooke had said to follow the road down the side of the town hall. No problem. But as she turned into the street that led to the base of the mountain, she skidded to a halt.

"Bugger. Bollocks."

Jareth Hicks was walking towards her.

She thought about turning back, except he'd already seen her. Besides, for some bizarre reason she got a good vibe from this guy. He was tough, though with an air of defiant charm she couldn't help but appreciate. Plus he was ex-military and didn't ask too many questions. He could be useful.

But as he got closer, she saw his eyes were fixed on the ground and his jaw rigid. When he was a few steps away, giving every impression he wasn't going to stop, she moved in front of him.

"Hey. It's me." She waved her hands in front of his face. He stopped, shooting her only a brief glance.

"Yep. It's you." He raised his head, looking past her towards the centre of town. "Where are you running off to this time of night? You got yourself in trouble again?"

"More than likely." She tilted her head to catch his eye, and as she did he smiled. "I'm sorry about before. You okay?"

He stuck out his bottom lip, play-acting. "I'll live. My pride will too, just about. And I apologise as well. Last thing you want is some guy jumping on you when you've come away for peace and quiet. Well, you know, as peaceful as it gets for people like us, I guess."

"People like us?"

He considered her out of the corner of one eye. "I'd say we're similar, me and you, Alice, Acid, whatever you want to be called. We both have dark pasts we'd rather not talk about. Can both handle ourselves when we want to."

"When we need to, you mean."

"I don't know. Looked to me you enjoyed teaching those sons of bitches a lesson the other night. Something in your eyes."

She lowered her chin. "In my eyes?"

"Yeah. A glimmer of delight, let's call it." He paused, both eyes on her now, trying to get a read once again. He shook his head. "Well, anyway, like I was saying, maybe we're too similar. We'd end up killing each other."

He laughed, like it was a joke, but the thought had crossed her mind. Not least the fact – his negative experiences with the army notwithstanding – he was still ex-military. He might profess his hatred for the US Army and the good old CIA for what they did to him, but you don't spend two decades intrenched in a certain code just to about-face and take a new ethical path. This was something Acid knew all too well. She looked up at Jareth, already pissed at herself for what she was about to say.

"I need your help." She lowered her voice as she spoke. "My friend, Spook, has gone missing and I think the Cheetahs might have something to do with it."

"Those guys? But why?"

Acid glanced around, squinting into the shadows on both sides of the street. "She's gotten friendly with this girl, the daughter of the mayor, the guy who's missing. They came to me, asked if I'd help them look for him. I said no. But I've been talking with the local PD and they've placed the Cheetahs as prime suspects in the mayor's disappearance."

Jareth stared at her, his expression one of confusion. "Didn't we already suspect they were involved? Digging graves up in the mountains days after the mayor goes missing. It all points a certain way."

"You don't seem shocked."

"Nothing shocks me these days."

"And you're not bothered? A military man like you?"

"*Ex*-military. These days I follow my own path. And my own set of rules."

Jesus. It was like he'd read her mind earlier and was now weaving his way in.

No.

Stay focused.

She stiffened. "My friend is in danger. I know it."

Jareth sighed, his shoulders relaxed. "You know, one of those rules I just mentioned is that in times of conflict I ask myself a simple question. What would my daddy do in this situation?"

"And what would he do?"

"He'd tell you to go fuck yourself," he replied. "My father is a well-respected man in some areas of his life, but a total shitbag in others. He doesn't care for anyone except himself and certainly wouldn't help out a stranger. Even one who was – what was it we said – kinda scary-looking but hot as hell?"

Acid felt her cheeks burn and gritted her teeth.

No.

Stop it.

Really!

She sniffed. "So you won't help me. Great. Thanks a bunch."

"Hang on. Let me finish. I answer myself that question, then I make sure I do the exact opposite. That way I know I'm nothing like the bitter old fuck."

Acid looked up. "So you will help me?"

Jareth let out another heavy sigh, more dramatic and pointed than before. "Well, you caught me on the hop just now. And another of those rules of mine is to know when it's time to say 'fuck it' and move on. That's a big one for me."

Acid chewed on the inside of her cheek, trying to stay calm. Time was ticking away. "So...?"

"All right," he said. "I'll help you look for your friend. But we aren't going blazing in like a couple of hotheads. We need to get a plan together first."

She kept her eyes on his as a smile formed. "Blaze in where like a couple of hotheads?"

"Well, the Cheetahs' clubhouse, of course. I'm assuming that's where you're heading. But I still don't see why they'd take your friend if—"

"A plan is great. I love a good plan." Acid called back, already striding down the street, the energy of a thousand tiny bat wings fluttering up her spine and down her limbs. At the end of the street she paused and gestured for him to follow. "Come on, soldier boy, let's show these damn bikers what we're made of."

Chapter Sixteen

Pushing through wet leaves and navigating treacherous terrain, Jareth led Acid up the side of Crow Mountain. They stuck to the same track he'd found a few days earlier, the one that snaked around the mountain away from the town and came out on a ledge a hundred metres above the MC's clubhouse. When he'd first discovered the Street-walkin' Cheetahs' headquarters, he was struck by how idyllic it appeared, log-built and sitting in its own grounds surrounded by luscious greenery and chattering wildlife. A far cry from the clubhouses he'd encountered in Oakland or Santa Cruz. Indeed, the headquarters of most of these organised crime gangs (which is what they were, at the end of the day) were grim, shadowy buildings. In comparison, the Cheetahs' place was an idyllic country retreat.

Not that there wasn't danger here. Until two days ago, Jareth had never had any run-ins with motorcycle clubs. Yet he'd heard enough stories about how they conducted themselves, and their approach to anyone who threatened their way of life, to know that you screwed with them at your peril.

So what the hell are you doing here, champ?

He stopped to wait for Acid to catch up. She was a few feet behind him, negotiating her way around a particular handsy tree hanging out over the path.

"How you doing over there?"

She snapped off the intrusive branch and bent it back on itself. "Oh, I'm peachy." She glared up at him with a dark expression. But on making eye contact, a smile escaped her. She looked away. "Piss off."

Ah, yeah.

That was why he was doing this.

Because she'd asked him to.

She got up to him. "How much further is it?"

"Not far." He peered through the moonlit undergrowth. They'd almost reached the highest point of the path, where it levelled out. He beckoned her to look. "See there how the track winds down the other side? It comes out around the back of the Cheetahs HQ. There's plenty of tree cover, meaning we can get down there and scope the place out without anyone seeing us. *If* we're careful."

"Hey. I'm always careful." She pushed past him.

Jareth watched her as she dealt with a spiky flowering shrub, stamping down on its prickly branches to clear a way. She was a piece of work and no mistake. But he'd be damned if she wasn't the most enigmatic and fascinating person he'd met in a long time. Most people were full of pretty words with empty meanings. They spent so much time overthinking life they never had a chance to live it. But not her. She spoke her mind and seemed to act purely from instinct. He liked that. It was refreshing. It was also dangerous.

He traced her route through the spiny undergrowth and joined her on the ledge overlooking the clubhouse. "From what I remember, there's a courtyard out front with a fire pit and a big seating area," he whispered. "It's a decent enough night. I'd suggest we get in position as soon as possible."

"Then what?"

"We wait. Once they're all out front partying, we can sneak in the back. Go in through the bike store."

"Easy as that." She glanced up at him, her expression showing him what she thought of his idea.

"You got a better plan?"

She turned back and muttered something. Sounded to him like, *Not without a couple of decent semi-automatics.*

"What did you say?"

"Nothing. Forget it."

They headed down the sloping track in silence until they got to another area of dense vegetation where Jareth took the lead, pushing back the encroaching foliage and holding it aside for Acid to pass through. Like he might have done at the door of a fancy restaurant in different (very different) circumstances.

A couple of decent semi-automatics.

Jareth had never met a British person with an interest in firearms. He'd worked alongside British soldiers, but that was different. Brits didn't go for guns the way Americans did. Especially not women.

To shift the unhelpful thoughts from his mind, he cast his gaze up into the night sky. The air was clear and over in the east the sliver of a new moon shone down from its inky backdrop. Over to the right he spotted Orion and then the Great Bear, constellations he remembered from childhood. Back then, to the young Jareth, they symbolised the vastness of nature, of opportunity and grandeur. Now they made him think of other things. The last time he'd seen the stars this bright was in Afghanistan, the night before the ambush. Perhaps one reason he'd been kicking his heels in LA for so long. With its perpetual smog cover, there was zero chance of seeing the stars.

The low rumble of music drifted up to them and, as Jareth stopped to focus on the noise, he heard shouts and peals of gruff laughter. They were close.

"There," he said, peering through the trees. "Can you see? Down to the left."

He stepped around the back of her and rested his hand on her shoulder. The clubhouse lights were on and there were already people sitting out front. From this viewpoint it was hard to make out faces, but they were all decked out in the emblematic trappings of their tribe: long hair, beards, faded denim and leather.

"The place is grander than I imagined," Acid whispered. "How many of them do you think there are?"

Jareth did a quick scan of the courtyard. "I've encountered maybe ten different members since I've been in town. But there could be three times that amount. At least. I make seventeen bikes parked up over there. Doesn't mean there aren't more of them. See the bike store around back? That's our way in. You ready?"

He tightened his grip on Acid's shoulder. She didn't flinch. If anything, she seemed to lean into him. But as she twisted around a second later, her face was stern and her eyes cold.

"I'm ready," she said. "Let's get down there."

Walking side-on, to better steady themselves on the steep incline, they shifted down the last stretch of the uneven path until they got to the base of the mountain.

Here the terrain was flat, but there was enough foliage and tree cover they'd remain unseen while they worked out their next move.

"Looks like the party has started," Jareth whispered, as he parted the branches. From this position they could see most of the courtyard, where more Cheetahs had assembled, along with some of their women-folk who were giving as good as they got in terms of the loud jeers and laughter filling the air. The fire pits had been lit and someone had turned the thrash metal music coming from the stereo all the way up.

Acid edged up beside him to see. "I can't see Spook," she whispered. "But they wouldn't have her or the mayor out on display. We need to get inside."

Jareth moved his focus away from the courtyard to the bike store and garage on the opposite side of the building. There, too, a light was on – a bright, raw halogen bulb attached to the back wall, which sent long spindly shadows stretching across the garage forecourt.

Goddamn it.

Some of the shadows were moving. Cheetahs working on their bikes, perhaps. The other option was they kept their supplies back there and it was someone rolling out a keg. But either way, the area wasn't safe.

With his eyes on the garage, he didn't look at Acid as she rasped the words, "Ah, shit."

"Don't worry," he whispered. "We'll wait it out."

"No. Jareth."

Her voice sounded strange. And as he turned, he understood why. His gaze darted from her eyes to the large hunting knife held at her throat, then to the angry face of the man with no neck standing behind her.

"Sonofa—" Jareth instinctively raised his hands as something hard shoved into his kidneys.

"Looks like we've found ourselves a couple of peeping Toms," a voice behind him snarled. "You two fuckheads gluttons for punishment?"

Jareth didn't take his eyes from Acid's. "It's not like that," he said. "We were just…"

"Just what?" The one called Turtle spat, pressing the blade against the thin skin where Acid's jaw met her neck. "Spying on us?"

Her eyes burned with an intensity that enlivened and worried Jareth in equal measures. "We don't want any trouble," she said, despite her face saying different. She locked eyes with him and gave the briefest of nods. "We were out for a walk, that's all. It's a pleasant night. We fancied a moonlight stroll."

Turtle grinned a hideous grin. All grubby teeth and gums. "Bullshit, bitch. We know your kind. Always making out that— Unff."

He reeled back as Acid elbowed him in the face. It was a risky move, but Jareth saw it coming where Turtle hadn't. As the sharp edge of Acid's humerus bone connected with the biker's nose, Jareth twisted around and grabbed hold of the pistol held against him, pushing it to one side. In the same movement he struck the blade of his hand into the man's Adam's apple, sending him staggering away, spluttering for air. In the confusion, he grabbed for the hand holding the gun and clawed at the fingers around the handle.

"Go to hell," the guy snarled in his ear. "I'll fucking kill you."

He held on with all he had as they wrestled against each other. Jareth was a big guy, almost six-four when he didn't slouch, but his sparring partner was just as big. Strong, too. Add dangerously pumped to the mix and all signs said this wouldn't be an easy fight. A fist to the face caught him unawares and knocked the focus out of him. The rich dark greens of the forest swirled around him, but he didn't go down. In fact he felt stronger than ever as the powerful, numbing adrenaline made itself known in his system. But where was the guy? Where was the gun? Disorientated, he spun around, seeing Turtle standing in front of him with blood gushing down his face. Then he saw Acid, with the sharp point of the knife blade against the nape of Turtle's neck. One vicious movement and she'd sever his spinal cord.

She had him.

Jareth grinned. *Nice work.* But Acid was shaking her head. She yelled at him, but the words were muffled, almost incoherent. He felt a presence behind him. A hand gripping his shoulder. Then his head collided with something hard and heavy, and as the earth rushed up to meet him, all he thought was, this isn't part of the plan.

Chapter Seventeen

With a hand on her upper arm and stubby fingers digging into her flesh, Turtle bundled Acid out into the open. Behind her she heard Jareth mumbling something about everything being okay, but he was semi-conscious and not making a great deal of sense.

"You don't have to yank me around so much," she told Turtle. "I'll come quietly."

"Shut your damn mouth, bitch."

She did, but not because he'd told her. As the bats nibbled noisily at her synapses, she scoped the area; clocked the building to the left, the courtyard spanning out in front of them, the tables, chairs and fire pits with what appeared to be the entire membership of the Streetwalkin' Cheetahs sitting around them. She counted over thirty, before they got to the clubhouse and a fat man with a bulbous scar running down the length of his face approached them.

"Johnny? Turtle?" he yelled, swaggering over. "What happened to you guys? Who are these folks?"

He was older than the others, mid to late fifties if Acid

had to guess. He wore an oil-smeared bandana around his head and the expression of someone who held more resentment than reason.

"Found ourselves some snakes in the grass, Beau," Turtle told him. "These are the two fuckheads who jumped Lance and me the other night over at Al's place."

Beau regarded Acid with a curled lip. "You been causing trouble for my brothers, huh?

"That's not how I remember it," she replied. "We didn't want any trouble then and we don't now. I'm looking for my friend and—"

"We want to speak to the manager," Jareth mumbled, as he was shoved into her. He had a large gash on his forehead and blood was running down the side of his face.

She nudged him. "All right, Jareth. Calm it down. You okay?"

"Uh-huh."

"Pieces of shit, the both of 'em," Turtle said. "They've disrespected me not once, but twice. That ain't cool, Beau. You know it. We need to show them what happens to people who disrespect our club."

Beau frowned. "You serious?"

Turtle appeared around the side of her. "Damn right, I'm serious. We're the Streetwalkin' Cheetahs, for Christ's sake. We would never have stood for shit like this before Vince took over. You know it. I know it."

"But Vince said—"

"Fuck Vince," Turtle yelled, before throwing his gaze around the assembled masses and lowering his voice. "Fuck him, Beau. I'm serious. He ain't here, so I say we do this like we used to. Back when the Cheetahs had some fucking balls in their pants."

"I don't know, Turtle."

"Fucking hell, Beau. Have we all gone soft around here? I say we need this. Good old-fashioned fire and brimstone shit. An eye for an eye."

Jareth, who had now roused himself, stepped forward. "Come on, guys, let's talk about this. Look at the two of us standing here. We ain't your enemies. We're a couple of old rockers ourselves, trying to keep our heads down and our hands clean. If we got in your way, it was by accident and we apologise. We got hauled in by the cops that night, didn't mention you guys once." His voice sounded deep and rough. But if he was attempting to mirror these gruff bastards to make a connection, it wasn't working.

"Save your words, hotshot," a voice barked, and Jareth stumbled forward, the guy shadowing him, Johnny, having shoved him from behind. "I agree with Turtle. Show these punks how we do it, Beau. Show them the Cheetahs aren't to be messed with."

Acid remained still, as a million chaotic thoughts swirled around in her psyche, each one fighting for governance. Johnny was armed and standing behind her a few steps over to her left. If he was aiming the gun at Jareth, she'd have time to grab it from him before he turned it on her. He was a big guy, but no one could hold onto a weapon if you hit the right pressure points. That part was easy. The only issue was he might shoot Jareth.

Could she risk it?

Would she?

She closed her eyes and sucked in a deep breath, trying to ignore the bat chorus chattering in her soul.

You can do it.

You're invincible.

Do it!

She chewed her bottom lip, scanning her gaze across the

assembled bikers for signs of weapons – guns mainly. Once she had Johnny's piece (an old Glock 17, by the looks of it) she could handle any blades or chains coming her way. The Cheetahs stared at her like they wanted her dead but none were noticeably armed. That didn't mean much. It was unlikely they'd favour a holster or open carry.

"All right, fine," Beau said, albeit in a reserved tone. "Let's go."

"The plank?" Turtle asked, his voice rising.

"Nah. We do this clean. Over on the wasteland. Go on."

"Suits me fine," Turtle said, pulling Acid off her feet as he dragged her over to a patch of barren land to the right of the clubhouse. "Time to pay the piper. Bitch."

He pressed the hunting knife against her back as they walked. She felt the sharp point through her jacket, piercing her skin. It wouldn't take much effort to slide the sharp blade past her ribs and into her heart. This Turtle guy had proven himself to be sluggish and unwieldy, but she couldn't risk an escape attempt. Not yet. Instead, as he bustled her over to the centre of the wasteland, she worked on keeping her heart rate down and her mind quiet. Despite all the chaos and turmoil she'd gone through these last two years, she still trusted her instincts.

"On your knees," Turtle growled, kicking the backs of her legs.

She dropped heavily onto her knees, but no pain registered. She was beyond pain. She was beyond feeling anything. A heady concoction of manic energy and hormones fizzed in her system as they pushed Jareth to the ground beside her. She heard the familiar slide-click of a box mag meeting the well of a pistol.

"Sorry, babe," Jareth whispered. "Guess I fucked this up."

"No, this is on me," she replied, staring forward. "I got you into this mess."

"Hands on heads, motherfuckers," a voice told them. It might have been Beau. It certainly wasn't Turtle, because if she looked out the corner of her left eye she saw him standing with his chubby arms folded over his barrel chest.

"Well, shoot," Jareth whispered. "I had you down as one of those people who never admitted they were wrong."

"First time for everything."

She knew what he was doing. If they properly considered their predicament they'd be shitting bricks, so distracting oneself with cynicism and humour - the way Jareth was doing - could be a big help. It wouldn't stop them getting their brains blown out but might keep them calm long enough an idea might show itself. Besides, wasn't everything in life a distraction from this moment – the crushing realisation of our own mortality?

She scanned the area, searching for an escape. Over to her left, Turtle was waving a pistol in his hand, aiming it at her head, pretending to shoot. He saw her looking and lowered the piece, grinning over the top of it. He was too far away. She'd never get to him before he fired. She'd never get anywhere. Turtle carried on grinning at her, perhaps guessing what she was thinking. Willing her to try it anyway.

She leaned into Jareth. "Thanks a lot, by the way," she said, speaking out of the corner of her mouth. "You sure know how to make a girl feel special."

He turned to look at her but got a clip around the back of the head for it. "Eyes front."

Behind them, Beau was now engaged in a pathetic oration, telling his 'brethren' how important it was for them to keep their status and show the world they were still a force to be reckoned with. Something like that. She was trying not to listen.

"What do you mean?" Jareth whispered.

"Couple of old rockers?" she said. "Old? Speak for yourself, buddy."

He snort-laughed softly down his nose. "I was trying to build some bridges."

"I know. Didn't work though, did it? Fucking hell. After everything I've been through, I'm going to die here, in a bloody forest." Her foggy breath bloomed out into the night air and she looked up at the sky. It was beautiful and clear, the earlier clouds gone and the ice-white crescent moon clearly visible over the treetops.

Jareth leaned against her. "You know, you never did tell me your story."

She rolled her shoulders back. The bats told her no. To keep quiet. But maybe it would help. A death bed confessional. She cricked her neck to one side.

"Up until two years ago I worked for an underground organisation called Annihilation Pest Control."

Against the backdrop of Beau's droning voice, she heard Jareth whistle. "*Annihilation Pest Control.* I take it you weren't dealing with actual rats and the like. So what was it, high-end assassinations?"

"Bingo."

"Was it legit? A government-controlled unit, I mean?"

"Absolutely bloody not. We did it for the money, baby."

Out in the gloomy forest she saw the faces of her past. Caesar and Spitfire. She caught herself smiling at the memory but shook the images from her mind.

No use being bloody sentimental.

Not now.

Jareth sniffed. "Makes sense, I guess. With everything you've said. Man, that's huge."

Acid turned to him, but he didn't meet her gaze. "Listen, Jareth, I—"

"Shut your damn mouth," Turtle screamed. "Beau. It's time. Get this done."

Beau stepped to the side of them, waving a pistol. "All right. Who's going first?"

Acid's heart smashed through her ribs and landed like a led zeppelin in her guts. This was it. She was about to be executed. She glanced around, searching for a way out, something she could use. A rock, a piece of wood. But the ground was bare. She had nothing.

She had stared death in the face many times over the years, but she'd never felt this vulnerable, this devoid of options. She closed her eyes, willing Jareth to do something as they waited for the inevitable. What she wouldn't give for the old push dagger she used to conceal in a secret compartment in her belt. What she wouldn't give to be the younger, more fearless version of herself. That ruthless she-wolf could get out of any scrape in which she found herself.

"Do me first," Jareth called out.

Acid opened her eyes. "No. I'll go first."

"Enough," Beau hissed, waving the pistol from one to the other. "If that's the way you want to play it, how about l choose? And I think we'll start with… you. No… you." He stepped in front of Jareth and raised the gun. But before he pulled the trigger, the noise of motorbike engines spewed through the clearing. Beau hesitated, glancing up over their heads as the noise of the bikes grew closer and then came to a stop a few feet away. A low murmur erupted from the crowd that had assembled to watch.

"Motherfuc— Vince!" Beau moved the gun behind his back. "I didn't think you'd be home until the weekend."

Acid twisted around and lowered her hands from her head. Two Harley Davidson bikes had parked on the edge of the wasteland. The men riding them dismounted in unison, and the shorter of the two marched over.

"What the fuck is this?" he yelled. "Beau, you want to tell me what the hell you're playing at here?"

The man looked to be in his late twenties, with long dark hair and a smattering of stubble that enhanced his razor-sharp cheekbones and fine jawline. He glanced around the scene, at Acid and Jareth, and then back to Beau.

"These fuckheads were spying on us," Beau said. "Plus they beat up Turtle and Lance the other day. We agreed that was disrespectful and they needed to be taught a lesson."

The younger man looked to the heavens as if he couldn't believe what he was hearing. "Jesus, Beau. What have I been trying to get across to y'all? Fuck!" He stepped around the front of Acid and Jareth. "Is Beau here correct? You been spying on us?"

"No. Not exactly," Acid replied. "My friend has gone missing and we were told the Cheetahs might know where she is."

"You think we have her?"

"Maybe. The police think it too."

"I see." He glared up at the assembled throng. "And do we?"

Acid followed his gaze to see the assembled Cheetahs rippling with shrugs and shakes of the head.

"Jesus Christ. I go away for a few days and the whole

town descends into chaos." He glared at Acid and Jareth. "Get up, will you?"

Glancing at each other, they got to their feet.

"What's going on?" Jareth asked.

"My own fucking club doesn't understand a word of what I've been trying to teach them, that's what." He blew out a sharp breath and waved it away. "It's a long story. Club business. Listen, I'm sorry about my brothers' barbarous actions tonight. That's not what the Cheetahs are about. Not anymore. Guitar, get over here."

"Yes, brother?"

Acid looked over as the other man approached.

"Take these people into the clubhouse. Get them a beer or a shot or whatever they want." He bowed his head at them. "I'll be in shortly and we can talk some more. Right after I have a quiet word with these dimwits."

He turned his attention to Turtle, approaching him with a raised fist as the fat biker backed away. Acid opened her mouth, about to protest, when the larger of the two new arrivals mumbled something and set off towards the clubhouse, beckoning for them to follow.

"Hey. Wait. Guitar, is it?" Acid asked, striding to keep up. "Who is that?"

"Vince Elway," he grunted, without looking around.

Acid glanced behind her at the young biker currently up in Turtle's face, then back at Jareth who was holding his hand to his head. "How you feeling?"

"I'll live."

She pouted at him. "As the adrenaline leaves, the pain begins."

"You said it." Then, calling after Guitar, "I take it Johnny Depp over there is head man around here?"

"That he is," Guitar replied, still not looking back.

"Club President. Ever since his old man died end of last year."

"He seems like a decent guy."

"Who said he wasn't?"

Jesus, Jareth, quit while we're ahead.

Acid shot him a hard stare, but he kept on.

"I heard a few stories, is all. Heard you guys were bad news."

Guitar stopped and looked at the ground. "Yeah? Well, you heard wrong. Now, how's about you two shut up and I'll get you that drink."

He strode off once more, leaving the two of them in his wake. Acid looked at Jareth and shrugged. "Cup of tea for you?"

"The hell with that," he replied. "I think we both deserve something stronger. Come on, let's find out what the hell these guys are all about."

Chapter Eighteen

Guitar was slow and steady as he reached over the back of the bar, returning with half a bottle of Wild Turkey in his oil-stained fist. Here, in the warm glow of the clubhouse, Acid thought he looked younger than he had outside. His long hair had hints of salt and pepper but was still thick, and his beard was full and neatly groomed. He placed the bottle on the counter and, with the same restrained movements, reached over with his other hand, this time grabbing up four tumblers, one hooked on each of his long fingers.

"Here ya go," he said, walking to the round table next to the bar and slamming the bottle down. "I guess we're welcoming any old body to the clubhouse these days." He placed the glasses alongside the bottle and Acid pulled one to her.

"I take it you aren't too happy about us being here."

"Don't matter what I think. Vince is the president and that's how it is. He's a good man and I respect his judgement," he said, before lowering his voice. "Even if he does have some crazy ideas for the club."

"I've got to say I'm amazed to be sitting here," Jareth told him. "I figured the two of us would have a deficit of brains right about now."

Guitar regarded him with pale, watery blue eyes. "Might still be true. Stupid of you coming sniffing around our clubhouse. It's a sacred space, man."

"Fair enough. But like Acid said, her friend has gone missing and we were told you might have something to do with it."

Guitar let out a low growl and dragged the bottle of bourbon towards him. "A lot of my brothers are old school, know what I mean?" He screwed off the cap. "They're set in their ways. Don't understand why we have to change how we operate when nothing was wrong in the first place. But since Vince took over, he's got other ideas for the club. Wants to take the Cheetahs into the twenty-first century."

"Meaning?" Acid asked, eyes on the bottle.

"Mainly that we go legit. No more guns or drugs, or any other illegal shit. Some of the boys, Turtle and Lance included, as well as Beau, they don't agree with what Vince is trying to do."

He poured himself a large slug of amber and waved the bottle over Acid's glass.

"Please." She watched as he poured her a drink, willing him to keep pouring. "And they want to sabotage his plans?"

"Something like that. But you saw them, they're a bunch of dummies. They'll sit up and play nice soon enough. Once they see Vince's ideas are working out for us."

"Will they?"

His response was a low grumble. Good enough for her. She took a sip of the drink and held it on her tongue. It was spicy and delicious and the burn on her throat as she swallowed felt like home. Guitar offered the bottle to Jareth, who accepted the drink but stopped him before he poured out any more than a single measure.

"So what does legit mean exactly?" he asked, sniffing his glass.

"He can tell you that," Guitar muttered, nodding towards the door.

The three of them turned to watch Vince approach the table. He had the sort of walk that made people pay attention.

"Welcome to the Streetwalkin' Cheetahs' clubhouse," he said, as he got nearer. "You might be the first civilians we've had in here. First one's we've invited in, at least." He laughed and slapped Guitar on the back. The older man didn't flinch. He didn't laugh, either.

"Civilians, huh?" Jareth said, raising one eyebrow as he met Acid's gaze. "How about that?"

She ignored him and watched Vince spin his chair around and sit astride it. A clichéd move, but he pulled it off.

"So what are your names?" he asked, looking Acid dead in the eye.

"You can call me Acid," she told him.

"Acid? Nice." They stared at each other, each with a smirk on their face. He turned to Jareth. "And you, friend?"

"Jareth. Jareth Hicks," Jareth said, shooting Acid a look as he shook Vince's hand. "Pleased to meet you. And thank you. For saving our necks back there. I was saying to Guitar here, I thought we were goners."

The smile on Vince's face fell away. "Don't worry. I've been giving those overzealous pricks a damn good talking to. They won't bother you no more. I'm trying to tell myself Beau was only messing with you, playing the big man in front of the boys. He wouldn't have actually pulled the trigger."

"That so?" Jareth said. "They sure seemed thirsty for blood. That Turtle guy especially."

"Turtle has got a bad attitude, but he usually toes the line when you call him on it. Shit, what're you going to do – poor son of a bitch has got Klippel Feil syndrome. Motherfucker's got no neck."

Acid took another large gulp of bourbon. "You know what they're saying about the mayor, don't you?"

"What's that you say?"

Jareth held one hand up as if in warning, but she ignored it.

"The police think you've got something to do with his disappearance." She gripped the tumbler tight as the bats screeched in her ears. "And I saw some of your boys digging a shallow grave up in the mountains. Got to say, it looks rather suspicious."

Vince slammed his fist on the table. "Fucking cops. How is anyone supposed to make a clean living when you've got every prick in town trying to drag you down? They think we hit Donovan?"

Acid nodded. "What about what I saw?"

"Guns. We still had a surplus of stolen rifles, and rather than sell them off I wanted to get rid. So I asked some of the guys to bury them, along with all other remaining contraband, up in the mountains where no one would find them. That's what you saw." He grabbed at the Wild Turkey and glugged a mouthful straight from the bottle before wiping his hand across his mouth. "See, I've been wanting to go legit for a long time. Me and my pop talked about it a lot before he died. Before he was murdered by Satan's Bastards."

His face dropped and he looked away. Acid glanced at Guitar. "A rival MC," he growled. "They killed our prez, Vince's daddy, end of last year."

"I was enraged for a long time," Vince told them through gritted teeth. "My brothers all wanted revenge and I did too, of course I did. But we'd already come so far. I couldn't destroy what he'd started. My father was an intelligent man and a forward thinker. He'd grown tired of a life of crime and murder. So rather than go to war with the Bastards, I chose peace. I chose reason. And I made a pact with myself that there'd be no more deaths. No more killing." He ran his fingers through his hair. "Listen, guys, I'm not trying to make out we're saints – at all. The Cheetahs have done some bad shit through the years."

At this, Guitar huffed out something approaching a laugh. "You said it, brother. Brutal times."

"Brutal times, but different times. Bygone times," Vince added. "Our long-term plan now is to open a couple of bars, couple of garages too. Maybe a diner as well, fuck it. Point is, we do it clean and we learn to enjoy life again. Get back to being a motorcycle club rather than a bunch of gangsters. We've amassed enough green over the years that we can get by without all the stress and strain that comes with running that sort of business."

"It's admirable," Jareth said. "But I can see why some of your men are antsy about the idea. It's a big change."

"If you ain't changing, you're staying the same, though. Right?" Vincent's eyes lit up as he spoke, like this was the most profound thing anyone had ever said. Maybe it was. "Sure, some don't like it, but they'll have to learn to or leave. We've got enough trouble right now without infighting in the club."

"You mean the local cops?" Jareth asked, saying it before she could.

"The Cheetahs are being persecuted," he replied. "Which is why I can't be too harsh on my wayward brothers out there. We got to be careful. Stick together. There's a lot of people in town gunning for us right now. Hunger and his goons especially."

"We can relate to that," Acid said. "They threw us both in jail the other night. Real pricks about it, too. That Chief Hunger, I did not get a good vibe from the guy."

"He's a piece of shit is what he is," Guitar growled, and knocked back his drink.

Vince slid the bottle over to his buddy without looking at him. "I take it you had it in your head we'd kidnapped your friend. Or worse. Same with the mayor."

"You can see why."

"Sure. Thing is, me and old Doug Donovan were good buddies once upon a time. Way back in school. Before we embarked down very different paths. But he's a decent man. I'd never do anything to hurt the guy. In fact, I appreciate what he's trying to do with the town. I hope one day we might be... not friends, perhaps, but allies." He stood and stretched, looking at Jareth as he did. "Turtle said you were working at Al's place. You heard of a fellow named Raymond Glick?"

Jareth shook his head. "Should I have?"

"Maybe. He's a big-time developer—"

"—and a total shitbag," Guitar muttered into his glass.

Vince grinned and brushed his hair behind his ears. "Couldn't have put it better myself. He's been trying to get his hands on my land for the last two years. See, I own all this. From the clubhouse all the way down to the river. Which is the exact spot where Glick wants to build a big old luxury hotel and spa complex. Been leaning on me pretty hard recently. Trying to start a war between the townsfolk and the Cheetahs. If anyone's behind these rumours about us doing the dirty on Donovan, it'll be that son of a bitch."

"But the mayor *is* missing," Acid offered.

"So I hear. Guitar and me were out of town the last few days, but I got word through. Terrible business. I hope he turns up okay. Got a daughter, you know."

"I'm aware," Acid said. "She was with my friend. She's missing too."

"No shit. I can see why you got your heads all in a twist about it. Shit is getting weird." Vince's hand came up and he teased at the long stubble under his bottom lip, thinking. "How long have they been missing?"

Acid gripped her glass. Less than twelve hours? Less than six? She coughed. "I'm not sure. There's still the possibility they're lying low somewhere. Spook was rather annoyed at me, you see, and…" She trailed off as the realisation dawned on her.

Shitting hell.

Had all this upset and chaos been nothing but a product of her own mania-induced paranoia? Normally she caught any disruptive thoughts before they took hold. But not always.

Stupid bloody cow.

She'd dragged Jareth into a potentially dangerous and volatile situation, and for what reason? Because she'd found Spook's beret? It was hardly a smoking gun. Spook Horowitz was scatty at the best of times, but full of excitement the way she was she may have dropped it, or had it fall from her bag without realising it. The point was, there were plenty of workable explanations for what had happened. Acid closed her eyes, hit with the image of Spook and the mayor's daughter snuggled up in bed together. She'd seen how they'd been looking at each other.

Fuck. Fucking hell.

She'd allowed that prick Hunger and his wet-arsed deputy to wind her up. She'd sided with cops, for heaven's sake. And now here she was cosying up with an ex-special forces soldier, too. What would Caesar have thought of her?

As Acid was pondering her own pathetic nature, she felt something nudge her leg and, raising her head, clocked Jareth's look.

He tilted his head to one side, gesturing towards the door. "Well, our friends clearly aren't here and we've taken up enough of your time." He got to his feet. "We really do appreciate your hospitality, Vince – and you, Guitar – but it's been a long night. We'll leave you boys to it."

Vince raised the bottle of bourbon, pointing the end at Jareth. "Least we can do after what we put you through. You seem like good people, our kind of people. I hope you find your friend. I say we keep praying they really are lying low somewhere, but I'll send some of my boys out at first light all the same. See if they can spot anything."

"Thank you," Acid said, and stood. "I'd like to say it's unlike my friend to do this, but it's not. She's always getting herself into some kind of trouble. Bloody pain in the arse. She'll turn up soon enough."

"*Bloody pain in the arse,*" Vince mocked, giving her a sly wink. "Got to love a British accent. Especially on such a fine lady as yourself, Acid."

She pursed her lips. "Quite the charmer, aren't you, Vincent?"

"I do my best."

"I bet you do."

"All right, we should get going," Jareth said, reaching for

Acid's arm. She dodged away from his hand but acquiesced all the same, following him over to the doorway.

"I can get some of my boys to drive you home, if you'd prefer it," Vincent called after them. "It's a decent walk back into town."

"We can manage. Thank you," Jareth called back.

At the door, Acid stopped and turned around. "I'm in one of the cabins down by the side of the post office in town," she said. "Fifth down from the main street. If you hear of anything, you'll let me know?"

"Will do," Vince answered. "You people take care now."

Chapter Nineteen

Jareth didn't speak as he and Acid left the Cheetahs' clubhouse behind and began the long walk back into town. The clock in his head told him it was around ten-thirty, but he felt so wired he knew he wouldn't be able to sleep for some time. Following his instincts, he led them through a thicket of trees, and was pleased to see those same instincts hadn't let him down when it brought them out by the river. Jackpot. It would be much easier to navigate their way into town this way, rather than taking the path through the forest.

"You want to talk about it?" he asked, staring in front of him.

"Talk about what?"

"Oh, nothing. Just that you used to kill people for a living."

"Ah. That." She made a hissing sound, like someone had squeezed all the air from her. "Do you mind if we don't?"

Jareth raised his chin. "Cool. No problem. I mean, it's

probably a really boring story, anyway. I've met plenty of elite assassins over the years. They were all dull as shit."

She let out a snort of laughter but stopped herself as quick. "Can we not? Please. I know you've probably got loads of questions, but I just want to go home and forget about tonight. I feel like such a bloody arse."

He looked down at her. She wasn't kidding. Her sassy countenance was now drawn and surly. Those bright, intense eyes had glazed over. "You all right?"

"No. Not really. Gah! Fuck!" She tipped her head back and screamed into the night sky. "What a bloody idiot. I let my imagination get the better of me, let the demons win. I shouldn't have dragged you into this."

The venom coming out of her was tangible, only it was all directed inwards. "Don't be so hard on yourself," he told her, and meant it. "You were worried about your friend. That's normal."

"I almost got us both killed."

"You heard what Handsome Harry said back there. The guy was only trying to scare us."

"Handsome Harry? Something you want to tell me?"

"Something you want to tell me?" She looked up at him and the glaze lifted from her eyes. One eyebrow twitched. "Are you jealous?"

Jareth looked straight ahead. "I don't get jealous. But anyway, back to the plot. You were right to follow up if you were concerned. It's what I would have done. And I came with you of my own accord, so don't beat yourself up about that either."

She didn't respond and a heavy silence fell over them once more. This time it carried on for the best part of ten minutes as they made their way around the largest section of the mountain, and another five minutes after that. The orange glow hovering over Blackfell Ridge was in sight before Jareth tried again.

"It's not a problem, by the way," he told her.

Still no response.

"Your past, I mean. Sure, when you first told me I was a little taken aback – or at least, I would have been if I didn't have a fucking pistol pointed at my skull. But maybe it's like Vince said, we've all done bad shit in our lives, right? I certainly have. 'Let he who is without sin cast the first stone…' and all that. I take it you're no longer an employee of Obliteration Pest Control?"

She looked down. "Annihilation Pest Control. And no. No one is."

"Okay, so—"

"Listen, Jareth, I mean it. I don't want to talk it about it. It's gone. It's not who I am anymore."

"And who are you now?"

"A fucking idiot who doesn't know her tit from her elbow, if tonight is anything to go by." She shook her head. "I'm so angry at myself for letting my imagination get the better of me. It's not like me. Or at least, it wasn't. Who bloody well knows these days?"

Up ahead, Jareth could now make out the outskirts of the town and the Blackfell Tavern, the only other bar to rival Al's place. The lights were on and he could hear the dull rumble of music.

"You want another drink?" he asked. "We can talk some more. Sounds to me like it might help. Let off some steam."

"Easy as that?"

"You never know."

"Yes, I do, Jareth." She turned to him, shoulders back, hair whipping across her face with the movement. "I should have realised. I should have sensed it coming on and acted accordingly, but I didn't."

He held his ground, kept his voice calm. "Should have sensed what?"

"Normally I would. I always used to, at least. When my moods drifted too far into the red, I'd take myself away. Let my system reset. Shit, that's what this little holiday was supposed to be all about. Yet somehow I've let the bats get the better of me. They've led me astray, when once they were allies." She screamed again, this time low and guttural, coming from deep inside of her. "My mind used to be so sharp. But now I'm seeing trouble where there isn't any. Fighting shadows. Tilting at windmills. You know, I used to tell myself that trouble followed me wherever I went, but that's not true. It's me. I'm the trouble."

Jareth leaned back. He saw it now. The dilated pupils, the way her eyes flickered from side to side as she was talking, the fact she hadn't blinked once this whole time. She wasn't well. She was having some sort of episode.

"Acid, it's okay," he offered, holding his hands out. "Why don't you come back to my motel. It's just around the next bend."

"No."

"Shit. No. For rest, I mean. I think we both need a decent night's sleep."

"Oh, no. No, no, no. I know what you're trying to do—"

"I'm really not."

"And yes, it'd be great. I'm sure of it. It's what my ego and the bats want more than anything right now. Oh, how I'd love to lose myself in you for a few hours. But I can't. I won't. I'm bad news, mate. Always have been. I'll just drag you down with me. I promise you that. Shit. I can't cope with this… life anymore. I need to get back to the UK. Move to the country. A nice little cottage in a sleepy village full of old dears. That'll do me. Spend the rest of my days doing jigsaws and watching soap operas. It'd be best for everyone—"

"Acid. Stop."

He grabbed for her hand, but she pulled it away. "Leave me alone. I'm serious." She set off marching towards the town, her wild hair bobbing up and down with each step.

"Wait a second," Jareth called after her. "I wasn't suggesting that. I wouldn't. Not when you're… You know…"

"What?" she spun around again. "When I'm what, Mr Colonel Fucking Soldier Boy?"

"When you're clearly upset. That's all I meant."

She hissed out a sigh. "Whatever. I'll see you around."

"Where are you going?"

"Back to my cabin. Wait for Spook. She probably got back while I was running around like an idiot telling myself I had to save her. She's an idiot too, of course, but she's also responsible. More than me. She'll be back once she's calmed down."

Jareth gave it a beat, tried again. "Let me walk you home."

"I need to be alone. I'm going to get packed up and go to the airport as soon as I talk to Spook." She dipped her head. "I'll see you around."

He raised his hand and smiled, but she'd already turned her back and was walking away. "Yeah. See you around, Acid Vanilla."

He waited until she'd put a hundred metres or so between them, wondering if she'd glance back. She didn't.

"Another goodbye," he muttered to himself. Then he rolled his shoulders and strolled back into town.

Chapter Twenty

Spook Horowitz might have been a more responsible person than Acid, but everything was relative, and right now she was acting anything but responsible. After leaving the police station, she'd gone back to Cynthia's place to take stock and work out the next move in finding her new friend's dad.

With what the cops had told them, Spook's first instinct had been to go to the Cheetahs' clubhouse, see if they might find clues there, but Cynthia had quickly quashed that idea. Not because they were dangerous, she'd explained, but because she knew for certain they would never hurt her dad in the way Hunger had implied.

"The new president of the Cheetahs is a guy called Vince Elway," she'd explained, the two of them sitting cross-legged and facing each other on Cynthia's bed. "He and my daddy grew up together. They were friends. When he took over as president, he came to see Daddy. He stayed for dinner and they sat up for hours talking about their plans for the town, putting the world to rights. Vince is a nice guy."

Spook had questioned it at the time, offering the fact she'd met a lot of nice guys over the years who'd turned out to be total shitbags.

"I know. But I got good vibes from him. He was talking about how he wants the club to go legit. Wanted my daddy's help in getting some licences and permits. For a bar and a garage. Reputable business."

Even with the niggle still there in the back of her mind, Spook had to admit Cynthia had a point. Especially as she also had to admit there was something weird about the way the chief had acted when they went to see him.

"He's got it into his head the Cheetahs are involved and that's stopping him looking for the real culprits," Cynthia continued. "Maybe Dad banged his head in the crash and wandered off into the forest. Maybe we find who this G person is and we find my dad as well. What I'm saying, Spook, is that I don't believe G refers to Donny 'Guitar' Rivers, and if that's the case, I don't trust the local cops to find my daddy. Which is why we need to do our own investigation."

Investigation.

Spook had liked that word. It had filled her with that same tingle of nervous energy she'd felt when she first met Acid. And on most of their adventures since. After Acid embarked on her solo mission of vengeance, leaving Spook to pace the floor in their Soho apartment, she'd missed that feeling. It was the sense of being alive, of being involved in something important.

So despite her trepidation, she'd chosen to trust Cynthia's judgement. If she wanted to ignore the cops and search for Mr Donovan her way, then that's what they were going to do. Which was why the last thing Spook and Cynthia were interested in on this chilly night was being snuggled up in bed together. And why they were now standing outside the rear entrance of Blackfell Ridge town hall, armed with a screwdriver and a mallet they'd appropriated from Cynthia's dad's toolkit.

"You sure this will work?" Cynthia whispered, as Spook took position in front of the door.

"I hope so," she whispered back, jamming the screwdriver into the side of the lock. "Look how old this doorframe is. Either the lock will give out or the wood will. Here, give me room."

Cynthia stepped back as Spook smacked the hammer down on the end of the screwdriver.

Damn, it felt good. Made her feel strong and bold and so very grown up (even if she only knew what to do because she'd surreptitiously Googled it ten minutes earlier whilst Cynthia was in the bathroom).

She brought the hammer down again, levering the screwdriver against the doorframe as the wood groaned with a pleasing splintering sound. A final whack of the screwdriver and she felt the lock give way.

"We're in." Grabbing hold of the door handle, she looked back at Cynthia. "You ready?"

"Let's do it."

Spook eased open the door and was greeted as expected by a stream of raucous beeps. An alarm system counting down.

"Come on." They ran inside and over to the panel of switches and flashing lights positioned at the foot of the stairwell opposite.

"Here, let me." Cynthia switched on her torch and shone it on the slip of notepaper she had in her hand. "Seven-three-two-zero." She reached up and jabbed the code into the illuminated rubber keypad and the place fell silent.

The two women looked at each other in the glow of torchlight and Spook felt another twinge of excitement rattle her body.

"Second floor," Cynthia said, moving around the side of the stairwell and starting to climb.

Spook made to follow her but stopped. "Shit."

"What is it?"

"My beret. I just realised. I must have left it somewhere."

Cynthia turned and shone the torch in her eyes. "So?"

"Nothing." She shrugged. "It's just… I hate losing things."

Cynthia sighed and moved the torch away from her and up the stairwell. "Come on, Spook, we haven't got time for this."

And there it was.

In that one pathetic display of inept gawkiness (because who gives a shit about a damn beret when your dad's gone missing?), she felt the power shift between them. She'd enjoyed being the one in control, but she'd been stupid to think it could last. Cynthia was cool as hell. Why would she look up to someone like her?

"Spook!"

"Sorry. I'm coming." Moving effortlessly back into the role she'd been playing since kindergarten, she chased her friend up the stairs and ran into her on the next landing. Cynthia had turned the torch off and was standing at the end of a long corridor. Large glass windows ran down one side, revealing the town square below; and on the other, four identical oak doors stretched down the landing, set apart in equidistant formation.

"Can't risk anyone seeing the torch," she whispered, as Spook adjusted her stance, attempting to claw back any level-headedness she might have once had.

"Sure. I was about to say the same."

"The mayor's office uses all these rooms, but my dad set himself up in the end one." Cynthia said, setting off down the corridor and whispering back at Spook. "It's smaller than the other rooms. He said it was important for the mayor to stay humble. And that his team worked a lot harder than he did, so they should have the best offices. He's always like that. Selfless. Kind."

She sniffed and Spook placed her hand on her shoulder. "He sounds like a great man. I can't wait to meet him."

They got to the end door and Cynthia tried the handle, glancing at Spook in the moonlight coming through the windows. "Locked."

A bristle of energy ran up Spook's spine. It didn't make her feel too proud of herself, but it felt good all the same. "Don't worry, Cynth. I've got this," she whispered, something of her earlier confidence returning.

This door was made from newer, harder wood than the previous one but using the screwdriver as a chisel she was able to breach it. Once inside, they closed the door behind them and Cynthia switched on the torch. The cone of light shone into the room, revealing a large rectangular desk covered with green leather and a new iMac sitting on top.

"Reckon you can hack into this one too?" Cynthia asked.

"You bet. Let me see."

Spook switched on the computer and moved around to the other side of the desk to see what she was dealing with. But before she had a chance to sit, Cynthia was grabbing at the sleeve of her sweatshirt.

"Wait, look at this." She was facing the corner of the room, shining the torch on a piece of paper she'd lifted off the desk.

"What is it?"

"A letter asking for a meeting with my dad. To discuss a project. But look here." She held it up to show her. "Look at the logo. Glick Developments. Glick. G."

"Shiiit," Spook whispered, prolonging the inner vowel sound until her breath ran out. "That's got to be it."

"Do you think this guy, this…" she scanned to the bottom of the letter "…Raymond Glick, knows where my daddy is?"

"I think we need to speak to him and—"

Spook froze. She'd heard movement. Holding her breath she held her hand up to Cynthia as the floorboards creaked in the corridor outside. A second later the door burst open to reveal two large, shadowy figures silhouetted against the window behind them.

Spook and Cynthia cried out in unison, grabbing at each other as the figures advanced on them.

"Leave us alone," Spook shrilled, holding the screwdriver up.

"Dumb little bitches," a man's voice growled. "Sniffing around where you shouldn't. Come here."

Their screams grew louder as the men grabbed for them. Spook held her ground but one of them clasped her wrist and twisted it until she dropped the screwdriver. He followed it up with a sharp thrust of his knee that dug into her lower back and dropped her to the floor. Then he rasped in her ear.

"What are you doing here?"

"Go to hell."

The man twisted her arm up her back, forcing it against

the joint. "If you want to see tomorrow, I suggest you start talking, bitch."

"Okay, okay," Spook stammered through the pain. "Please, don't hurt us. What do you want to know?"

"You can start by telling us who you are and why you're here," the man said. "And just so you know, the first answer you give that I don't like, you'll regret ever opening your mouth."

Chapter Twenty-One

What a total shitshow. But that was it. Decision made. Jareth Hicks was out of here.

An assassin, for Christ's sake.

What the fuck?

The thing was, Jareth had been speaking the truth earlier. All that, 'he who is without sin' crap. But now, alone and with time to consider what Acid had told him, the implications of her words hung heavy.

"I mean, what the hell am I supposed to do with that information?" he asked a balled-up pair of boxers, before chucking them into the yawning mouth of his holdall. "Infuriating woman."

And sure, she was attractive, funny, exciting to be around, but what she'd told him tonight was concerning on too many levels. Besides, Jareth had made another pact with himself – to never again leave his heart out for the birds to peck at.

Be bold, be honest, but don't give too much of yourself.

That was his mantra now.

Acid might have gotten into his head, but he wouldn't wait around for her to destroy his heart. The way women like her always did. It was time to move on. To pack up and get out of Dodge.

Goodnight, Vienna.

Elvis has left the building.

Although it was probably best to wait until morning, he reasoned, as a yawn overcame him, wiping the dark thoughts from his mind momentarily. He was too exhausted to make any sort of movement and, besides, the first train out of Blackfell Ridge wasn't until eight.

Moving his holdall to the floor, he lay back on the bed and placed his arms behind his head, immediately regretting it as the pungent smell of stale sweat hit his nostrils. Damn it. He sat up again and swung his feet onto the thin carpet. Looks like he was getting a shower.

He ambled into the bathroom and switched on the light to be met with a ghostly vision of himself in the mirror over the sink.

"Well, shit."

Normally Jareth was okay with what was reflected back at him, but tonight he turned from the mirror in dismay. He looked damn old, is what he looked. The grey hairs at his temple were more evident than ever, and the way the halogen light bounced off the scar on his forehead made it look grotesque where once he'd thought it cool. Though the addition of the new scab courtesy of Johnny Loose Fists didn't help none either. He hauled his damp t-shirt over his head and threw it onto the floor before unbuttoning his jeans and slipping them off. The boxers and socks followed and, once naked, he turned back to the mirror, examining his chest muscles and biceps. Ever since his heart attack he'd been taking it easy in terms of the gym and such, but he still had decent tone and size. Not too big. But hard. Strong. Something going for him, at least.

Grabbing a towel from the rack, he draped it over the side of the sink before stepping into the bath and twisting the dial on the shower unit.

"Motherfucker.

He gasped as the ice water hit his body, but forced himself to stay calm, using the experience as a training exercise rather than an annoyance. A few more seconds and he'd relaxed into the chill of the water. A few seconds more and it ran warm.

Of course, he could have showered in the morning, but a part of him – the regimented and disciplined part, the part the military had honed over the last twenty years – wouldn't allow it. What self-respecting man goes to bed smelling like a goat's asshole?

He closed his eyes and put his head under the water, letting it run over his hair and into his mouth as he pondered what was next for *Jareth Hicks, the Civilian.* The ex-soldier and free spirit who only had to answer to himself. Who could go anywhere and do anything.

He knew from experience that direction was more important than speed in this life, but when every direction looked too much like an escape route, it was hard to know which one to pick. Either way, he'd have to return to LA for a while, get his house in order both literally and figuratively. He'd paid until the end of the year at the Princess Grace Apartments, but after that he'd get the next plane out of there. Go to South America maybe, or Europe. Somewhere he'd never been before. Somewhere with no memories.

"*Sometimes you want to go… Where nobody knows your name…*" He sang loudly into the stream of water, para-phrasing the old theme song from Cheers.

But no more private security work. That was for sure. There was nothing like losing one of your buddies and suffering an almost fatal heart attack to put a guy off that line of work. He switched off the shower and grabbed the towel from the sink, wrapping it around his waist before stepping out onto the tiled floor.

He was about to wipe the steam from the mirror and go in for a closer examination when he heard a knock on his room door. Immediately his head shot up and his focus shifted to his hearing, listening for any voice or sound that might follow. The knocking went again, a heavy thud in the middle of the door. Sounded like they were using the heel of their hand.

"Who is it?" he called out.

No answer.

"Hello?"

Nothing.

With his nerves already shot to pieces, his head spun with possibilities. None of them good. Moving slow and silent, he crab-walked back into the bedroom, eyes scanning the furniture and floor for something to use as a weapon. His eyes fell on the lamp, which was standing proud and unassuming on the nightstand. It would have to do. Kneeling beside the bed, he followed the electrical cord to the wall and pulled out the plug. After winding the plastic flex around his fist, he got to his feet and, holding up the lamp, approached the door. The knocking went again.

"All right, keep your panties on."

The words proved fateful. As Jareth yanked at the door handle, the exertion freed the towel from around his waist, and it fell to the floor at the exact moment the door opened. Standing in the glow of the motel's neon signage was Acid Vanilla.

Of course it damn well was.

She looked him up and down without reaction. "Am I disturbing you?"

"Not really," he replied, making to cover himself with the lamp. "How did you find me?"

She shrugged. "Knew you were staying at this motel, so I asked the guy at reception what room the tall soldier was in. He was all too happy to oblige." She narrowed her eyes, whispering, "Appalling security in these places. I could be here to kill you."

He ignored the comment. "Well, I'm surprised to see you again so soon. Or ever again."

She rolled her head back. "Yes, well, I couldn't sleep. Can I come in?"

Before he had a chance to reply, she shoved past him into the room. He saw now she was carrying an open bottle of red wine.

"Make yourself at home," he told her, after she'd already sat on the edge of the bed. Looking both ways outside the door, he closed and locked it, then turned back to the room, finding Acid drinking straight from the bottle. As she lowered it from her mouth, he saw her teeth were stained with the stuff. "Am I right in thinking that's not your first bottle?"

Her eyes rolled back in her head. "I might have had another half bottle knocking around." She waved the fresh bottle at the lamp still gripped in his hands. "Were you expecting someone else?"

"Can't be too careful." He scooped up the towel and walked over to the sideboard facing the bed. There, he placed the lamp down and wrapped the towel around his waist. As he turned back he saw Acid had been watching him the whole time, a sly smirk playing across her wine-stained lips.

"Don't get dressed on my account, sweetie."

He walked over to her. "You okay? You seem a little wired."

"I'm absolutely tickety-boo, colonel soldier man." She peered into the bottle. "Spook's still missing, by the way. Don't know where she is. I've walked all around town but can't find her. But you know what? Screw her. Screw everyone. The whole fucking world can go to hell." She swigged back another gulp of wine.

"Easy, tiger." He reached for the bottle and she let him take it. "Why don't I get some glasses and we can talk about this?"

Her response was the kind of shrug one might receive from a sullen teen, but he took it as affirmation. Walking back into the bathroom, he picked up the two glass beakers next to the sink, eyeing his reflection in the now clear mirror as he did. He didn't look any better. He blew out his cheeks as Acid called from the other room.

"Bloody well hurry up, will you? I'm parched."

He gave his reflection a withering look and then headed back into the room. It was going to be one of those kinds of nights.

Chapter Twenty-Two

Cynthia and Spook hugged each other close, whimpering quietly into the darkness as the Ford Transit they were in lumbered and lurched over rocky terrain. After being thrown around by the shadowy assailants, the two women quickly realised their compliance was needed if they were to stay alive.

So they'd sung like overzealous canaries, telling the men who they were, why they were sneaking around in the dark. All in the hope they might let them go. Spook had been hopeful it was all a silly misunderstanding. That, heavy hands and angry faces notwithstanding, the men were security guards, tasked with keeping the town hall safe from night-time prowlers. But no. As soon as she'd finished explaining, the men had dragged her and Cynthia out of the office, through the building, and bundled them into the back of the waiting van.

Twenty minutes later they were still on the road, although now it seemed they were on some sort of track rather than smooth tarmac. Spook narrowed her eyes into the gloom, but with no light back here it was difficult to see much. Beside her, a folded blanket sat atop one of the wheel arches and a half empty bottle of water was rolling about by her feet.

"Where do you think they're taking us?" Cynthia whispered.

Spook held her friend tighter but didn't answer. She didn't know where they were going or what would happen to them when they got there. The only thing she knew for certain was they were up to their eyeballs in shit, and it was her fault. Again.

"Did you hear them muttering to each other when I mentioned my daddy and that letter?" Cynthia went on.

Spook had. "I think one of them mentioned the name Glick. Him being worried about something or other. I didn't hear too well, but sounds to me like we stumbled upon something important." What she didn't add was that finding this important piece of information might also be what got them killed. She sat upright. "I think we're stopping."

They listened, neither of them daring to breathe as the engine was switched off. Cynthia let out a soft wail as the van rocked from side to side, the men climbing out of the front seats and slamming their doors shut. Her wails grew louder as a lock clicked open and the double doors at the back of the van swung wide.

"Please," Cynthia cried. "We don't know anything. We won't tell anyone. We were just... We were..."

"Hey," Spook said, grabbing her hand and squeezing it. "Keep it together. We're okay."

The two men, still shrouded in the night's darkness, clambered into the van and scooped up two hessian sacks from the floor of the flatbed. "Put these on," one of them said. "And don't try anything cute, you hear me?"

The two women did as they were told. Because what else could they do? Despite this, a part of Spook hated herself for submitting so easily. She thought of Acid. What would she do in this situation?

"Can you tell us wha—"

"Shut the fuck up."

Firm hands grabbed her ankles and dragged her from the van. She felt the cool chill of the night air permeating her clothes as she was bustled to her feet. Once upright, those same hands gripped her upper arms, thumbs and fingers digging into her skin, shoving her forward. Beneath her feet she sensed the soft give of grass before the toe of her shoe met with a kind of step or doorway and the ground turned to stone, and then wood, and then to something softer. As they whipped the sack from her head, she looked down to see a large red and black rug with a distressed pattern of floral swirls.

She was standing in the lounge area of a wooden cabin, not dissimilar to the one she and Acid were renting in town. In front of her was a table surrounded by four chairs and, beyond this, two doors led off from the main space. Again, similar to the layout of her own cabin, although she noticed the windows on both sides of the room had heavy shutters across them, blocking out any view or way of placing their location. A wood-burning stove stood in the corner to her left, and overhead a single naked light bulb cast the room in a pale glow. She startled, sensing a presence beside her, but it was Cynthia, still with the sack over her head. One of the men whipped it away, leaving her hair tangled and dishevelled. She brushed it from her face, taking in the scene with wide, terrified eyes.

"It's okay. I'm here," Spook whispered, shuffling closer.

"I said shut the fuck up, didn't I?"

Spook startled as the gruff men bustled past them into the room. It was the first time she'd had proper eyes on them and she was surprised to see they looked nothing like she'd pictured.

They were both tall and broad, probably in their late thirties (although Spook was terrible at ageing people), but despite their brutish manner they were well dressed and clean-cut. Nothing like the red-eyed, bearded mountain men she'd been imagining. They both wore their hair super short in an army-style cut and one of them had a scar on his chin. It was he who pulled out a phone from his pocket and swiped it open.

He pointed at Spook and Cynthia and then at the table. "Sit."

The women exchanged a nervous glance before scurrying over and taking a chair beside one another.

"Now don't move and keep your mouths shut. Understood?" The man with the scar beckoned to his friend. "Travis, if they move, you know what to do."

"Sure do." The second man – Travis – reached around his back and pulled a pistol from his belt. He pointed it their way. "You sit tight now, girls."

From her seat at the table, Spook watched the man with the scar – clearly the one in charge – as he paced up and down with the phone at his ear. As a voice sounded over the line, he stopped and leaned against one of the window shutters.

"Hey, it's Jackson. Yeah. Bit of a problem. Travis and me went to the office like you said. Yeah, yeah, it was there. We got it. But we also discovered a much bigger problem in the shape of the mayor's kid and her little girlfriend."

He glanced over at them, nodding along to whatever the person on the line was saying. "Understood. Fine. See you then."

Spook scanned the room, searching for clues of where they were, or why they were here, or for something she might use as a weapon. When her eyes landed on the end of Travis' gun, she stopped looking.

Ah, man.

Who was she kidding? She might have enjoyed playing the big bold leader with Cynthia, but that was all it was — play-acting. She wasn't Acid. She was nothing like Acid.

Jackson hung up and came over to the table. He placed both hands on its edge and leaned forward.

"What's the plan?" Travis asked him.

He lowered his head. "Glick's on his way over. Said to put them in with the prisoner for now."

Travis nodded. The two women exchanged a glance.

"All right," Travis said, emphasising each word with a swipe of the pistol. "Get up."

Spook and Cynthia obeyed in haste and, with another wave of the pistol, Travis sent them hurrying to the door on the right. Once there, they stopped and waited in silence as he lumbered over and made a show of pulling a large brass key from his pocket. He eyed it and them with a flourish of delight before unlocking the door and shoving it open.

"Inside."

A shaft of light coned across the floor and up the back wall, revealing the room to be half the size of the main space. Spook also picked out the edge of a bed, a small table, and some feet. As her eyes grew accustomed, she saw someone crouching in the corner, their arms wrapped tight around their calves. When Travis pushed Spook and then

Cynthia into the room, the person got to their feet and barked out a hoarse cry.

"Cynthia?"

"Daddy!" The emotion in the young woman's voice lit up the room as she rushed past Spook and threw herself at the man. In turn, he wrapped his arms around her and squeezed like he would never let go.

Behind Spook, Travis mumbled something under his breath, but made no move to break up the tearful reunion. Spook heard the click of a light switch and a small bulb flickered into life overhead.

"I'll leave this on for now," Travis told them. "But I don't want to hear any bullshit out of you. You hear me?"

Spook blinked into the newly lit room at the man with his arms around Cynthia – who was still holding her so tight, like his life depended on it, that it made her pine momentarily for her own parents' love. He wasn't a large man, but even now, wearing torn and dirty clothes and with three days' growth darkening his chin, he had a commanding presence. He addressed Travis with a low, calm voice and eyes that were pleading but bright.

"What's going on, Travis?" he asked. "Why is my daughter here? If you've hurt her…"

"Save it," Travis replied. "She's fine. For now."

"Do you expect to get away with this?" Mayor Donovan asked. "Come on, Travis. You aren't a bad guy. Or a dummy. Let us go. We can make this okay."

"I said, save it!" he yelled, pushing Spook forward.

She turned to see him backing out of the room, jerking the pistol between them as he did. "Not a peep."

Mayor Donovan sighed, but held his hand up in a show of surrender. "Yes. Fine."

No one spoke as Travis left the room and closed the door behind him. Mayor Donovan waited for the click of the lock before holding Cynthia out at arm's length and fixing her with concerned eyes. "What the hell are you doing here?"

Chapter Twenty-Three

It didn't take Cynthia long to fill her dad in on what had happened. Spook listened as her friend spoke, resisting the urge to interject on one occasion when Cynthia had breezed over how easy it had been to hack into his computer.

It was easy. For Spook. Wasn't easy for most.

As Cynthia spoke, Mayor Donovan watched her with an open mouth and a deep frown rumpling his thick but well-sculpted brows. For an older guy he was good-looking, Spook supposed, but typical of many politicians of his age and background. His smile remained strong and his eyes crinkled at the corners when he talked, in that same way Clinton had perfected so well, and which all men in power had tried to ape ever since. His thick black hair was trimmed short and styled in a neat side parting. One other thing Spook noticed was that, despite surviving an apparent car accident, he didn't look too beat up. He had a graze on his forehead and two of his fingers had yellowing bandage wrapped around them, but that was all.

As Cynthia continued to fill him in and they exchanged

more hugs, more exclamations of love and relief, Spook shuffled over and sat on the side of the bed. The frame was old and creaked underneath her as she adjusted herself – maybe why the mayor was sitting on the hardwood floor. The mattress, too, was so thin she felt the thick coil of a spring digging into her butt-cheek. She stayed put regardless, telling herself she deserved the pain, telling herself it would keep her focused.

Often throughout her life – especially when stressful events were encircling her – Spook would fall into the benign embrace of disassociation. In the past, this wasn't too much of an issue. Wandering around with a vague smile on your face whilst all your classmates at the MIT were swallowing bottles of Adderall and Ritalin didn't endanger anyone. Nor did the fact Spook didn't shed a tear for either of her parents when they died, choosing instead to put her focus on comfort eating and Anime box sets on both occasions. But ever since she'd met Acid Vanilla and her terrifying and surreal world of elite killers and global conspiracies, she realised how dangerous this character trait was. And she'd realised it mainly because Acid was always there to call her out on it.

For Christ's sake, Spook, focus!

She could almost hear her friend's voice in her head. Husky and well-spoken, and always with a healthy undercurrent of sarcasm. Right now she was probably asleep on the other side of town. Or drunk in some bar. Either way, she wasn't here. She wasn't coming to save them. She didn't even know Spook was missing.

Focus, kid. Focus.

She shifted on the bed, the spring digging deeper into her flesh, and watched Cynthia as she continued with her tale. She seemed buoyant now, with her daddy, and he too appeared strong and stoic in the face of so much uncertainty. But that didn't mean they were out of danger. It didn't mean that thug with the gun wouldn't burst in at any moment and drag them outside to execute them.

"Stop that," she whispered to herself. "It does not help."

Nor did it help to tell herself this was all her fault. But it was. Partly, at least. She'd gotten cocky, believed she was untouchable. But she wasn't Acid and she never would be. She wasn't cool or brave or sassy. She was an awkward tech-nerd with dubious social skills and an unhelpful ability to stick her head in the sand when things went wrong. And yes, she was also super-brainy and hardworking, but those traits hardly transferred well to high-pressure situations. She was useless here and had been an idiot for believing otherwise. Acid would have overpowered those guys as soon as they took the sack off her head. Or she'd be working on an ingenious plan of escape. All Spook could do was sit and wait, hope some bright idea might burst through the fog of doubt clouding her brain.

"You were wrong to take this on yourselves." Mayor Donovan's words drew her attention back to the room. "These people are dangerous."

She raised her head. "How do you know? Who are they?"

The mayor turned to take her in, as unease trickled down her spine.

"This is Spook," Cynthia said, placing her hand on his chest as if to stop him from attacking her. "She's my friend. She's been helping me."

"Helping you? Damn it, Cynthia." He staggered over to the wall and leaned his back against it, arms folded. "How is this helping anyone? You should have left it for the police to take care of."

But Cynthia was defiant. "We went to the police. But Chief Hunger was pretty dismissive. Acted like it was all a big chore for him."

Donovan frowned. "What did he say?"

"That he was dealing with it. That we should stay out of it and let him do his job. But like I told you, he has it in his head Mr Elway and the Cheetahs are involved. Except we all know that's not true, so what happens then? You remain here all dirty and beat up? What are these people planning on doing with you?"

The frown deepened, but now with a sense of defeat sagging his shoulders. "I don't know," he said. "But I do know what their motivation is."

"Oh?" Spook said. "You want to enlighten us?"

He considered her again with steely eyes, giving her the impression he was about to snap. But whatever he was planning on saying, he must have changed his mind. Instead, he pushed off from the wall and walked over to the bed.

"Their motivation is money," he said, easing himself down beside her. "Money and power. Like everything in life."

"What do you mean?" Cynthia asked, coming over to the bed but not sitting.

"The men who brought you here, Travis and Jackson, they work for a man called Raymond Glick."

Spook and Cynthia exchanged looks. "Glick Development," Cynthia whispered.

"We found a letter in your office," Spook added.

"He's a real estate developer," Donovan went on. "Hotels, golf courses. He's a multi-millionaire. From Texas originally. He's got a chain of luxury hotels all across the world, in areas like Blackfell Ridge where guests pay top dollar to be surrounded by idyllic, unspoilt country. That's his hook apparently, the juxtaposition of high-end luxury and amazing scenery. He's been wanting to build a hotel and spa complex on the edge of town for the last few years, and as soon as I became mayor he was all over me like a rash. But the land he wants to build on is owned by the Elway family. After his father died, Vince became the sole owner. Glick wanted me to help him get it, use my position to lean on Vince and the Cheetahs. Then he wanted me to push through the relevant paperwork for land and building rights. When I told him I wouldn't, he turned nasty."

"But I don't get it," Cynthia said. "Why kidnap you? What does that achieve?"

"Come to me, *Princesa*." He reached for his daughter's hand and pulled her to him. She nestled down between him and Spook. "Glick asked me to meet him up on Crow Mountain. Said he had some important items he wanted to run by me. Something 'mutually beneficial' were his words. But when I got there it was only more of the same, wanting me to use my position to help him get what he wanted. His men were with him, acting tough, like I care. Glick offered me a large sum of money. A bribe. I told him no. I told him he was to get out of my town and never come back."

"And he didn't like that?" Spook asked, leaning around Cynthia.

"No. He did not. As I was driving home down the mountain, I realised I was being followed. A Dodge pickup. It got up close, then rammed into the back of me. I tried my best to out-manoeuvre whoever it was, but they forced me off the road and into a tree. I must have banged my head and passed out. When I woke I was in the back of a truck, with my arms tied and a sack over my head."

"Those evil fuckers," Cynthia gasped, before catching herself. "Sorry, Dad. I didn't mean to—"

He waved it away. "It's what they are. Though maybe evil is the wrong word. I think it was an impulsive act on Glick's part, but now he can't back down. Or he's planning to use me as leverage somehow."

"What's going to happen to us?" Cynthia asked.

"If I'm pronounced missing officially, they must elect a new mayor. Perhaps one that Glick has more control over. After that, who knows."

Spook turned away. "But even with a new mayor in place, he can't allow you to be found, can he? He kidnapped you. He kidnapped us. We all know too much." She trailed off as the words took form and slammed her in the guts. She lowered her head. "They're going to kill us."

"No. They won't," Donovan said, getting to his feet. "I won't let them. And no matter what you think of Chief Hunger, he is the law around here. He'll keep looking for us. He won't let these people get away with this."

"Wait…" Spook said, lifting her head. "You hear that?"

The three of them looked at the door as voices drifted through from the other side. Then laughter and jeering and the sound of the outer cabin door slamming shut. Spook and Cynthia got to their feet and joined Mayor Donovan in the centre of the room as a key rattled in the lock.

"It's okay," Donovan whispered, raising a protective arm in front of Spook and Cynthia. "I'll handle this."

But as the door swung open, his arms dropped to his sides and all the fight drained from his muscles. Two men were standing in the doorway, both of them wearing the familiar uniforms of law enforcement. The skinnier of the two men stepped into the room and placed his hands on his hips, chewing on the end of a cigar as he regarded the three of them.

"Hell's bells, Mayor," he said with a devilish grin.

"Looks like you've found yourself up shit creek without so much as a paddle. Or a boat."

"Hunger," Donovan gasped. "You bastard."

Chief Hunger tutted loudly and wagged his finger. "Now, now, that's no way to speak to your chief of police." He lowered his voice, all the jovialness gone. "And I'd say you'd better start being a little nicer to yours truly, Mr Hotshot Mayor. Because right now I'm all that stands between you three chumps and a long walk off a short bridge."

Chapter Twenty-Four

Jareth sipped at his wine as Acid paced the floor of his motel room. It was the first drink he'd had since getting out of hospital and it was a lousy one to start with. But regardless, it was much needed. Acid hadn't stopped talking since she'd burst into his room ten minutes earlier, prowling up and down like a caged beast whilst he sat in the chair next to the bed trying to keep a lid on his own emotions. Without taking his eyes off her, he took another sip of wine, this time holding the liquid in his mouth for a few seconds in the hope that doing so might relinquish some deeper flavour notes than the initial hit of vinegar. But no. It still tasted like hobo wine. Not that Jareth was any kind of wine connoisseur, but he had tastebuds.

"You know you're a hard man to read," Acid told him, stopping abruptly and meeting his gaze head on. "Unlike any military man I've ever met."

He laughed. "You've met a lot?"

"Some. In my old line of work I went up against plenty

of mercenaries and private security. Many of them were ex-military. I found most of them to be soulless shits with zero personality and even less of a sense of humour."

"Aww, and I'm not a soulless shit? That's so sweet."

She snorted and went back to pacing. "I don't think so, actually. You're kind of cool, in a laid-back kind of way." Then, stopping once more: "Aren't you scared of me?"

"Should I be?"

"Maybe."

"Has someone hired you to kill me?"

"No."

"Then why should I be scared? Besides, fear is a pointless emotion. Over the years I've learned to channel those feelings into a different response. I don't get scared, I get resourceful."

"Thank you, Tony Robbins," Acid cried, lolling her head back and speaking to the ceiling. "But you're right. I used to be like that. Still am sometimes. Other times I'm just a real fucking mess."

Jareth held the glass to his lips but didn't drink. He didn't react either. She was testing him. Or sizing him up. Either way she'd have to do better. "Why do you think that is?" he asked.

"Piss off. I'm asking the questions."

"Oh, I didn't realise this was an interrogation."

She spun around and grabbed up the bottle from the nightstand. "Nothing bloody well fazes you, does it?"

This time Jareth's laughter was genuine. Genuine, but bittersweet.

"It used to," he told her. "Hell, there was a time everything fazed me. My old man, friends, teachers. Girls, especially. I was what you might call an angry young man when

I was growing up. Even more so when my dad screwed me over and forced me to enlist. But after a while I realised by pulling so far the other way, the only person I was hurting was me. I had an amazing mentor in my first commanding office. A guy called Oswald Bates. Captain Bates. He taught me a whole lot about being a good soldier, but also about being a good man."

Acid had slowed her pacing. She walked over and sat on the bed, filling her glass from the bottle and waving it at him. "Go on."

He stared into the centre of the room, looking at nothing in particular but seeing plenty. "I guess over the years I learned real peace of mind comes from accepting your circumstances. The only way you get a clear head is by acceptance, and the only way you survive in high-pressure conditions is by keeping a clear head. That applies to everyday life as well as in wartime. You get all caught up in your thinking you make mistakes. Overthink every single option until you get to the point you don't know what's up or down. So I made a pact with myself to never get caught up in any drama. To walk away whenever I felt the slightest bit off kilter. That way, I take control of my own destiny. No point waiting around for someone else to do anything for you. You got to do it for yourself. That includes your happiness."

"Happiness?" Acid muttered. "What's that again?"

"You should try it sometime."

"I'll pass. But the clear head thing I understand. I used to think it was that simple."

"What changed?"

She gulped back a mouthful of wine and rolled her eyes dramatically. "Every fucking thing changed."

Jareth stood and walked to the window, easing open a

flap of curtain for a view of the parking lot. An old guy in a red plaid shirt and a beat-up Stetson was John Wayne-ing his way down the street opposite, but that was all.

"Are you expecting someone?" Acid asked.

"Hope not," he replied, not turning from the window. "But you can't be too careful. It pays to stay clear-headed, but it pays to stay alert just as much."

Behind him Acid scoffed. "There's always a caveat."

"What do you mean?"

Turning, he saw she was now lying on the bed, propped up on her elbows. "Life. You think you've got it all worked out, then something happens that rocks your ideas off their bloody foundations." She sat upright. "Two years ago I thought I had it all worked out. I'd wanted out of the killing business for a while and I saw my chance. It wasn't ideal, and it was damn risky, but I was savvy enough and had money saved so I could disappear."

"And I take it things didn't go to plan. What happened?"

"Spook bloody Horowitz happened, that's what." She looked away. When she spoke again, her tone was steady and her voice low. "My leaving didn't go down too well with my boss."

"Oh?"

She looked back and her eyes were shining in the light, a film of tears threatening to break free. "Let's just say, he sent me a message I couldn't ignore."

Jareth returned to the chair. "You're really worried about this Spook girl."

"I am. I know she's a grown-up and I don't give her enough credit sometimes, but... Well... She's like family, I suppose. All I've got."

Jareth didn't react, but it was a surprise to hear those

words. He didn't have Acid down as the sentimental type. But then, wasn't everyone sentimental if you dug deep enough, hit the right vein. He'd known grown men who were tough as all hell, happy to kill boyish insurgents without missing a beat, but show them a photo of a wounded dog and they were in more bits than the afore-mentioned insurgents.

"Tell me about you," she said. "What's your story? The real one, I mean."

He looked at her and smiled. "It's not very interesting."

"Try me. It'll help me get out of my head if nothing else." She tapped her glass against her temple. "Clear it for me, Colonel."

Jareth sat back, feeling the soft embrace of the armchair around his aching muscles. "I told you some of it already. My dad was a local cop. A real piece of work who forced me into signing up. Either that or I went to jail. I wouldn't have lasted five minutes. Not when the other guys found out who my father was. So the decision was kind of made for me." He took a big gulp of the wine. It was starting to taste a little better. "At first I hated being in the military, especially as I was sent to Afghanistan straight away. But over time, with Captain Bates' help, I saw a future for me. I've always been a tenacious sonofabitch, but the army helped me hone that stubbornness into something more practical. Then, half-way through my third tour, I woke up with a sack over my head, taken to a CIA black site in the middle of the desert. I was told they were recruiting a new task force and needed the best of the best. Told me my name was on top of their list. Although I suspect now that was them tickling my balls."

He paused, waiting for a response, but none came. He drained the glass of wine and saw his hand was shaking.

Shit.

He hadn't talked about this stuff in so long, but he still felt the memories in his body, tightening his shoulders. He didn't have to close his eyes to see the flash of the explosion in front of him. He smelt the burnt flesh as though it had just happened. Tasted it, too.

He turned his attention back to Acid. "I became a captain in Delta Force in 2006. We were a Black Ops unit, off the books and ultimately answering to the CIA. It was tough and bloody, but I believed what we were doing was worthy. And it was, by and large. But then around the end of 2017, life took a turn." He had an urge to get to his feet, to go to the window and distract himself from the words coming out of his mouth.

He stayed where he was. No point running from this.

"You know, I loved my team, but I got frustrated at all the bureaucracy and bullshit. Under Bates I felt I'd found my calling. I believed with enough hard work, coupled with my intellect and tenacity, I'd blaze a path to success. But with Walker I fast came to the realisation I'd only achieve success if I learned to play the game. His way."

"Walker was your commanding officer at Delta Force?"

"Yes, ma'am. A real piece of shit. A hard-nosed CIA guy with something close to bloodlust driving him. Wanted to get those Arabs at any cost. His words." He risked another glance Acid's way. She was sitting upright with the bottle of wine between her thighs. Her eyes were now wide and startlingly alert.

"He's the reason you left the military?"

"Yup. The reason I'm no longer a colonel. Why I can't – and won't – call myself that. Ever again." He surveyed her face, but she didn't flinch. She was a tough cookie, this one. She kept on staring at him, waiting for more.

Well, shit.

It looked like he was going to go there.

After all this time.

"We'd been searching for this Taliban commander for a couple of months. A man calling himself Jaladdin. Single moniker. Like Prince or Madonna. Anyway, the CIA intel said he was holed up in this apartment block on the edge of a small town in the Khost Province. Walker was fucking ecstatic. He couldn't wait to take this guy out. Only, it wasn't going to be him doing the dirty work, of course." He leaned forward and reached for the wine. Acid handed over the bottle without a word and he poured himself a large glass. "I knew there was something up. Just an instinct I had, something in my belly. I wanted to wait, get eyes on him before we moved. But Walker wouldn't have it. I even tried going over his head, but Walker defied his commanding officer too, ordered we move in." He puffed his cheeks out. This was hard.

"It was a trap?"

"Uh-huh. The Taliban knew we were watching and booby trapped the entire place. Walker had gotten bad intel. The apartment block wasn't a Taliban stronghold, it was a civilian home. There were families still living there. Only these Taliban pricks had set up IEDs around the place without the residents' knowledge. My buddy was first in, a guy called Andrew Polchek. Polly. A good man. He was newly married. Had a boy, one year old. He kicked open the first door and the blast took half his face off and most of his torso. He died in my arms. Same way he does every night when I close my eyes."

Acid's hand hovered over his. "Shit. I'm sorry."

"It is what it is. War, right? It's a shit business. I pulled my men out of there straight away, but the damage was done. We'd fucked up. The same bomb that killed Polly killed a mother and her newborn daughter. Three lives wiped out. For nothing. Jaladdin wasn't even in the town. Only, Walker wasn't going to let that derail his career. Or his cause." He knocked back the entire glass of wine, didn't even taste it. "The son of a bitch threw me under the bus. Wrote in his report it was my call to go in that night. The government couldn't have the CIA linked to that mess, so that was what they wrote on every report. After that, Delta Force was disbanded and they gave me an ultimatum. Another one. Retire now, go quietly, or be court martialled for violations of the Uniform Code of Military Justice. You know, they wouldn't even grant me leave to go to Polly's funeral. I was so angry I punched Walker out in front of his entire team. Got myself a dishonourable discharge for that, but it was worth it. Almost. So, here I am. Wandering around trying to work out what the hell to do next. Some story, huh?"

Nothing registered on Acid's face. "Those soulless shits."

Jareth felt the tension leave his shoulders. "Ha. You said it. I've been doing a bit of private security since then. But I don't know whether I'll go back to it after this." There was something about the way she was looking at him, made him consider spilling all. But he decided against it. For another time, maybe.

If there ever was one.

This Acid Vanilla sure was a cool girl, but she was as messed up and broken as him. In anyone's book, that was a recipe for disaster.

"You know, there's one thing I keep meaning to ask," he said. "What the fuck are the bats? You keep mentioning them."

Acid reached again for the bottle of wine, almost empty

now. She poured herself a glass, then drained the bottle into Jareth's.

"It's how I talk about my condition," she said, pulling her legs up onto the bed. "It's a rare form of bipolar. Lots of ups, not many downs, but the ups can get *really fucking mental* if I don't watch myself. It helps me function better if I visualise these heightened moods as bats. It's a long story, but it works. Most of the time."

Jareth had a compulsion to move onto the bed beside her. "Makes sense," he said. "I think." He stayed where he was on the chair, but his weight had instinctively shifted forward onto his feet. Alert, but for different reasons.

"For a long time I put my faith in the bats," she continued. "They made me feel strong and unhuman. In a good way. A useful way, at least. I wonder now whether it was their presence that allowed me to do what I did. The bats were in charge, so I wasn't the one killing people, not really. God, it sounds ridiculous when I say it out loud."

"No," Jareth said. "It doesn't. You have to get yourself in a certain mindset to kill someone. I've heard people get to that point in all kinds of ways. For me I just switched off. Let my training take over. I was like fucking RoboCop or the Terminator when I was in the field. Which is why I think I needed to push myself to be more caring when I was out of it. That was easier. I simply did the opposite of whatever my father would do. I usually found that was the right thing."

"I've never met anyone like you, Jareth Hicks."

He shot her a look and saw her pull back, like she'd shocked herself with the statement. But she let it ride. No caveat this time. No cynical aside.

"I could say the same about you, Ms Vanilla."

"Don't." She looked away. "I'm a total nightmare. I've spent my whole adult life living in some kind of suspended persona and now I don't even know how to be normal. If I even can be."

"Hell, who wants to be normal?"

"Yeah, yeah, I know. But after the life I've had, I wonder if that's what I need."

Jareth moved to the bed and shifted around to face her. "Way I see it…Whatever you ain't changing, you're choosing."

Acid leaned back. "Wow," she whispered. "That's kind of deep."

"But true, right?"

She nodded, not taking her eyes from his. Her pupils were dilated again, though now for a different reason he hoped. She leaned closer. "You're a good man, Jareth Hicks."

He followed her lead. "I try to be, but I'm not. Not really. And this is wrong, you know that." He leaned in regardless. "I don't let my heart get involved anymore. It's safer that way."

"Oh sure. I'm exactly the same."

"This is a bad idea, Acid."

"*Such* a bad idea."

Their lips were inches apart. The room fizzed with electric energy. But really there was no room. There were no walls, no floor, no motel even. Time didn't exist. Nothing did. They were two lost souls floating in space. Then her lips were on his. Soft and warm and moist. He kissed back as she grabbed him around the neck, breathed her in as she pushed him down onto the bed.

Two lost souls.

Floating in space.

The last thought that passed through Jareth's mind before lust and impulse overtook him was that for a bad idea it sure felt good.

And it had been such a long time.

Chapter Twenty-Five

Chief Aldous Hunger III was not a man who could be bought. No siree. Not a chance in hell of anything like that happening.

So when the big Texan first approached him, saying he had an offer he couldn't refuse (or words to that effect), Aldous's first instinct was tell him to go to hell. Then he met the man in person and decided his response ought to be more tactful – not least, as there was something altogether unsettling about Mr Raymond Glick. He was a tall man, almost seven feet tall, and had played basketball in college before getting into real estate and exchanging his sneakers and shorts for a briefcase and check book. But it wasn't Glick's imposing height that made people wary of him, as much as the strange way he had of looking at them side on. He'd ask a question and then stare without blinking, waiting while the other person spilled their guts and told them things they never intended. It brought to mind a book Aldous had read a few years back on negotiation techniques, where this method was mentioned often – a way of staying quiet and not being afraid of awkward silences so the person you were dealing with would keep talking. Weaponised silence, they called it. It sure was apt terminology.

So even before Glick had shown his hand, Aldous already had a fair idea who he was dealing with. Raymond Glick was a man used to getting what he wanted, ready to strike down those who got in his way. He explained to Aldous how he'd found the perfect site for his new development and hoped the chief of police might help sway the local landowner's decision to sell. He followed up by explaining how he'd make it worth his while, offering a mighty 'fixer's fee' as he called it, plus shares in the development when it was built. Aldous was set to make at least six figures a year if all went to plan, four times what he made now. Add that to the money he'd been promised for getting the Cheetahs to sell, and he'd be set for life. More than that, he'd be damn stinking rich.

He hadn't counted, though, on the new mayor being such a stickler for protocol, or how quickly Vincent Elway would take over the presidency after his father was killed.

But these things were sent to try him. And new plans were now in place. The question was no longer, would the hotel complex get built? But, how quickly could they start breaking soil? It was a shame Donovan had to get caught up in all this, but it was his own damn fault. If he'd accepted Glick's offer, none of this would have to happen.

Stupid, pious bastard.

Aldous was still pissed at the way his new business partner had taken Donovan out without his input, but the way Morris Wade explained it, it was a spur-of-the-moment decision. Wade was Glick's right-hand man and almost as menacing as his boss. But whereas Glick's shtick was all dark, brooding threat, Wade was upfront and abrupt.

"In our line of work," Wade had told him. "You don't offer payment to government officials and have them refuse. Looks bad on everyone. We had to send him a message, try to change his mind."

Of course, it hadn't worked out that way, but the actual outcome was even better. After Donovan was knocked unconscious in the crash, Aldous had suggested they bring him here, to the old police hunting lodge, and keep him tied down while they worked out how to best leverage the situation. It was now a matter of working out what to do with him once their plan had been actioned and Wade was in situ as the new mayor. But Aldous Hunger III, being the smart son of a bitch he was, had an idea.

"I should have known you'd be involved," Douglas Donovan snarled as Aldous, followed by Trooper Crawford, strode into the room. "This has got your vile stench all over it. But you won't get away with this. I swear it."

"Save your breath, Doug," Aldous told him. "We've already got away with it. Crawford, you want to do the honours with *Mr* Donovan?"

"With pleasure." Crawford lowered his satchel to the floor and removed a quart bottle of whisky. "Here you go, Mayor."

He chucked the bottle at Donovan, who caught it with one hand.

"What the hell is this?"

"We thought you might like a drink. To ease the pain, as it were."

"You lousy bastards," he cried, scrambling to his feet, still holding the bottle. "You run me off the road, lock me up, kidnap my daughter. I promise, if you hurt her at all, I'll kill the both of you… What the fuck?"

He'd been making to lunge forward, but he was barely upright when the flash of Aldous's mobile phone camera pushed him back.

Letting a wide grin spread across his face, Aldous examined the shot. He was by no means a professional photographer, but the framing was perfect, as was the tableau. On the screen, the (soon to be ex-) mayor of Blackfell Ridge was lunging forward with a bottle of whisky in his fist. His clothes were torn and dirty, and with his wild hair and red eyes, along with the smear of dark stubble, he looked like one of the drunks you'd find out on the edge of town. Certainly not a man fit to govern.

"Tut, tut," Aldous said, showing him the screen. "You appear a little – dare I say it – unhinged, in this one, Dougie."

He gave Crawford the nod, and he reached back into the satchel, pulling out the envelope containing the photos they'd had developed. He handed them to Aldous, who shook them out of the envelope and flipped through them, pleased once more with his handiwork, and his damn fine plan. He held each one up in turn to Donovan, delighting in the realisation blossoming on his grimy Latino face.

"See here? That's your office, ransacked, with bottles and drug paraphernalia strewn all around." He stepped closer to give him and those interfering little bitches a better look. "And this one? Your home office. Same story. Holes punched in the walls, smashed liquor bottles. Smears of your own blood. Damn, it sure looks like you went medieval on the place, my friend."

"You bastard!" Donovan snatched for the photos, but Aldous pulled them away. "No one will believe you."

"Won't they? I'd say once you show up — maybe in a couple of months or so, depending on our timescale — there'll be a new mayor in town. One who will sign off on a major new deal, to bring untold wealth and prosperity to the town. In the meantime we leak these photos, let people know what kind of person their old mayor really is. A man who gets so blind drunk he smashes up his home and the town hall before driving his car into a tree and wandering off without a care in the world." He handed the photos back to Crawford. "I mean, some might believe you. But I wouldn't count on it. Y'see, Doug, they might tolerate you now, with your bright teeth and good head of hair. But you ain't one of them. Are ya?"

"Racist pig." It was the Latino daughter scrambling to her feet, with eyes like fire. "Not everyone is like you. They'll believe us."

Aldous laughed. "With the entire police force claiming different? With our reports filed and part of public record?" He lowered his voice. "Listen, Donovan, I'm doing you a favour here. For you and your little girl. I have no idea what Glick is planning, but this way you get to walk away from this. And walk away you should. Far away. If you know what's good for you."

It was a bold move, Aldous knew it, and there was a lot could go wrong. But he'd be long gone before anything went awry. Soon as he got what he wanted from Glick, he'd move away from Blackfell Ridge for good. It was back to civilization for Aldous. But not LA. Never again. He'd try Malibu, perhaps. Portola Valley. Rub shoulders with some real class and leave Donovan and Elway, and all these other meddling pricks, for Glick to deal with.

"You horrible motherfucker!"

It was the daughter again, coming for him now with her

claws raised and her teeth bared. She got within a few feet before Crawford stepped in and a swift backhand sent her stumbling into the wall.

"Cynthia! You bastard. I'll kill you."

Before Aldous could react, Donovan was on his feet, arcing a fist through the air and catching him on the side of the head. The impact vibrated his skull, but the muscle memory of countless barroom brawls had him lashing out in retaliation. His flailing fists connected with something fleshy as he fought to focus. He heard shouting, high-pitched screams, Crawford's voice telling someone to, "Back the fuck away." Aldous raised his head, trying to regain control over his balance before a heavy blow to the guts bent him double and something sharp slammed into the middle of his back, sending him to his knees. Through the red mist clouding his vision, he saw Crawford pushing the two girls away, the two of them coming at him like snapping turtles. Aldous pushed off the floor before Donovan got in another attack. He was on one foot and one knee, ready to stand, when a deafening bang reverberated through the room and the whole place froze.

Raising his head, he saw the two girls and Crawford staring at something behind him. Staying low, he twisted around, noticing first Donovan at the side of the room, the whisky bottle still clenched in his fist, then the enormous figure silhouetted in the doorway.

"Howdy there, folks," Raymond Glick said, striding into the room, a pistol in his hand. "I'm sorry to spoil all the fun, ladies. But I need to break up this little pyjama party."

Chapter Twenty-Six

Spook couldn't remember a time she'd seen a man duck to get through a doorway. The large Stetson the man was wearing probably had something to do with it, she thought, but then he took it off (holding it to his chest, like she'd seen men do in old movies when greeting a priest or someone of the opposite sex) and he appeared to grow bigger still. His head seemed huge, with a mane of thick white hair cut short around a square cranium. But it wasn't only his head. His hands were as big as boiled hams, making the gun he'd just fired look like a toy in comparison. Everything about him was huge. Including his imposing presence. As he turned away, side-eyeing them with a steely gaze, an unfriendly smile spread across his bulbous fish lips.

"Seems we've got ourselves a slight problem," he growled.

Even if he hadn't been pointing a pistol at her and Cynthia, Spook would have taken an instant dislike to the man. He had something of the night about him, something dark and clammy and sinister. She couldn't take her eyes off him as he clicked his fingers and another man appeared by his side.

"Take this, will you?" he said, handing him the pistol, holding it between two fingers like it was something unpleasant he'd peeled off his shoe. The man took it and placed it in the pocket of his suit jacket. Both men were wearing suits. The giant (who she assumed was Raymond Glick) wore a silvery grey two-piece that shimmered as he moved, whilst his slightly less giant (but still equally menacing) counterpart wore a more subdued blue number.

"Please, Mr Glick," Cynthia's dad started. "Let us go. Let my daughter and her friend go, at least. They are no concern for you. I'll sign off building rights. Okay? I was stupid to turn down your offer. But I see now."

"Save it, Pedro," Glick told him. "Things have moved on a lot since then."

Although too terrified to take her eyes from Glick, Spook sensed everyone in the cabin had now turned to face him. The corrupt chief, the horrid bastard trooper, Cynthia, her dad – they were all hanging on the big man's word. He had that kind of presence.

"Crawford," the chief said. "Show Mr Glick the photos."

They all turned as the corrupt trooper strode over and placed the incriminating shots into Glick's catcher's mitt hand. He remained poised, profile-on as he regarded the chief. "Hunger, what is this?"

"That's our way out of this, once Wade is in place at the town hall and we've gotten rid of those pesky Cheetahs once and for all. I've had an idea too about how we do that. See, I've heard recently they're trying to go legit. Open a couple of bars and the like."

Glick ran an impatient tongue along his top teeth. "And?"

"How do they do that without licences and permits?" Hunger went on, his voice rising. "They can't, is the answer. Soon as they realise they've got no livelihood around here; it won't be too much longer before they sell up and move on. Then building the complex is just a matter of time."

"Vince would never give in to you people," Cynthia's dad told them, barking the words with venom. He was a good man and his presence buoyed Spook; she just wished she could find her own voice. But her throat was as dry as Acid's wit, and if she opened her mouth she feared she might throw up.

Acid...

Where was she now? Did she even know she was missing?

Spook closed her eyes, trying to stay calm, trying to stay logical and analytical as she went over what she knew. This was difficult enough without sleep or sustenance, but doubly so when your legs were shaking uncontrollably. She knew Acid was pissed at her, but she wouldn't leave without saying goodbye. Would she? Not after everything they'd been through together.

No.

No, no, no.

Don't think like that, Spook told herself. Acid is still in town. And if that's the case, sooner or later she'll be out looking for her. Acid also knew about Mr Donovan's disappearance and that Spook was helping Cynthia look for him. If these bastards had indeed trashed the mayor's home and office like the photos showed, then Acid would put two and two together. Word travelled fast in places like Blackfell Ridge.

"Find us, Acid," she whispered hoarsely at the floor. "Please find us."

"Vince Elway is a decent man," Cynthia's dad went on. "A man of honour. A man of his word. Better than the likes of you. He won't sell. Never. That land belongs to him and his father before him."

"Yeah, and look how that worked out for the old fucker," Glick replied.

Spook raised her head to take in the mayor, seeing his expression morph from rage to shock and then to horror. "What do you mean?" he asked.

"I mean, I've been after that land of theirs for some time. And you must understand by now, Mr Donovan, I am a man of means and I always get what I want. I had hoped that paying that rival club to bump off Elway Senior would have left the club in ruins and his son no choice other than to sell up. But it seems the kid has more heart than I gave him credit for. Stupid bastard."

"You're behind Jacob Elway's murder?" the mayor gasped.

"I like to think of it more like I'm removing the crap from out of my path. Same way an excavation vehicle removes obstacles to the laying of new foundations. And unfortunately for you people," he said, waving his hand at Spook and her fellow captees, "you're also in my path."

An unexpected yelp escaped from Spook's throat.

"We aren't in anyone's path," Donovan replied, speaking hastily, without taking a breath. "I'll sign whatever you want me to, I swear. Get me the papers. I'll do it now. Please."

"Please, sir. Let us go."

Spook glanced over to see there were tears rolling down

Cynthia's face. She so wanted to go to her, to hold her, to tell her Acid was coming for them and soon all would be well. But she couldn't do that. It wasn't true.

"You don't need us," she said instead. "We're not in your way. Listen to what he's telling you. I mean it, we—"

Glick rounded on her, his enormous face red with a fury that almost knocked her off her feet. "I don't remember addressing you, missy," he yelled. "And I'd suggest you do yourself a favour and shut your pretty little trap. Before I do it for you."

He straightened up, rolling his shoulders back and adjusting his jacket as he did.

"Mr Glick, sir," Chief Hunger said, stepping between them. "What about my plan? The photos? We've got leverage here. They aren't going to be a problem."

"Leverage?" Glick replied. "You call that leverage? This is big business we're doing here, Hunger. We can't have loose ends. Can't have anything coming back to bite us on the ass. Besides, I've got a much better idea for how we get rid of these folks and take those long-haired biker boys down in one fell swoop."

"Oh?"

"What you were trying for with your rumour-mongering in town was… adequate, I suppose. But we can't make anything stick without evidence. If we want to frame those sons of bitches, then we need a body. Or better still, three bodies."

"No," Cynthia cried.

"You can't do this," her dad yelled.

Inside Spook was a typhoon of spiralling emotions, most of them synonyms of one another. Fear ruled. It threatened to engulf her as she listened to Glick's words. Next, a weird sensation bubbled in her chest, making her feel as though she was about to burst into tears. But no tears came. She sucked back a deep breath and held it in her chest, tried to summon her inner Acid.

Stay strong, kid.

Stay strong.

Glick placed his Stetson on his head, twisting the brim into position as he considered Spook and Cynthia in turn. "You girls were stupid to get involved," he told them, before turning to Mr Donovan. "And you were more stupid to turn down my offer, Mr Mayor. But there's nothing I can do about that now."

Spook saw the chief and Crawford exchange furtive glances. "Are you serious about this?" Hunger whispered to Glick. "Will it work?"

"Of course it'll work, you damn fool," came the reply, spat out the side of Glick's mouth. "Their lives will be all the leverage we need to take down those bikers permanently. Once they see what we've got on them, they'll sell up sharpish. They may be a bunch of cretinous heathens, but they aren't stupid. They'll not risk getting arrested. You told me yourself, there's a list a mile long of suspected felonies linked to that club. We add murder and kidnapping to that list and I'd say their riding days are over."

Spook watched the chief, watched as his face told her the penny had dropped. "Fine. We do it your way," he said. He stepped in front of Glick and turned his back on Spook and the Donovans. When he spoke again his voice was low but still audible. "How we going to make it seem like the Cheetahs killed the three of them?"

"Well, my friend, that's easy," Glick replied, his voice loud and booming, happy to be heard. "We take them up the mountain, to that place you were telling me about."

Chief Hunger's back went rigid. He shot Crawford a look. "You mean…?"

"That's right." Glick stepped around him, locking eyes with Mr Donovan as he spoke. "These idiots are going to walk the plank."

Chapter Twenty-Seven

Acid was awake but in that warm and dreamy state of near-sleep where nothing mattered and everything was well. And maybe it was. Despite the wine and the fact her mania had reached a real crescendo over the last forty-eight hours, she felt rested and calm. She was back in her body. Grounded. It was nice. For the first time in a long time she was happy to be alive. Happy to be her.

Generally, when she awoke naked with another human being beside her, she'd get up and get gone as soon as possible. But not today. Opening one eye, she saw Jareth was lying with one arm up over his head. Nuzzling into his side, she breathed in his musky aroma, shivering as her body recalled the previous evening's activities. It had been a meeting of minds as well as bodies, a cosmic and orgasmic experience that had gone on for hours. At one point towards the end, she even told herself she'd fallen for him.

Bloody hell.

She cringed inwardly at the memory. That was the wine

and the mania talking. Had to be. She didn't do love. Case closed.

But it didn't diminish how good the sex had been, or how much lighter she now felt. Reaching over to the nightstand to see the time on his watch, her arm barely got across his broad chest. She brought it back, lightly scratching his skin with her fingernails as she did.

"Huh?" He jolted awake and grabbed her wrist, already in fight-or-flight mode.

"Hey, it's me," she purred. "Don't worry."

He glanced around, eyes wide and breath held tight in his chest. "Shit, Alice. Sorry. I was having a… I think I was…" He shook his head. "Sorry. Bad dream."

"Don't worry, I understand," she told him, as they sunk back into the soft embrace of the bed. "Your friend again?"

Jareth shrugged and stared at the ceiling. He didn't want to talk about it. She understood that, too. He turned his head to look at her. "Damn. Aren't you a sight for sore eyes?"

She snorted at that one. Couldn't help it. Habit. But for some reason the way he said it sent another shiver through her. "Stop that, Romeo," she told him, covering his eyes with her hand. "And don't look at me like that."

"Like what?" he asked through laughter.

"You know."

She sat upright, making no move to cover her nakedness with the sheet. She might not have been as lithe or toned as she once was, but she liked her body (even if she wasn't always too keen on what went on inside of it). It had served her well over the years. In many ways.

"Last night was incredible," Jareth whispered, his hand caressing her back. "We don't have to get up yet, do we?"

She tensed at his touch, wasn't sure why. Maybe because

she knew what he could see, what his fingers were so softly tracing the outlines of. The scars of her past. She turned back, but it wasn't pity she saw there in his features. Quite the opposite. He grinned that wonky smile of his and his eyes twinkled with an air of mischief.

Jesus, man.

Give a girl a chance.

He patted the mattress and winked.

"No. Sorry," she said, sucking back all her emotion. "I need to find Spook. I'm sure she's fine, but still…"

Jareth's face fell, but into an expression of seriousness rather than prissy disappointment. He wasn't a game player. She liked that about him, too.

"Sure," he said. "You've got to do what you've got to do."

She reached back and snaked her fingers through his. "We can do this again, though. Once everything is settled. I'm here until the end of the month. So… It'd be good to see more of you."

She hated herself the second the words left her mouth. And the way she'd said it – *It'd be good to see more of you* – like some pathetic bloody idiot, desperate for a boy's attention. She coughed to cover it, but the damage was done. In turn, Jareth was breathing heavily through his nose. He pulled his hand away and stared into his palm as if it held all the answers.

"I'm still leaving," he said, not looking up. "I told you that. Nothing's changed."

"Oh. Right." She braced herself, as though a rifle butt had smashed her in the chest. "Of course you are. I forgot. And I don't blame you."

"We could stay in touch, maybe?" he said. "Who knows where'll we be in six months."

She turned and gave him the sort of smile that concealed all one's demons. "Doubt that would work. But it's cool. This was nice. Needed. Let's keep it that way."

He smiled that smile again. She turned back before it pulled her in. "I need to freshen up."

She whipped the covers off her legs and swung them onto the floor before striding across the room into the bathroom. At the door she had the urge to turn back, toss her hair over her shoulder with a sultry look, give him the whole bit, show him what he was saying goodbye to.

The bats said yes. Her guts, too. But for once her head won out. This was a dead end and it was pointless going further. Besides, she had to find Spook and apologise. That was her focus now. Not her emotions. Not Jareth Bloody Hicks. Once she was washed, she'd tell him thanks for a wild time and she'd see him around, never intending to set eyes on him again.

Like she always did.

———

AND SHE'D MEANT it too. Every word. Acid Vanilla didn't do big farewells. She had no time for them. And she certainly had no time to pine for ex-soldiers.

So when she was back at Jareth's door two hours later, banging the heel of her fist on the wood, she should, by rights, have been angrier with herself. On a normal day she would have been. But on a normal day she would never have returned to his motel room. It was gauche and needy and not the way she operated.

But today wasn't a normal day.

"Now I know something is wrong," she spat, as Jareth opened the door to see her leaning against the frame, gasping for breath. She'd run all the way from the centre of town.

"Acid? I was literally on my way to the station." He held up his hand to show her the leather holdall. "What's going on?"

"Do you think Vince was bullshitting us?" She barged past him as a chorus of bats screeched across her nervous system. Once inside the motel room, she spun around to face him. "Do you think they're behind this?"

A million chaotic and contradictory thoughts were crashing together in her mind.

Who to trust?

Who to believe?

She pulled Spook's beret out of her pocket and held it up.

"She's gone, Jareth, nowhere to be found, and she wouldn't do that, not without leaving me a note. Or something. Someone's taken her or... Or... Fuck! I have to find her."

She was talking ten to the dozen, trying to keep up with her spiralling moods.

"All right. Let's calm down," Jareth told her, closing the door. He placed his holdall on the bed and walked over to her. "Can I?"

He held his arms out and she launched herself into his warm embrace. But it didn't help. Her fists were clenched tight. Manic energy tingled through every cell in her body.

"I saw smashed glass and blood everywhere," she mumbled into his chest. "They broke the doors off the hinges... But Spook was with her... The mayor's daughter... They're in trouble, I know it... I have to find them. I have to."

Jareth moved his hands to her upper arms and stepped back. "Acid," he said, lowering his head to look her in the eyes. "I need you to take a breath and slow down."

"Fuck you."

She pulled away as the bats screamed in her head.

Jareth held his hands up. "Hey, I'm on your side, remember? Cool it." He kept his hands raised, not taking his eyes from hers. "What's going on?"

"I went back to our cabin, but she wasn't there and there's no sign of her having been back since yesterday. So I took a walk around town, and as I got up to the town hall I saw police cars outside and a lot of commotion. I heard from one of the locals that the mayor's office had been trashed and that the same thing had happened at his house. I got the address and raced over there and she wasn't kidding. I slipped past the cops and got in through the back door. The place was a real mess. Blood up the walls, broken bottles everywhere, holes in the plasterboard. Do you see?"

She glared at Jareth, waiting for the penny to drop.

Why wasn't he getting this?

"If Spook was anywhere, she'd be with the mayor's daughter, Cynthia. And my best guess is they'd been staying in that house. So either they were there when it was trashed and caught the brunt of whatever went down, or someone's trying to make it look that way."

"How do you mean?"

"I don't know. It was something about the place didn't sit right. It felt staged, like a film set of a break-in rather than an actual one. If whoever did it was looking for something in the mayor's house, they wouldn't have trashed it like that. There'd be drawers askew, sure, papers strewn around, but not the blood, not the broken glass. And likewise, Spook and her friend are both small. There's no way they'd have put up enough fight to cause all that damage. So what's the story?"

Jareth was silent for a long time. Too long, if you asked the bats. They were demanding blood. Demanding she do something. Anything.

"We should go to the cops," he said. "See if they can throw any more light on this."

"Seriously? That's your plan? Are you fucking high?"

Suddenly she wondered why she'd come here. Then she remembered it was for this very reason. He was calm, considered, could help her silence the bats and think strategically. But now that she was here he seemed too calm, too considered.

And it was jarring with her brittle mood.

"No, I'm not high. And I'm not saying we sit back and let them take over. Or fob us off with more talk about the Cheetahs. Clearly this is fresh evidence that happened recently, perhaps last night. If they still think it's Vince's crew, we can tell them categorically they're wrong. That we were with them last night. It might push them into investigating other avenues."

"Fucking hell." She shoved her hands on her hips. "Other avenues? You sound like a bloody cop."

Jareth grimaced. "It's not like that. But do you want to find your friend or not? I know the local cops aren't up to much, but they know the area better than we do. They know the places your friend might be." He stepped up to her, put his hand on her shoulder. "Listen, I'm going to stay and help you find her, but you've got to help yourself as well."

Acid made to shrug his hand off but stopped herself.

She looked away. "Fine. We'll go see the bloody police. But we go now, okay?"

"Sure," Jareth said, squeezing her shoulder. "You lead the way."

Chapter Twenty-Eight

"Where's Hunger?" Acid asked, slamming her palms down on the wooden countertop. "Where's the chief?"

The young deputy behind the desk got to her feet. "Ma'am, you need to calm down. This is a police station and you're causing a scene."

"I'll cause a bloody great big one if you don't get the chief out here this minute. My friend is in trouble. I know it. And I'm sick to the back teeth of being told to *calm down.*" She flinched as Jareth gripped her arm.

"My apologies about the outburst," he said, stepping in and giving the young cop the full charm offensive. He leaned over the desk. "My friend here is upset, as you can see. But that's because she's mightily concerned. Her travelling companion has gone missing and we believe it's linked to the mayor's disappearance."

The deputy watched them both without comment, her mouth stuck in a downturned arc. "I see," she said. "If you both take a seat, we'll ask you to——"

"You can stick your damn seat up your arse," Acid

yelled. "Spook is out there somewhere and I need you people to take this bloody seriously."

"What the heck is going on out here?" A door opened and a man poked his head out. The friendly but ineffectual Deputy Brooke. "Oh. It's you two."

Acid jutted her chin his way, not backing down. "Are you investigating the break-in at the mayor's house?"

He stepped around the side of the door and leaned his back against it, giving the deputy behind the desk a nod of reassurance. "Why don't you both come through?" he said. "We can talk better in here."

Acid couldn't resist a glare at the young deputy as she passed by the desk, feeling satisfied when the woman dropped her gaze away first. Brooke hurried inside his office, holding open the door as she and Jareth stepped in.

"Please, take a seat," he said, letting the door swing shut and waving his hand over the two chairs in front of his desk.

They sat and Acid waited as Brooke edged around to the other side and got comfortable. A hundred questions bubbled in her chest and throat but she stayed quiet, waiting for him to proceed.

He grabbed a pen from his desk tidy and peeled back the top sheet from the notepad in front of him. "First of all," he said. "Let me assure you we're doing all we can to get to the bottom of this mess."

"*This mess*," Acid spat. "Is that what you call three missing people and the mayor's house and office being ransacked, a bloody mess?"

Brooke raised his head, his prominent Adam's apple rising and falling. "I'm sorry, Miss, erm…?"

Acid sniffed, sensing Jareth's eyes on her. "Vandella. Miss Vandella."

"Miss Vandella. Of course. I'm sorry for sounding flippant. That wasn't my intention. And I agree, these break-ins overnight add an extra layer to the case. As soon as I speak with Chief Hunger, we'll be setting up a new line of enquiry."

"Oh, piss off. Are you kidding me?"

"Acid," Jareth whispered through gritted teeth. "Keep a lid on it." He leaned forward. "I'm sure you can appreciate, Deputy, that we are very concerned about what's happened to Aci— Alice's friend. It isn't in her nature to disappear. And as far as I can gather, no one has seen her or the mayor's daughter since yesterday. Right after they were in here talking to you, I believe."

Brooke placed his pen down without writing a word. "What are you implying?"

"I'm not implying a thing. But you can see how it looks. If I was someone investigating their disappearance, I'd find it kind of odd that the last people to see them alive are now dragging their heels looking for them."

"Hey," Brooke replied, pointing at Jareth. "You watch what you're saying. I know everyone is a little antsy right now, but don't forget who you're talking to." His finger quivered in the air.

"And who am I talking to?" Jareth asked, his voice low and authoritative. "I thought you were the second in command of this police department. A man who vowed to uphold the law in his town. Yet, right now all I can see is a man scared to act without Hunger's say so. Now tell me, Deputy, am I far off the mark?"

A ripple of heat energy shot through Acid, which she did her best to ignore. It certainly wasn't unpleasant, but it was inappropriate given the circumstances. She sat tight. Brooke chewed on his bottom lip and picked up his pen.

"Those are choice words," he told Jareth, leaning back

in his chair. "But I'm going to choose to ignore them. I get why you fellows are upset but, like I told you, we're doing all we can."

"Where's the chief right now?" Acid asked.

Brooke's eyebrow twitched. A tell if ever there was one. Jareth had seen it too, because he leaned forward again. "Do you even know where he is?"

"Chief Hunger's whereabouts are of no concern to you."

Jareth didn't let up. "Come on, Deputy. I see how uncomfortable you are right now. But I also believe you're a good man. What aren't you saying?"

Brooke opened his mouth, then shut it again. Holding up his hands, he said, "I'm sorry I can't be more help to you presently. This is a police matter and I assure you we are doing all we can. If we hear anything, you'll be informed forthwith."

"Fuck you and this red tape bullshit," Acid jumped out of her chair and onto her feet. "You're useless. All of you. Absolutely bloody useless."

She lunged over the desk. But before she reached the terrified deputy, an arm wrapped around her waist, halting her trajectory.

"Alice. No."

She gnashed her teeth, clawing the air as Jareth pulled her over to the door. "Get off me."

"Stop that, you're not helping."

"Get her out of here. Now," Brooks said. "I mean it. I will not be talked to like that."

"I'll talk however I want, you procedure-humping piece of shit," she yelled, digging her nails into Jareth's arm to wrestle free. "Let me go."

But Jareth already had the door open and was shoving

her back through it into the reception area. "We have to leave. This is not helping."

Brooke prowled after them. "I promise you; I'm doing all I can."

"We know. Thank you," Jareth called back, still dragging her away. "Apologies for this."

Acid elbowed him in the chest. "Doing all you can? Nah, mate. Not good enough."

"Out."

Jareth yanked her through the reception area before grabbing her around the waist and carrying her out onto the street.

"Get the hell off me," she snarled, smashing her fists down on his back. "I mean it, Jareth."

He walked a little further before complying with her wishes. They stood facing each other, breathless and tense in the early morning sun. Jareth's nose was bleeding where she'd caught him with a sharp elbow.

"*You* need to calm down," he told her.

"I am calm."

"Really? You want to tell your face?" He straightened up, placing his hands on his hips like a disappointed parent. "What the hell did you expect to achieve doing that? Poor bastard would be within his rights to throw you in jail after that little outburst. And you know what, I wouldn't blame him if he did."

"He knows something. I saw it and so did you."

"Yes. Maybe I did. But he isn't going to disclose anything while you're screeching at him."

"Screeching? Jesus. What, like a harpy? Like a witch? Sexist pig."

"Ah, get a grip, will you?" His hands went to his head, running his fingers through his hair. "Fuck me."

"I already did. Wasn't that great."

"Wow."

She waved him away with a violent flick of her wrist. "Just get lost. I'll find Spook myself, even if I have to burn this entire town to the ground. I'll find her. Me. Because that's the only person I can ever rely on."

"I've abandoned all my plans to help you today. For Christ's sake, Acid, I'm on your side. And I think the same – something is rotten in Denmark and Brooke seems to know more than he's letting on. But there's a right and a wrong way of going about things."

They were only feet apart. Acid had a sudden urge to grab his big stupid face and plant her lips on it. It would shut him up, at least. Instead she spun around, striding away from him as fast as she could.

"Acid, wait." He caught up with her in a few bounds, moving around the front of her and walking backwards as she marched on. "You're right. I do think there's something he's not telling us. So let me talk to him, all right? Calmly."

She stopped. "What? Man to man?"

"Not exactly. But I do think I've a way I can get through to him. Get some better answers than the ones he's giving."

"Yeah?" She stared deep into his eyes and a vague sense of relief washed over her. He was looking out for her. He really was on her side. Not for the first time since they'd met, it surprised her how good that felt. Still, it didn't stop her from folding her arms petulantly and tilting her head to one side. "What do you have in mind?"

"Wait here," he said, already heading back to the station. "Give me five minutes. I'll be back."

Chapter Twenty-Nine

Deputy Brooke was still standing in the reception area when Jareth re-entered the police station. And still wearing that same dour expression on his face, like he was planning a one-way trip to the rope store. He registered Jareth's presence with a weary nod.

"You got a minute, Deputy?" he asked him.

"I think you've had your minute, sir. I'm busy."

Jareth lowered his head. A display of surrender, making himself smaller, lowlier, in the police officer's perception. "I'm aware things got heated just now," he tried. "I came back to offer my humble apologies. But I wonder also if I might talk to you. Soldier to soldier." He glanced up as he said this last part, to catch Brooke's reaction. Pride. Written deep on his face.

"How did you know?"

"Us military men recognise their own, right?" he replied. "Now, I'm aware my friend and I have been royal pains in the ass this morning – and you're a busy man who has given us more than our fair share of attention – but I've a few questions still bothering me, and I'd be so grateful if you could help answer them."

The part about recognising one's own was true – to a certain extent – and Brooke had a certain way of carrying himself that hinted at a military past, but the framed photograph Jareth had spotted on the windowsill had helped a great deal, too. It showed a much younger Brooke, dressed in full army uniform with an older man and woman, no doubt his folks, standing on either side of him. Most likely it was his graduation day from the academy. The kid in the photo wore that same expression of pride Brooke exhibited when Jareth had mentioned his military background. Not that the flush of emotion remained long. A second later, his face crumpled into a worried frown and his shoulders sagged so much they were practically non-existent.

"Five minutes," Jareth added. "Then I'll be out of your hair forever."

He held eye contact with the deputy, allowing a grin to form. Letting him know – *you can trust me*. Letting him know – *I'm on your side*.

"Fine," Brooke said. "Five minutes."

Jareth didn't need telling twice. He strode across the reception area and into Brooke's office, sitting in the chair he'd vacated a few minutes earlier.

"Z Company 671 Base Support Battalion," Brooke said, closing the door and moving around his desk, easing himself into the large leather chair. He gestured at the photo on the window ledge. "That's me at Leonard Wood. After that I did two tours of Afghanistan, first at a COP and then an FOB. Kandahar and then Delaram. I'd like to say I saw a lot of action, but I got off kind of lightly. The Taliban had retreated by the time I got there. I worked hard though, and I always say those years made me who I am. I had been thinking about staying on after my second tour, making a career of it, but then my mom got sick and I decided a lateral move to the local PD was my best option. Got a young family now, but I still miss it. Made some good friends out there." His eyes misted over and he shook his head, frowning away the memories. "What about you?"

Jareth kept his smile in place. "Similar. I trained at Fort Sill and was in Hellman's at the start of it all. Those were hard times. I saw things I don't ever want to talk about. But I made a career out of it. For a time, at least." He sat forward, considering what he said next. Pulling rank right now could go either way. "Eventually I made colonel. Then soon after that I was head-hunted. By an off-the-books unit called Delta Force."

Brooke whistled. "I heard talk about you guys, but I thought it was rumours mainly. What was that like?"

"Well, you know, I can't talk about it."

"Yeah. No. Of course. Shit. Delta Force. Black Ops. Man, that's intense." He gripped his fists together over his desk. "I bet you saw some stuff."

"Oh yes. Saw some crazy stuff." He wasn't being flippant. But he wasn't allowing himself to think about any of it, either. His reactions were surface level. For Brooke's benefit. It worked. The Deputy Chief's whole manner relaxed as he unclenched his hands and held them out, palms up. You didn't get more of a subconscious display of openness than that.

"What can I do for you, Colonel Hicks?"

Jareth didn't correct him. Instead he looked away and sighed, like what he was about to say was hard to articulate. He moved his head from side to side, chewing the inside of his mouth. "The thing is, Deputy. I've spent a lifetime learning how to read people. Picking up on tics and tells and the like. And when we were in here before, something wasn't sitting right with me." He turned and fixed Brooke in the eyes. "You're an honest man, I can see that. And a good cop. But I can see something's playing on your mind."

"How do you mean?"

"Well, stop me if I'm wrong, but I get the impression you aren't happy about what's going on in your town. When we were asking before about the mayor, you seemed somewhat agitated, like you know more than what you're letting on."

"I don't know what you're talking about. As I told you, this is police business and—"

"Oh, come on, Brooke. That all you do? Toe the party line? Say what Hunger tells you to say? And what's the deal with that guy, anyway?"

"He's chief of police. That's his deal."

"Fair enough. So, tell me about Raymond Glick."

That hit a nerve. Jareth clocked the recoil behind his eyes, the way his jaw stiffened. "Raymond Glick?"

"You know who he is, right?"

"Yeah. I know him. Of him. He's a property developer. A big shot from out of town." He kept his tone steady, but the curl of his lip gave him away.

"Are he and Hunger close?"

"I'm sorry, Colonel. I've got nothing to say about Chief Hunger or Raymond Glick. If that's all you wanted to ask me about, then…"

He trailed off, glancing at the door as if to end the conversation. But Jareth didn't move. He didn't speak either. Didn't intend to until Brooke gave him more. Something useable. Either that or he'd have Jareth escorted from the building. But he didn't think he'd stoop that low. Brooke was a decent guy, but decent guys didn't fare too well in corrupt environments. He needed him to see that.

Ten seconds went by as the two ex-soldiers faced off against one another. Jareth narrowed his vision, eyes boring into Brooke as a palpable discomfort bloomed in the air between them. He had no intention of breaking the silence.

After another ten seconds, Brooke broke eyeline and sat back in his seat. "Damn it," he whispered, scratching at his neck. "But you didn't hear this from me, all right?"

Jareth shrugged. "Didn't hear what, soldier?"

Another sigh drifted over the desk. Brooke let his head fall back, as if the answers were in the yellowing ceiling tiles above. He stayed that way and sighed a little more, demonstrating to Jareth how stressful this all was.

Yeah, yeah, pal. We get it.

Now spill.

When Brooke lowered his head, his face had a hardness to it that was new. Like he'd realised the implications of what he was about to do. Either that or he was waking up to the truth.

"Listen, Hicks. Before I say anything, understand I've no evidence of any of this. I don't know if I'm right or wrong or what the hell is going on. But something has been bugging me. You're right about that."

His eyes widened, but if he was waiting for Jareth to respond, he'd be waiting forever. Instead, Jareth raised his chin a touch. Enough to make the nervous deputy continue.

"Hunger and me don't get on too well. He keeps me and the other local cops at arm's length. The only person he really confides in is Rex Crawford, a State Trooper. I don't like him and I'm sure he's got his fingers in a lot of dodgy pies. You get me?"

"Sure do. But what about Glick? I spoke with Vincent

Elway yesterday. He thinks Glick has something to do with the mayor's disappearance. Or at least, that he's behind the chief's obsession with the Cheetahs and their possible involvement."

Brooke grimaced. "Shit. I know Hunger has had meetings with Glick recently. In fact, I saw them together this morning. I don't know what their story is and that's the truth of it, so don't ask. But I know Glick wants to build a hotel complex out on the edge of town and that there are two people standing in his way. Mayor Donovan and Vince Elway."

Jareth was watching him with the trained eye of a field negotiator. He was telling the truth, but he was also scared. "What do you think's going on?"

Brooke gave one of those thin-lipped smiles that said everything it needed to. "I don't know what to think. But I heard Hunger on the phone the other day, speaking in hushed tones. Heard him mention the Cheetahs and Mayor Donovan and said the word 'leverage' a few times." Releasing another dramatic but no less heartfelt sigh, he got to his feet. Jareth watched as he walked over to the window and picked up the graduation photo. "I've been struggling with what to do for a few days. This is a small town, you know. A peaceful town. We're not used to this sort of shit."

"What sort of shit is that?"

"You know, corruption, lies, kidnapping, threats on people's livelihoods. And their lives."

Jareth folded his arms. "That what you think's going on?"

"Don't you? Jesus Christ."

"You think they've kidnapped the mayor, along with his daughter and our friend?"

He placed the photo down but remained staring at it. "I

know it sounds ridiculous. And if it is true, I can't work out what the hell reason there is behind it."

"Leverage. Like you said."

"But to do that they'd have to pull off something big and drastic. And illegal." He turned to Jareth and his face was more drawn than ever. "You don't think they'd…? No. He's the chief of police, for God's sake. He wouldn't. He couldn't."

"Do you have any idea where they might be?" Jareth asked. But Brooke was staring off into the middle distance. Whatever the poor bastard was seeing, it had sent him pale. "Brooke. Do you know where they might have taken them?"

He snapped out of it. "I'm not saying the chief is definitely behind this, just that—"

"Enough fucking around," Jareth told him, controlling his anger, but with an energy to his voice it would be hard to ignore. "Anywhere you can think of. You know the town better than us."

Brooke sat back (or rather, slumped like a sack of shit) into his chair. Poor bastard. Jareth felt for him, he really did – knowing all too well what it was like to serve under someone you mistrusted as much as you disliked – but this was no time for playing nice. When he still hadn't answered the question, Jareth got to his feet and loomed over the desk at him.

"Deputy Brooke. We need your help."

He glanced up, but without fear or trepidation in his face. Just a deep sense of resignation. He looked like a cheap balloon that someone had let all the air out of.

"There's an old cabin half-way up Crow Mountain," he said. "It's owned by the police department for training exercises and whatnot. But we've not used it in a while. Shit. I had it in the back of my mind these last few days, but kept putting off going up there. I mentioned it to the chief. Saying the mayor might have wandered off with a concussion after his crash and stumbled across it. But he told me to sit tight. That he was handling it. And despite this niggling little voice in my head, I did just that. Guess I got too used to the easy life behind a desk. Fucking pussy."

"Don't be too hard on yourself. You're stepping up now."

"Am I? I'm still sitting behind this stinking desk."

"Where is this cabin?"

"The old Pine factory on the far side of town. There's a track opposite that winds up the east side of the mountain. It's kind of overgrown and hard to access. But you can walk it easy enough."

"And you think that's where they are?"

"I don't know. But it's where I'd look if I didn't have Hunger watching my every move."

He was telling the truth. Jareth held out his hand to him. "Come with me. I'm heading there now. See what I can find. Would be good to have a lawman on our side."

"I can't."

"Don't worry about my friend. She's got a temper, I know, but she's just worried. She'll calm down once she's clear you're not trying to block us."

Brooke regarded him through watery eyes. "It's not that. I already told you, I've got a young family. A wife and a small boy. They need me in one piece. I'm sorry. I'm not cut out for heroics no more." He looked down, finding the notepad in front of him real interesting all of a sudden. "Hell, who am I kidding. I never was. I'm not like you. I'm not brave or experienced. The war was all but over when I got there. I was nothing but a base caretaker. The most action I saw was when an IED blew up a truck that was in

237

our convoy one day. We thought we were under attack, but it was a historic bomb. There was a lot of shouting, a lot of scared young men, but apart from the unlucky bastards who were in the truck we were fine. The enemy was long gone."

"Doesn't mean you can't help us now. Escort us up to this cabin."

"I'm sorry." He didn't look up. "Like I say, you didn't hear this from me. But if you are going up there, be careful."

Jareth straightened. "Okay. Thanks, Brooke. You're a good man."

"I'm a fucking coward."

Jareth went to agree but held his tongue. Brooke had his reasons for not wanting to put himself in danger. Difficult to hear from someone tasked with protecting Joe Public, but there it was. Jareth turned and headed for the door.

"Good luck, Colonel," Brooke called after him. "Keep me informed of any news."

Jareth didn't reply. He was already out the door and striding through reception to the exit. Outside, Acid was leaning against the side of a grocery store.

"You took your time," she said, as he got close.

"Time well spent."

"You've got information?" She stood upright. "You know where they are?"

"Not for definite, but I've got a lead. An old cabin up in the mountains. Brooke thinks the same as Vince, that Glick is going for a land grab, playing him and the mayor off against each other." He stopped short of telling her that might include framing Vince for murder, but he needn't have spared her. The look in her eyes told him she'd been thinking exactly that.

"We've got to get up there," she said, already in motion.

"They've been gone at least twelve hours. Time isn't our friend."

"And what do you plan on doing if you find them?" he asked, catching up with her as she veered down the next street. "If Hunger and Glick are prepared to kidnap the mayor, they aren't going to give him up so easy. I'm guessing Glick will have robust security around him."

"Good." She didn't let up. Didn't look at him. "Then we annihilate every single one of the fuckers. Any way we can."

He'd expected something along those lines, but actually hearing her speak that way stirred up conflicting emotions in him.

He shook them away. Not the time.

He got up to Acid and grabbed her arm. "Hey, wait a minute."

"What?" She spun around, as good as gnashing her teeth at him. "Why are you dragging your damn heels?"

"If we're going up there, don't you think it might be shrewd of us to get our own security? Maybe find some fire-power, too?"

"What do you mean?"

"I mean," he said, rubbing the side of his finger over his bottom lip and sighing, "that despite my better judgement, I think we should pay Handsome Harry and the Cheetahs another visit."

Chapter Thirty

Acid danced from foot to foot, hands clasped in white balls of fury. It felt to her as if Jareth had been talking for hours. But that wasn't unusual. At times like this, when the bats had taken over, Acid had trouble concentrating on anything other than the job at hand. Right now she was a woman of action, driven only by the vehement bloodlust in her system. She had a target. She knew who she was up against. And if that odious prick Hunger and his cronies had hurt Spook, she'd cut their fucking heads off

"So can you help us or not?" she asked, stepping in between the two men. "We need guns and any men you can provide. Hunger and Glick have our friend. And the mayor and—"

"We *think* they do," Jareth butted in. "I mean, it looks likely, but we still have to step careful. He is the chief of police, after all."

"Oh piss off," Acid told him. Then, darting her attention back to Vince, "You heard what Jareth said, it's likely they're going to pin this on you."

"I see that," Vince replied. "And I don't like the sound of it, but I get what Hicks is saying. We have to be strategic."

Acid threw her arms up along with her eyebrows. "Fucking hell. Am I the only one with any balls around here?" She stepped back to take the men in. "Okay. Fine. I'll say it. What we're all thinking. They're going to kill the mayor and our friends and make it look like the Cheetahs did it."

They were standing around a large table in the back room of the Cheetahs' clubhouse, the room they used for 'official club business'. It was just the four of them. Vince and Guitar on one side of the table, Acid and Jareth on the other. She leaned over and banged her fist so the table shook. Why weren't they getting this?

"They're going to frame you for murder," she yelled. "Don't you bloody well care?"

Vincent shot her a grin. "Locking me up won't mean that piece of shit gets his hands on my land. Not once the state gets involved. Besides, even if he does try to frame me, I doubt he'll make it stick."

"Yeah, but he might not work it that way," Jareth said. "It only takes Hunger leaning on one or two of your crew. Turtle, for instance. They get him to make a statement supporting the cop's narrative in exchange for immunity or a payoff, and suddenly all eyes are on you. I imagine they've a lot to throw at you once you're in a courtroom, right? So they offer you a choice: sell the land to Glick, let him build his hotel, or you and your men go to prison for the rest of your lives."

"See?" Acid spat. "You need to help us so you can help yourselves. Get ahead of them on this."

Vincent closed one eye, rocking back on his heels. He didn't seem to be taking this seriously.

"They're going to kill my friend," she said, stepping in front of him. "And yours. Mayor Donovan. Neither of them deserves to die for the sake of a fucking hotel. Please, Vince. Help us."

He glanced at Jareth, then back at her. "I can't guarantee my men are going to be into this," he told her. "I've spent the last half-year trying to convince them going legit is the best way forward. No more guns. No more violence. Now you want me to have them light up the mountain, take on the local cops."

"Not local cops," Jareth told him. "One corrupt cop. I spoke to Brooke, his deputy, earlier. The man knows there's something fishy going down regarding Glick and Hunger. He just can't prove it. Yet if we pull this off, he'll be a good ally, I'm sure of it."

"Oh, cool. You're asking me to make allies out of cops now, too?"

"Come on, Vince," Jareth continued, placing a hand on Acid's shoulder, giving it a squeeze before she ran her mouth off. "Think of this as you helping clean up your town. We get the mayor back safe, then that's good for you. We get rid of the people trying to frame you for murder, I'd say that's even better."

Vince let out a laugh, doing that thing with his eye again, like he was squinting into the sun despite them being in a dark room. "You talk a good fight. I suppose." He turned to Guitar, who up to now had been standing with his head bowed, listening. "What do you think, brother?"

The older biker lifted his head. "I think we got to stop these sons of bitches," he said. "Sounds to me like this is a life-or-death situation; but it's about principles and honour just as much. We might have travelled down nefarious paths, but we always conducted ourselves honourably and on our own terms. We had a code. Everything we did, good or bad, had a just reason. Your daddy knew that. You know it. But these bastards are trying to make us look like a bunch of fucking barbarians. No. Not going to happen." He stepped forward and placed a fatherly arm around Vince. "We got to stop them, brother. We got to help these people."

Vince met Acid's gaze, the devil alight in his eyes. "That's what I thought he was going to say." He sniffed, serious now. "All right. Guitar, take Johnny and Bobo up to the storage unit and bring back half a dozen nines and an armful of grenades, what we can carry on foot. No rifles or anything too big. Meet us by the east side garage in thirty minutes."

"Will do." Guitar gave Acid and Jareth a nod as he shuffled past them out of the room.

Acid watched him go, then turned back to Vince. "Half a dozen nines? Grenades? I thought you'd gone legit?"

Vince brought his shoulders up around his perfect jawline. "We still got a small stockpile. Tiny, really. Shi-it, what's a guy to do? Everyone needs a little firepower, especially when you got people like Chief Aldous Hunger the fucking third running the show."

"Just legit enough," Jareth added.

"Exactly," he said, pointing an oil-stained finger at Jareth. "Just legit enough. I like that. Good one, brother."

"You're doing good work here with your club," Jareth told him. "But it always helps to have insurance, right?"

"Jesus." Acid rolled her eyes so they both saw. "Sorry to break up the mutual appreciation jerk off, or whatever this is, but do you think we might come up with a plan? The vague outline of one, at least?"

The men turned to look at her, the same supercilious expression twitching on both their faces. It made her want to smash their heads together but, as it was, she closed her eyes, shutting them out while she made peace with the dissonance screeching in her head. When she opened them again, they were still looking at her.

"You all right?" Jareth asked.

"Absolutely," she told him. "Just getting my game on and all that. Don't worry about me, sweetie. I'm ready. Are you?"

Jareth let out a soft chuckle. "Never a dull moment with you, is there? So... a plan?"

"I know the cabin you're talking about," Vince said, drawing out an invisible mountain side on the table in front of him with his finger. "Guitar and I will go with you. That should be enough backup without giving ourselves away. We don't need too many bodies confusing matters. We can ride up the path to around this point without being heard. From there, we travel the last five hundred metres on foot. My suggestion is we approach the cabin on a wide trajectory and come at them from the far side. Hunger and Glick both strike me as arrogant bastards, but that's a good thing, makes them vulnerable." He waved a finger in Acid's face. "But I need you to calm it down, missy. I can see you're chomping at the bit to take these guys out, but I meant it before, I want to go legit. That means no killing anyone, unless we have no choice. We get the option of capturing those fucks alive, then we take it. Let the authorities deal with them. Agreed?"

"Spoilsport," Acid muttered.

"Maybe. But that's how we roll or you're on your own. So, agreed?"

"Agreed."

"Okay then," Jareth said, giving her shoulder another squeeze. "I'd say that's a plan, wouldn't you? Let's go get these bastards."

Chapter Thirty-One

Acid gripped her arms around Vince's waist, her forearms reading the rigid muscles running down his sides as she pressed her cheek into the rough leather of his jacket. He smelt good, of dirt and sweat and cologne. As they approached a steep incline he leaned back and his hair whipped in her face. She turned her head to one side, catching sight of Jareth a few metres away, riding on the back of the second bike with Guitar. As their eyes met she sat upright, putting some distance between herself and Vince, gripping her thighs tight around the Harley's engine instead.

"How much further?" she yelled into Vince's ear.

"Almost there," he replied, turning around and letting off the throttle. "In fact, I'd say it'd be a good idea we stop anywhere here."

He waved his VP down and brought the bike to a stop next to a row of tall pine trees that stretched up into the mountain.

"The trees here will provide us with enough cover so we

can approach undetected," Vince told her, kicking down the jiffy stand and dismounting. "They'll keep the bikes hidden as well."

He offered her his hand, but she ignored it. She clambered off the bike and, once on firm ground, ran her fingers through her wind-matted hair. As Jareth walked over, she zipped her leather jacket all the way up and gave him a nod.

"Are you okay?" she asked, instantly hating the gooey way her voice sounded. She sniffed. "Are you ready, I mean?"

"Damn it, Acid. You keep asking me that. Yes, I'm ready."

"Well, then… good." She dug the heel of her boot into the earth. "It's just… I feel like I dragged you into this. It's a fucked-up situation and I don't want you to get hurt because of me."

"Hey. Listen," he said, trying to make eye contact. "I'm doing this because people are in trouble and I might be able to help them. I'm doing it because I want to."

She squinted up at him and brushed the hair from her face. She wanted to tell him thank you, that he was a good man and she was glad to have met him. But she didn't.

"The track ends round about here," Vincent said, appearing beside her. "But Guitar knows the way. Right, brother?"

"I know this old mountain like the back of my balls," the gnarled old biker called back, flipping open the storage box on the back of his bike. He removed a large sack and brought it over to where Acid and the others were standing. Looking for all the world like a heavy metal Santa Claus, he shoved his hand inside and pulled out a Glock 17. He held it out to Acid, handle first. "Here you are, miss. I heard you were a good girl this year."

"Well, you heard wrong," she said, accepting the pistol, unable to disguise the glee soaring through her. "But thank you. It's been a while since I held one of these babies."

It was like shaking hands with an old friend. She released the magazine. It held a full complement of ammo, but raising her head she saw Guitar holding out a single round between his thumb and index finger.

"One in the chamber for good measure?"

"Ooh, you saucy devil," she purred, slipping into her old persona like she'd never been away. It felt good. It felt right. She had purpose again. Fighting the good fight (all right, perhaps not the *good* fight, but she was back fighting and that felt good enough). It was Alice Vandella who struggled with who she was. Acid Vanilla never had that issue. That woman was bold and strong. She was a survivor. Always had been.

"Lovely stuff." Acid shoved the magazine back and racked one into the chamber.

Then, taking the single bullet from Guitar, she removed the magazine once more to load in this final round.

Seventeen plus one.

The magic number.

She shoved the pistol into the waistband at the back of her jeans and popped the collar of her jacket. "Lead the way, big man," she told Guitar. But he'd already set off, beckoning them to follow with a wave of his hand as he disappeared between two bushy fir trees.

"Think that means he wants us to follow him," Vince stage-whispered, giving Acid a sly wink as he headed after his friend.

She watched him go, sensing Jareth was about to say something, but was glad when he didn't. This wasn't the place or the time for that sort of shit. She was Acid Vanilla in full effect, possessed entirely of righteous fury and with only two things on her mind. Rescue Spook and teach those bastards a lesson. Acid didn't do deep conversations. She didn't do love.

In silence they followed on behind, winding their way through the dense vegetation and grabbing onto the spiky branches, practically swinging from tree to tree as the path got narrower and the gradient steeper. By the time they reached a clearing and the ground levelled out, Acid was exhausted. But there was no time to rest.

Guitar moved to the edge of the clearing and parted the branches of a thick pine. "Up there," he growled. "You see it?"

Acid did. The cabin was bigger than she'd expected, standing on its own on a rocky ledge a hundred metres up the track. But it appeared to be deserted.

The door was closed, as were the wooden shutters covering the two windows on the front and side of the building.

"Are you sure this is the place?" she asked.

"That's the police cabin. They used to come here on shooting expeditions, back when a guy called Steep Jeffries was chief."

"Brooke said it hadn't been in use for some time," Jareth said, leaning over Acid to look, his chest against her shoulders. "Sure looks run down, but doesn't mean they aren't in there."

Acid slid the Glock from her waistband. "Only one way to find out, chaps." A rush of adrenaline rattled her bones as the bats grew loud. She checked on the others, giving Vince and Guitar a firm look. "Jareth and I will move around the far side of the building, scope out what we're dealing with. You two stay put, but keep us covered. Once we get in position, wait for my signal to move." She held up the Glock, comforted by the weight of it in her hand. "And yes, before anyone feels the need to add a bloody caveat, I agree, we do this quick and quiet. None of us wants the Feds involved, so let's keep the body count to a minimum."

Vince chuckled shrilly to himself. "This chick. Man, I love her."

Acid shot him a hard stare, but he didn't see and she didn't push the matter. Instead, she turned to Jareth who was admiring his own piece, just handed to him by Guitar. "Let's move."

Giving the cabin a wide berth, they crab-walked around it through thick undergrowth. Acid kept her gun held high and her breath tight in her chest. Back in her assassin days, she'd have been more mindful of her breathing when out in the field, aiming for a state of alert looseness, to better react to any eventuality. But all of that seemed a long time ago. She was out of practice and, besides, the stakes seemed so much higher today. If Spook was inside the cabin and a shoot-out ensued, she could be injured. Or worse.

No.

Stop that.

The bats screeched the thought away, filling Acid's psychology with an intense focus that made her feel super-human. As they got level with the edge of the cabin, she glanced back to see Jareth was right behind her, eyes fixed ahead. He held his own gun in two hands, close to his head. As he met her gaze, she jerked her chin towards the rear of the cabin where she'd seen a small window without a shutter.

Jareth saw it too, pointing a finger at his chest and then over to the left side of the window, then pointing to her and the right. Acid returned the nod and with guns poised, fingers tight on their triggers, the two of them spread out, approaching the window in two wide arcs and climbing up the steep terrain in silence. Acid reached the cabin first and flattened her back against the wood, conscious of her heart beating heavily behind her ribs. It had been a while since she'd had this many chaotic emotions filling up her system. Adrenaline, cortisol, a little dopamine, all topped off with that chaotic nervous energy she called the bats. She hadn't blinked in forever. Her entire body tingled with a super-alertness that, whilst hard to get a hold of, gave her comfort. She was complete. She was ready.

Jareth joined her at the window a second later and the two of them froze, eyes on each other across the void but focused only on listening. Acid shook her head. She heard no rumble of voices, no movement, not even the static hum of a mobile phone or CB radio.

It was no good. She needed eyes on the room. After a sharp three-count in her head, she stepped in front of the window, shooting a cursory glance through the dirty glass before shifting over to the other side. Jareth caught her as she got near and pulled her towards him.

"Anything?" he whispered.

She shook her head and he let go. With her taking the lead, they edged around the side of the cabin, and as they reached the front entrance she shifted her attention to the bottom of the slope. Vince and Guitar were waiting for her signal. She raised her fist, telling them to hang fire. Keeping her pistol drawn, she crept around the corner of the building and stepped up onto the raised porch. Another silent stride and she was at the front door trying the handle. It was locked.

"Let me."

Jareth sidled up and nudged her out of the way. Without

question, she moved to one side, allowing him room as he raised his leg and smashed a heavy boot against the door. It didn't budge, and no sounds came from inside. There were no gunmen bursting out trying to kill them. No Spook screaming for help. Jareth kicked at the door again and this time Acid heard a satisfying splintering sound. Two more kicks and the lower door panel snapped in half, leaving enough space she could snake her hand through and slide open the heavy iron bolt on the other side.

She called through into the cabin. "Spook. Are you there?"

No answer. She got to her feet and moved out of the way. Without support from the bolt, another boot from Jareth splintered the mortis lock clean out of the wood and the door swung open to reveal a dark cavernous space. Leading with the Glock, Acid slid promptly inside, keeping her aim high as she scoped out the room. A swift assessment told her it was clear of threat, and as her eyes grew accustomed to the darkness she saw a wide, open-plan room with nothing much in the way of furniture except a basic wooden table and chairs over to one side. A small kitchen was opposite, comprising of a solitary worktop and a fridge, on top of which sat a kettle and a jar of instant coffee.

"Spook?" she called out again. "It's Acid."

"No one's here," Jareth whispered over her shoulder.

Two doors led off from the main space. Without exchanging words, they took a door each, Acid going for the one on the left, the door that would have led to Spook's room if this were their cabin in town. With considered movements, they reached for the door handles in unison, both using their left hand, holding their weapons to their chests with their right.

A shared glance and they pushed the doors open, bursting into the rooms with guns drawn.

"Drop your weapons."

"Hands in the air."

"Don't move."

Bollocks.

Acid lowered her piece. Apart from a rickety old cot bed, the room was empty.

She turned to see Jareth in the doorway. He shrugged, but said nothing.

"Same story?"

"A dirty old bathtub and a mop bucket."

Her shoulders sagged. She'd been so sure she'd find Spook here, she hadn't contemplated other possibilities. Now she did, she was already out of answers.

"Fuck. Fucking hell."

"We must have missed them." It was Vince, him and Guitar standing out on the porch. As Acid moved into the main space, he stepped inside, peering about as he went. He ran a finger across the top of the table and held it up. "If they were ever here at all. Place is pretty dusty."

Acid shoved the Glock back into the waistband of her jeans. "What the hell is going on?"

"Acid. Over here."

She followed Jareth's voice into the room with the bed, finding him kneeling in the corner.

"Look." He pointed to one of the old floorboards. "See there, where the two knots look like to O's?"

Acid squinted at what he was showing her. "Yes. So?"

"Come closer."

Placing a hand on his back, she leaned forward to look, her stomach doing a backflip as she saw what was there. On either side of the two knots, someone had scraped rudimentary letters into the wood. An S and a P on one side and a K on the other. "Ah, kid," she whispered. "You were here."

"Acid. Jareth." The call came through from the other room, Vince yelling for them with a fervour in his throat she'd not heard from him up to now.

They strode back into the front room to find him and Guitar wearing the same grim expression.

"What is it?" she asked.

"Guitar here thinks he might know where they are," Vince told her, beckoning at his vice president to speak.

He sighed. "I saw tyre tracks outside just now," he said. "They appear to lead up the mountain. To where the Crow's beak formation juts out over the old quarry." He stopped and grabbed at his chin, pulling the grey wiry beard into a point before giving Vince a sideways glance.

"Go on, it's okay. Tell them."

"Well, it's just… It got me thinking about what's up there. About Glick and Hunger trying to pin the mayor's murder on the Cheetahs." He swallowed. "I think I know where they might be. But if we go there, we'll need to approach from the nearside of the mountain. It's a tough climb, hazardous too, but it's our only option if we don't want to be seen. But I suggest we're quick about it. Real quick."

"They're going to kill them up there," Acid said. A statement rather than a question. But she got an answer anyway.

Guitar nodded grimly. "I believe so. And in the most brutal and unpleasant of ways you can imagine."

Chapter Thirty-Two

Spook had been doing her best to hold it together, but the further the dusty old truck trundled up the mountain the more terrified she became. After being thrown in the back ten minutes earlier, she'd shuffled into the far corner, facing outwards. Knowing no one could sneak up or grab her from behind always provided some comfort. But not much. Not now.

Cynthia sat beside her, squeezing her hand with every bump and lurch the truck made. It helped a little.

But not much.

Not now.

The truck was a Transit, covered on all sides by aluminium panels and with a dim bulb over the back doors providing the only light. In front of the two women, Mayor Donovan sat cross-legged, his bruised face hanging low, but alert eyes (some might say fearful, but Spook liked to think they were alert) darting between the pair of them. Behind him one of Glick's men sat on the truck's wheel arch, an imposing rifle resting across his thighs. He hadn't stopped staring at Cynthia since they'd set off from the cabin, and the way his wet lips were twisted to one side troubled Spook a great deal.

"Don't worry, girls," the mayor whispered. "I'll make this right. I swear."

Over his shoulder, Spook saw their captor raise his head, fingers closing around the rifle barrel. "I thought you were told to keep your mouth shut."

Donovan shifted around. "Do you really think you're going to get away with this? I'm the mayor, for God's sake. People are looking for me."

The man's sneer twisted into a grimace, but one of pleasure rather than disgust. "Reckon they might find you, too. Soon enough."

Spook rolled her shoulders, hoping the nervous energy trapped there might dissipate. But it was the same story as before. Didn't help. As she shivered the fear away, she felt a trembling sensation in her belly. Like the worst turbulence she'd ever experienced. She'd only felt this scared once in her life. Back when she discovered there was a price on her head and that a deadly – but oddly monikered – assassin was coming to kill her. Spook had found her life in danger a lot since then (being in Acid's orbit since she'd spared her life and they'd escaped Paris, meant trouble was never far away), but those times she'd had her friend by her side, looking out for her, protecting her.

Walk the plank.

Glick's words bounded around the inside of her skull. He was speaking figuratively, she told herself. It was only pirates who made people walk the plank. Pirates from long ago. From the movies. As far as she understood it, there were no high seas near Blackfell Ridge.

Still, the summation that Glick's threat was merely a weird turn of phrase did little to ease her growing panic. She gripped Cynthia's hand as though their lives depended on it, exchanging worried glances and thin-lipped smiles while the truck bounced and pitched onwards. But whether or not Glick was talking in riddles, the subtext was clear. They were about to die.

The truck lurched to a stop, sending Mayor Donovan skidding into Spook and Cynthia.

"Hey, calm it down, dumbass," the man with the rifle yelled at the driver, slapping his hand on the side of the truck. "I'm riding loose back here."

The double doors swung open and a shard of light speared across the floor of the truck. Spook grabbed Cynthia, who grabbed her father, who grabbed Spook. They hugged each other close as the man with the rifle stomped down the truck.

"End of the road," he called back. "Out. Now."

Donovan kept his arms around Spook and his daughter. "Let these two go," he pleaded. "Whatever you're trying to achieve, it's me you want. It doesn't concern my daughter or her friend."

It was a noble gesture, but useless. Spook and Cynthia had seen too much, knew too much. Whatever walk the plank meant, it would be a shared fate.

"Get out the damn truck," the man ordered. "I won't tell you again."

Spook released her grip on Cynthia and her dad and shuffled on her butt towards the open doorway.

"Spook. No," Cynthia cried.

Spook looked back, giving her the most reassuring smile she could muster. "It's okay," she said. "I'm okay."

This despite her feeling like her insides had turned to

liquid. And not in the way people meant when they had bad guts or food poisoning. Her entire body felt like it was made of sludge. Her bones, her internal organs, her brain, the lot. A quivering mess held together by a thin layer of goose bumps. For once she had no disassociation going on, but it was hard to feel any kind of relief about that. How she'd loved to be detached from the situation right now. Especially as another man appeared in the doorway and grabbed her by the wrists, whipping her out of the truck and onto her feet.

"Stand there. Shut up."

Spook counted six men in total. The two original kidnappers, the rifleman who'd rode with them, plus three more who were now climbing out of a black Jeep which was parked up behind the truck. Up to now their personas and features had swum together in her panicked mind, filed under the heading '*Bad men to be scared of*', but now, as one of them dragged Cynthia from the van, she studied them more deliberately. If by some slight chance she survived what was coming, she'd need to identify them. And it sure helped to think that way. Of a future version of Spook Horowitz. One who was proud of herself for staying calm under pressure, for thinking ahead. And for surviving.

The men who had snatched them looked to be in their late forties. They had shaved heads, presumably to better deal with their male-pattern baldness, and were big and brutish. Their muscles rippled under thick layers of fat as they manhandled Mayor Donovan from the van and shoved him on the ground. Watching over them as they dragged the mayor to his feet was the man with the rifle. He was older than the other two, and not as heavily built, but with the same air of menace. He still had that lascivious sneer plastered across his face as he pointed the rifle at Spook and Cynthia, gesturing for them to move over to Mr Donovan.

They gathered in a line as the men from the Jeep swaggered up to them. Spook saw it was Chief Hunger and Glick, along with his henchman in the blue suit. She already knew Hunger's rat face, but up close in the daylight Glick appeared more imposing than he had done in the cabin. His skin was thick and greasy, like whale blubber, and his eyes were wide-set and unblinking. He looked like Arnie's Terminator if he'd landed on the set of Dallas rather than downtown LA. He considered his prisoners with a weird turn of his head, smiling out of the corner of his mouth.

"Jackson. Travis. Good work, boys. You as well, Trooper Crawford." He slapped the man with the rifle on the back. "Couldn't have sorted this out better myself. Top marks."

Spook shot this guy Crawford a look. Trooper? Another lawman. He was built like the Pillsbury Doughboy, with a pugnacious face and eyes that looked like slits under heavy lids.

"They were no bother at all," he said. "But this whole job remains dodgy as hell for me. I trust our arrangement hasn't changed."

"You'll get your money," Glick said. "You all will. But not until the mission is complete and I've got those deeds in my hand. So let's not get complacent, boys. This is not the time to congratulate ourselves. There's work to do."

"You motherfuckers," the mayor cried out, gasping the words as though they were his dying breath. "All this over a piece of land?"

"Now, now, Mr Mayor," Glick replied, clicking out the corner of his mouth. "Not just any piece of land. This prime location is what I expect to be my flagship resort. Out in the wiles of Montana. A haven of luxury and decadence at the foot of the infamous Crow Mountain. Who could want for more? And the whole shebang standing amidst a veritable garden of Eden. Green trees as far as the eye can see. Well... that is, until we build the golf course over yonder. We're going to have to lose a good few hundred acres of vegetation for that." He turned his entire body to take in Hunger, who was snickering silently beside him. "Call it progress."

"You really think the people of Blackfell Ridge are going to stand by and let you tear down their surroundings?" Mayor Donovan rasped, his voice hoarse. "You'll rip out the heart of the town."

"Don't matter what they think once I get those deeds in my hand," Glick said, turning only his head. "And you three are just the people going to help me get them."

"I don't get it," Spook pitched up, the confidence in her voice surprising her. "How will killing us help you get the land?"

Glick stepped back and raised his hands up to his chest, as if her question had shocked him to his core. But it was all for show. "Well, would you look here? The little China girl has a sensible question."

"I'm half-Malaysian, you rotten piece of shit." She spat the words out before she'd properly realised what she was saying, who she was speaking to.

But Glick didn't flinch. In fact, he found it amusing, giving her a wink and doing that horrible clicking noise out the side of his mouth. It only exacerbated Spook's anger, her senses of unfairness. So much so, that for once rage trumped fear.

"You won't get away with this," she told him. "You'll see. My friend will be looking for me. For you. And, shit, when she finds you, she'll... You'll... Damn it. You're going to regret this."

Glick stepped back, laughing with gusto at her outburst. Spook's entire body was shaking and she felt like she was about to throw up. She swallowed back a shudder of emotion.

Stay strong, Spook.

Tough like Acid.

"You've got some balls, missy, I'll give you that," Glick said, still chuckling. "And you know what? I'll answer your little question. How will... *disposing* of the three of you help me get the land? Easy. See, when your bodies are found on Cheetah land, my friend Chief Hunger here will arrest Elway and his crew for the murders. With the mayor's new zero-tolerance policy on crime, it stands to reason those nefarious bikers would have an issue with him. Old pals or not." Glick was pacing up and down in front of the three of them as he spoke, enjoying himself. "But before anyone else hears of these matters, we go to the Cheetahs and offer them an out clause. A simple choice. Sell me the land or go down for murder.

"Now, if my old memory serves, Montana is the only state where a condemned man's sentence is decided by the trial judge, not the jury. And wouldn't you know it, I am very good friends with not one but six members of the Montana State judicial system. Not to mention the governor of this fine state. An old golf buddy of mine. The upshot being, if those dirty bikers don't want to play ball and Elway's found guilty, he will fry." He stopped in front of Spook, looming over her and wrinkling his nose. "I don't think he's going to want to risk that, do you?"

She held his gaze. "My friend will kill you."

"Which friend?" He looked around at his cronies. "What is this little bitch talking about?"

Hunger stepped forward. "She means this fucking punk rock chick and her boyfriend. They've been a royal pain in my ass this last week. Good-looking chick, but a real mouth on her. Don't worry, though, she's ain't coming. And if she was, what the hell is some stupid woman and her lame ass boy toy going to do against all of us?"

Glick turned back to Spook. "That's what I thought. So there you have it, missy. We get the Cheetahs to sell, and in doing that we create a position that needs filling. And wouldn't you know it, we have the ideal candidate right here in the form of my worthy associate, Mr Morris Wade." He reached out and slapped the man in the blue suit on the shoulder. "After a shotgun election we'll swing it so Mr Wade takes over the reins as mayor of this fine town. Once in position, I don't think those licences and land rights are going to be too hard to come by. All in the name of tourism and the advancement of the town's economy, of course. It'll be an easy sell. I may even run for mayor myself later down the line. If all goes to plan."

He stepped in front of Cynthia's father, casting him in the shadow of a huge wolf grin.

"You evil bastard," the mayor hissed. "You'll pay for this."

"Oh, to hell with you, Donovan. You had your chance. But then, if you had accepted my offer I wouldn't have had this brilliant idea of getting Elway to part with his land. And now I have, it's time for us to initiate the first phase." He gestured up the track to where it disappeared around the top of the mountain. "Shall we?"

He looked to his men, giving them a brusque nod as rough hands gripped Spook's upper arms, hard fingers squeezing at her flesh. Along with Cynthia and her father, they bustled her forward, Glick leading the grim procession up the track. He'd only taken a few steps when Chief Hunger ran over and blocked his path.

"Mr Glick," he whispered, just loud enough that Spook heard him. "Don't you think it'd be better if we were far away from this when it happens? We don't want any ties to the crime scene."

Glick brushed him off. "The hell with that. I want to make sure this is done properly, so I can get my plans back on track." He strode off, leaving Hunger spluttering in his wake as they led the three prisoners up the winding path. Spook groaned and gnashed her teeth, trying to wriggle free with all she had. But it was useless, and after only a short time she gave in. Her captor was too strong and what the hell would she do even if she broke free? A deep sadness erupted in her belly and shivered up into her chest, manifesting itself as an existential wail. There was no use in denying it. They were screwed. Acid wasn't coming and Spook saw no way of escape. She was going to die here on this mountain. She was actually going to fucking die!

But as they moved further around the side of the mountain and the track levelled out, her existential sobs metamorphosed into a guttural cry of terror.

"No... No fucking way... Please... No!"

Up ahead the path came out onto a rocky ledge, and over to one side she saw the enormous edifice of rock and earth that protruded out across the ravine and resembled a crow's beak.

But it wasn't this that sent Spook's entire body into panic mode and had her hyperventilating.

A large wooden structure was bolted onto the ledge, with two steps leading to a small podium and a low railing running around its sides. From it a long piece of wood jutted out at a right angle to extend over the abyss. It looked to Spook like an Olympic diving board. Or what you might see on an old-fashioned pirate ship.

Shitting shitbags.

Glick hadn't been speaking figuratively.

It was a plank.

He was actually going to make them walk the plank.

Chapter Thirty-Three

Acid gripped onto the sinewy roots of the pine tree above, steadying herself as she leaned in to speak to Vince.

"Are you serious?"

He grimaced, dragging himself up over a sharp boulder that stuck out of the mountainside. "I'm afraid so. The concept was first dreamt up by a guy called Bartholomew Heap. Wild Boy Heap to his friends. And enemies. He was one of the founding members of the Streetwalkin' Cheetahs. The president, before my daddy took over."

"Wild Boy Heap," Acid repeated, glancing across and meeting Jareth's eye. "Sounds like the type."

Vince hauled himself up onto a wide ledge, where he remained panting until the others caught up. As Acid swung herself over, putting her faith in the sturdy tree root for support, he grabbed her hand and helped her up.

"He was certainly the type," he said. "I never met the man, but I heard all the stories. He was obsessed with the Cheetahs being like modern-day marauding pirates.

Outlaws, who did what they wanted, when they wanted, with who they wanted. I'm not saying I approve of his ways, or that he was a nice guy, but he got results. Respected and feared in equal measure. Sign of a good leader. There was a time the Blackfell Ridge chapter of the Cheetahs was the most feared and respected MC in the country. Maybe even the world. And the walking of the plank went some way in making that so."

"That's crazy," Acid mumbled, watching Jareth, making sure he made it up onto the ledge. As he swung his leg up over the side, he gave her a look of reassurance, along with that crooked smile. She turned back to Vince, giving him her full attention. "So they made people take a dive off the end?"

"That's about the long and short of it," Guitar told her, brushing himself down over on the other side of the ledge. "More than a hundred metres into the quarry below." He flattened his hand and mimed the fall, whistling as he did so and ending with a distressing splattering sound and spread of his fingers wide. Then, perhaps remembering himself, he sniffed. "Sorry, I didn't mean… I wasn't thinking."

"It's fine," she told him, the quiet iciness in her voice giving her a boost. For once, there were no troubling emotions to knock her off course. Acid Vanilla was in kill mode, and she meant business. She raised her head, taking in all three men. "It's not going to happen. Not to Spook."

"Damn right," Vince replied, wiping his arm across his forehead. "It sounds grim as hell, but I don't know anyone who saw it in use. Or know anyone who did. It was more of a legend, even when my daddy was a boy. A threat to keep their enemies in line. Like the nuclear deterrent."

"But it's up there still?" Jareth asked.

"Yup. I was there a few months back. Beautiful views of the town up on that ledge. And the entire structure is still as it was. I even sat on the end of the plank for a while. Feels like you're flying."

"I bet," Acid said. "Until you hit the rocks below."

He ignored her, throwing his attention up the last stretch of their climb. "It's a fiendish idea from Hunger and Glick, I'll give them that. Everyone knows about the legend of walking the plank and how it's linked to the Cheetahs' past. It wouldn't take much for the townsfolk and the authorities at large to make the connection and pin whatever happens on us. Bastards."

"Yes, well, like I keep saying," Acid said. "It's not going to happen. None of it."

She wasn't here for the history lesson and was glad when her two new friends left it there and pushed on ahead. Placing the toes of her boot into a foothold, she lifted herself up, grabbing onto more roots as she scaled the inverse incline. As was common in times of high stress, she was acutely aware of the thousand silent bat screams pushing at the boundaries of her psychology. But for now their screeches were perfectly in tune with her thoughts. The intense bristling emotion flooding through her veins felt good, like old times, when her manic energy only ever made her feel superhuman and invincible. The fizzing rushes of vigour buoyed her. She had tunnel vision, her thoughts trimmer and more focused than they had been in a long while. Step one was to get safely up to the next ledge above. There was no step two. Not yet. But that was how this worked. How you survived out in the field. The second your mind drifted off into theories about what might happen you were a dead woman walking. Simple as that.

"How we doing?" Jareth called out. From his voice, she placed him being a foot or two below her on the rock face.

"Almost there," Vince replied. "Let's keep it going."

Acid ignored them. They meant well, but right now she was a machine. With no time for platitudes or motivational bullshit. With her knuckles white from exertion and her fingernails broken and bloody, she grasped onto the next available hand-hold and hauled herself another half metre up the mountain. It was here where the main part of the ledge protruded out, meaning she'd need to crawl upside down for around two metres. Stretching her arm as far as it would reach, she grabbed her fingers around another tough root that snaked out of the ground and was visible all the way up over the ledge. She couldn't see which tree it belonged to, but the ones up here were hardy and tough and would bear her weight. Scrabbling for a foothold, she pulled herself along until both hands clasped the root. All those years of gymnastics training paid off as she scaled the overhanging rock, placing one hand strategically over the other and using her feet to nip at the root, pushing herself up. At the top, she let go of the root with one hand and reached for the ledge, but the rock she'd thought was a firm part of the structure of the mountain crumbled in her hand and she slipped.

"Acid!"

The voice could have been Jareth. Or Vince. Or even Guitar. It could have been her own inner voice, the bats screaming across her nervous system. She held on to the root with everything she had, scrambling her feet at the rocks below as she twisted in the air, desperately trying to regain control.

Fuck.

Pissing hell.

She held her breath. Every muscle and sinew of her body, every nerve ending and brain cell were now in tune, working together to right the situation.

"Come on, you bugger," she hissed. "Don't give up."

"Here. Take my hand."

She looked up to see Jareth had somehow managed to scramble above her to the summit and was reaching back down for her.

"I'm fine," she gasped.

"Don't be an idiot. Take my damn hand. Now."

She grabbed hold and he dragged her up over the edge. "I could have managed," she said, getting to her feet.

"Sure you could. But we haven't time to mess around."

As if to best serve this point, a scream echoed around the side of the mountain. Acid jerked her head to one side, frozen in a tableau of intense concentration as the screams continued.

"That's Spook," she whispered, already moving, already slipping the Glock out from the back of her jeans. "And she needs me."

Moving like a panther's shadow, she hurried up the spiralling track until it levelled out with the Crow's beak formation up ahead. Sticking close to the mountainside she slowed her pace, edging around the rock until she had full view of the area. She screwed her eyes into the sun, searching for the familiar outline of her friend but her attention halted instead by an ominous wooden structure in front of her.

She raised her weapon to her chest, watching in silence as a lone man stood on the mountain end of a rickety wooden plank. The man, who she assumed to be Mayor Donovan, was shaking as he shuffled along and the plank wobbled and swayed beneath him. A second man was standing on the platform, a gun pointed at his head, offering him an impossible choice. From this distance Acid couldn't tell for certain, but the gunman resembled that creepy prick Crawford, the state trooper who'd arrested her and Jareth a few days earlier.

Along with Donovan and the gunman, she counted seven more bodies. Most of them were dark silhouettes against the late morning sun, but Aldous Hunger III was easy to recognise with his weaselly profile and scrawny limbs. He was nearest to the edge of the precipice, bouncing from foot to foot like a kid queuing up for a roller-coaster. Beside him, standing tall and wearing a huge Stetson, had to be the man she'd heard so much about. Raymond Glick. He cut an imposing figure but was nothing she couldn't handle.

She froze as another shrill cry reverberated out over the cliff and, shifting her focus to the far side of the ledge, she saw Spook and Cynthia. They were some ways behind Glick and obscured a little by the trees, but that didn't mean she couldn't see the brawny forearms wrapped around their necks and the guns pressed against their temples.

It was Cynthia whose wails now permeated the silence, sobbing uncontrollably and trying to struggle free as her father moved further along the tottering plank. He glanced back over his shoulder, giving her what he must have hoped was a comforting smile. He didn't manage it.

"Move him in," Glick called out.

"No!" Cynthia screamed, her cries promptly muffled by a large hand across her mouth, yanking her back.

The mayor raised his head to the skies. "You won't get away with this, Glick. You kill me, my death will only help put you away. And you, Hunger. You'll pay for this. I promise you that."

Glick turned to Hunger, his broad shoulders shaking as he guffawed silently. The two of them were undoubtedly enjoying themselves. Grinning at each other as poor Mayor Donovan squirmed, laughing at his young daughter's distress. Acid gripped the Glock tight to her chest as the bats whispered in her head.

Kill them, they said.

Annihilate them all.

Donovan was half-way along the plank now, taking tiny steps. But that bastard Crawford (definitely him; she'd recognise those porcine chops anywhere) grabbed up a long branch and moved onto the plank, prodding him forward.

"Time to take a dive, mayor," Hunger called out, looking at Glick the whole time, the pathetic prick. But it proved to Acid once and for all who was running the show. Hunger kept going. More lame jokes. "How about a swan dive, mayor?"

With the branch stabbing into his back and the pistol aimed at his head, all Donovan could do was keep going to the end. Once there, he stared down into the quarry below. He looked calm, but who knew what was going through his mind. His hands gripped the material of his trousers in an attempt to stop them from shaking. It was a failed attempt.

Acid had looked death in the eyes on many occasions, and every single time she'd found the prospect ultimately shocking. It was as if, despite all the evidence to the contrary (and in her line of work, there'd been plenty of evidence), the human brain couldn't come to terms with the prospect of its own demise. Some of those times Acid had felt a strange, otherworldly stillness descend over her. Other times it was an all-encompassing sense of injustice. But always with a surge of regret and surprise. There were, of course, many more instances when the roles were reversed. When she'd been the one delivering death to a person's door. But every single mark she'd disposed of – whether it be a Russian gangster or a paedophilic priest – had that same look in their eyes. An almost arrogant air of bewilderment, a sense that it couldn't possibly be them that was about to die. Because how could that be? They were a thinking, breathing entity.

Right until they weren't.

Acid kept her eyes on Donovan. Poor bastard. You could read every holy book, every piece of existential philosophy under the sun, nothing prepared you for death. Not even sixteen years in the murder industry.

A silence had now fallen over the scene. Even the snickering Hunger had shut up, aware of the gravitas as Donovan balanced unsteadily at the end of the bowing plank.

Crawford looked back at Glick, who lowered his head in response. A signal to do it. With that, the greasy pig took a step forward, leading with the branch, ready to nudge the terrified mayor over the edge.

Acid adjusted her grip on the Glock, finger poised on the trigger

Kill them.

Annihilate them all.

She sensed a presence behind her. Felt a hand on her shoulder, knew right away it was Jareth. But before he had a chance to talk her out of it she set off again, moving stealthily, her finger quivering on the trigger of the Glock.

"Hey. Let's be clever about this," Jareth whispered close behind, matching her every step. "There's a hell of a lot at stake. One wrong move and… Acid!"

Jareth meant well. And she agreed with him to a point. But this was a high-pressure situation and the bats were in charge. Donovan and those girls would not die today. Not if she could help it. And if it had to be bloody and messy rather than clever and strategic, then so be it.

That was the way the bats liked it.

It was the way Acid Vanilla liked it.

Chapter Thirty-Four

"Help us! Please!" Spook surveyed the area with desperate eyes, praying someone – anyone – might hear her cries.

"Shut up. Dumb bitch," Travis growled, tightening his grip on her. "No one's coming to save you. And it's your turn next on the high dive."

"Fuck you," she spat back, a spike of adrenaline rushing up her spine and trumping any fear she'd been experiencing. This was zero hour. No returns. No going back. If Acid wasn't coming, Spook had to be her own hero. Had to try, at least. Summoning all her strength and courage, she struggled free from the man's clutches and smashed the sharp point of her elbow into his ribs.

The blow startled him, but only briefly, and wasn't powerful enough to make him release his grip on her. It sure pissed him off, though. The second he regained composure, he raised the gun and smashed the base of the handle into her face. The pain was immense. The sort of pain where you couldn't even make a noise. It felt like her cheek bone had shattered. An intense sensation spread through her cranium and into her sinuses. It was at once numbing but also the most pain she'd ever experienced. Finding her voice, she went to cry out but was unsure whether she made any noise. The world span three-sixty as the ground turned into the sky and rushed up to meet her. She gasped for air, dropped onto all fours, her glasses tumbling from her face.

And that's when she heard her.

"Rotten bastard."

For a split second, Spook thought the voice was in her head. But as she grabbed up her glasses and scrambled to put them on, she saw Acid on the far side of the ledge. The sight of her, dressed in black and with a pistol aimed and ready, sent a wave of pure relief shivering through Spook's body, turning her already fatigued bones to jello. But that was a good thing – staying low meant Acid had a clear shot of Travis. And she wasted no time in taking it.

The sonic crack of gunfire sent birds and wildlife scattering as Travis's head jolted violently to one side and a cloud of red mist burst out from a hole above his ear. Another shot to the chest sent him stumbling towards the edge of the cliff. That was Spook's cue. As Glick and his cronies opened fire in retaliation, she scurried to hide behind a small bush. Everyone was shouting at once, bullets whooshed overhead, ricocheting off the rocks and sending clouds of dust and gravel into the air. She heard Glick and Hunger yelling at each other, saw them running in the opposite direction as Acid moved up onto the mantle.

Take that, you pricks.

Through the chaos, Spook saw Cynthia's poor brave dad shuffling along the plank, heading for solid ground. She tightened her already tensed fists, willing him on. He'd almost made it. Another metre to go. But then his head jerked back and he dropped to the plank. Only metres away was Crawford, his gun still raised.

Cynthia screamed. "Daddy! No!"

Spook shot her attention to her friend, seeing her staring wide-eyed at her father. Back to Mayor Donovan, she saw he'd fallen face down. There was a whole lot of blood pouring out of him, but he was still breathing, hands gripping onto the sides of the swaying plank.

"Daddy. Please. No," Cynthia yelled again, gnashing her teeth and clawing at Jackson's arm as he dragged her away.

An urge shot through Spook. She wanted to cry out. To tell Cynthia it would all be okay. That her father would be okay. But before she had a chance, another gunshot surprised the words out of her. She looked up to see Crawford stumbling on the platform as more shots thudded into his chest and torso, making him dance like a possessed marionette figure before a final head shot sent him toppling over the edge into the quarry below.

"Take that and fuck you," she whispered, finding her voice. "You mess with me, you mess with my friend."

But it wasn't Acid. Spook saw now she had others with her, two long-haired men wearing biker attire, and another man with short hair. It was the younger of the two bikers who had shot Crawford.

"Spook, are you hurt?" Acid called out, seeing her edging closer. "Did they hurt you?"

"I'm okay," she replied. "But Mr Donovan. And Cynthia…"

The name had barely left her lips when she heard the poor girl's cries. "Spook. Help me."

Maybe it was Acid's presence, or the fact Cynthia had specifically called for her to help, but it awakened something inside of Spook. Without giving it another thought, she got to her feet. Over on the other side of the ledge the corrupt cop, Jackson, and Glick's guy, Wade, were dragging Cynthia away. Standing to her full height, Spook saw Chief Hunger and Raymond Glick side-stepping down the dusty track towards their vehicles.

"Acid," she said, as she got up to her. "They're getting away. They have Cynthia."

Acid gripped Spook's shoulder, giving it a good squeeze. "I see them."

She raced over to the edge, shooting as she went, driving the men into the dense undergrowth with a rain of bullets. Looking back, she yelled over Spook's head, "Shoot out the tyres on their vehicles down there. We need those pricks on foot if we're going to catch them."

Spook spun around as the guy with the short hair ran past her. He had his arm outstretched and was already firing at the trucks down below. He was a good shot, too. As Spook and Acid hurried over to the side of the ledge, she saw him take out the nearside tyres on both vehicles.

Acid pointed at the platform, at Mayor Donovan's prone form. "Is he dead?"

"I don't know," Spook replied, assuming the question was for her, not caring if it wasn't. "He looked in a bad way."

Acid's eyes were as glassy and intense as Spook had ever seen them. It was kind of scary. Kind of exciting, too.

"Okay, listen." Acid pulled a mobile phone from her pocket and handed it to her as the bikers joined them. "Go to him. Do what you can. Then get on the phone and ring the Feds. Tell them everything you know. Tell them we need medical attention up here, a helicopter, whatever. Tell them there are men with guns and we have a kidnap situation. That should speed things along."

"Come on," one of the bikers growled. "We need to move."

"But, Acid," Spook yelped. "If you leave me… I don't know if I can… I mean… What if they come back…?"

Acid shot a look down the track, then at Mr Donovan, then back at Spook. Her eyes weren't any less intense. "Listen, kid, you've got this." She grabbed her shoulder with her free hand. "I'm sorry that I didn't believe you. I should have, because you're always right. I need to remember that. But now I need to go get your friend back and you need to save the mayor. Can you do that?"

Spook gasped. She wanted to cry.

"Spook," Acid repeated, gripping her shoulder tighter. "Can you do that?"

"Yes."

"Good. Then go." Acid released her, running after the three men as they skidded down the sloping track following Cynthia and her captors.

"Be careful," Spook called. But if Acid heard her she didn't look back, didn't say what Spook had been waiting for. As she reached the bottom of the slope she took a left and, with her gun drawn and ready, disappeared into the undergrowth.

"Be careful," Spook whispered once more to herself. Then she flipped open the phone and readied herself to make the call.

Chapter Thirty-Five

With Acid and the Cheetahs close behind, Jareth pushed on through the trees. The sharp, unforgiving branches of the local pines and firs whipped at his face and skin, scratching and cutting at his flesh, but he hardly felt a thing. Adrenaline. It was one hell of a hormone. Up ahead he heard the muffled screams of the woman and that was all that mattered. If he could hear her, he could save her.

They reached a clearing and he paused to allow the others to catch up and to assess the situation. In front of him the track split into two.

"Anyone see which way they went?" he called back.

"No," Acid hissed as she reached him. "What now?"

He turned to Vince. "You know this area?"

"Sort of," he replied. "The two tracks run in parallel for a while and both lead to the same spot, but the one on the right veers off around the side of the mountain whereas the other cuts through forest."

"Both paths are hard to navigate, if memory serves," Guitar added. "Vince and me will take the right, you guys take the left. We'll be in hollering distance the whole time if you need backup."

"Cool. But let's try to do this with some stealth. Yes?" Jareth said, casting a side-eye Acid's way. "If you catch up with them, whistle and we'll come to you. They can't have got too far, dragging the mayor's daughter with them."

"Well, they're making good ground whilst we stand around talking," Acid snapped. "We need to move, soldier boy."

Before he had a chance to reply, she shoved past him and ran on ahead. "Acid, wait." He set off after her, exchanging a brief glance with Vince as he did.

"See you at the finish line, soldier boy."

"Yeah, yeah. Whatever."

He raced after Acid, catching sight of her as she got to a bend in the track and disappeared behind a row of pine trees.

"Acid," he rasped, over a dry throat. "Wait up."

For all his frustration, it was good to see her so in control. She was focused, streamlined in both thought and movement. This was her in battle mode and he knew that because he recognised it in himself. In highly pressurised situations, many people went to shit, but a select few thrived. They were the ones who joined the Special Forces, became Black Ops soldiers. Or elite killers.

She was waiting for him as he got around the bend.

"There," she said, pointing down the track to where Glick's henchmen were dragging their captive across an expanse of rocks. The poor woman was giving as good as she got, kicking and screaming and trying to break free, but the bastards weren't letting up. One of them had hold of her whilst the other covered their backs, brandishing a tasty-looking revolver.

Acid adjusted her stance and raised the gun. "Got ya."

Before Jareth had a chance to respond, she opened fire, hitting the guy at the rear on the shoulder. But from this distance it was a lucky shot and far from fatal. It also alerted them to their presence. The man leapt behind the cover of rocks, firing back in retaliation as the other guy dragged the mayor's daughter out of sight. The rounds whizzed over-head as Jareth grabbed Acid and propelled them both into the protection of the trees. Once there, they traded bullets with the gunman, but he was too far away to make any of them count. They were running down their ammo whilst his buddy got away with his captive.

No way.

Not going to happen.

Jareth stepped onto the path and dropped on one knee as the gunman moved out from behind the rock. He fired off two shots and made them both count. One in the chest, one in the head. He was on his feet and chasing after the woman as the bastard's lifeless body slumped to the ground.

"Nice shooting," Acid called out, keeping close behind as they raced down the track.

"Well, contrary to popular opinion," he hollered back. "I am kind of useful under these sorts of conditions."

"Yes, I suppose you have some uses," came the pithy response, the one he'd been expecting. But there was warmth in her voice. She couldn't hide it.

With weapons raised, they elbowed through a bank of spiky fir trees, coming out onto a wide space relatively clear of vegetation. Jareth barely had a chance to register the piles of felled timber before the brutal bang of gunfire filled his ears and a bullet whipped past his head.

Far too close.

"Over here," Acid cried out, dragging him behind a

pyramid of logs as a hail of bullets thudded into the wood on the other side.

They crouched, side by side, deep gasping breaths falling in time with one another as hot rounds splintered their makeshift shelter.

"Did you get a look?" Jareth asked.

Acid released the mag on her pistol. "Got him in view," she said. "Glick's guy in the blue suit. A hundred yards down the track."

"And the girl?"

"He has her under his arm," she said. "Going to be hard to get a clear shot."

Jareth gnawed at his lip. He was thinking the same. "What about the big boss man?"

"Didn't see him."

Jareth raised his gun. "I can't imagine him and Hunger have much of a plan other than to get far away. We can't let them do that. Glick's a powerful man with friends in high places. We need to end this. Now."

"I like the way you talk, Colonel," Acid said, nudging his arm. "It's hot."

"Seriously?" He turned to take her in. "You're saying this now?"

She arched one perfect eyebrow. "What? We can't have a little fun while we stop these creeps?"

She was on her feet and leaning around the side of the log pile before Jareth could stop her. It was a rash and impulsive move and drew more fire from the man in blue.

"Shitting hell," she said, hunkering back down beside him. "He's using the girl as a shield. Can't risk it."

"He's also using up his ammo," Jareth replied. "How many mags you reckon he's carrying, considering the fact he's wearing an expensive suit and these pricks didn't expect company?"

Acid squinted at him. "Doesn't pay to make assumptions, sweetie."

"Yeah, but I'd bet dimes on the dollar he's almost out."

"Well, we'll find out soon enough."

But before they had a chance to test that hypothesis, they heard new gunfire coming down from above them.

"Vince," Acid yelled out.

He and Guitar were running towards them, jumping over fallen logs and swerving around large patches of leafy ferns, shooting as they went. The man in blue shifted his position, stepping back to return fire.

"He's got the woman!" Jareth yelled out. "Shit—"

His eyes widened to burning point as he saw Guitar catch a piercing bullet in the neck. The man in blue must have been using hollow points because the shot blew Guitar's entire voice box out in a horrendous burst of blood and gristle. He tumbled to the ground as Vince hit the deck beside him.

"Motherfucker."

Jareth swung his aim at the man in blue, but there was still no clear shot. Regardless, he fired a couple of warning shots as a way of covering Vince's ass, allowing him to drag his fallen brother's body behind the cover of a large fern.

"Acid, you think you can—"

He turned, but she wasn't there. Not where he'd expected her to be, at least. A lightning assessment of the scene revealed her to be lying on her back, head and shoulders exposed around the side of the log pile. She had one eye closed in concentration and the tip of her tongue gripped between her lips as she steadied her aim down the track. Jareth halted. He didn't speak as he knelt at her feet.

She had this.

A second went by. The scene fell silent. Jareth tensed. He knew what he had to do.

As Acid pulled the trigger he got to his feet. As she fired again he saw Blue falter to one side, releasing his grip on the mayor's daughter as a flurry of rounds blasted his ankle bones into a thousand pieces. Before he had a chance to rectify his gait, Jareth fired one more perfect punishing shot, hitting the prick right in the middle of his smarmy face. The woman screamed as blood and brain matter splattered her. But Blue was dead. She was free.

"Good shooting," Jareth gasped, but Acid was already racing down the track. He followed, catching up with her as she grabbed hold of the young woman's shoulders.

"It's all right," she told her. "You're safe."

"M... My daddy?" she gasped through hysterical sobs. "Is he...?"

Acid glanced at Jareth who stepped forward. "We're not sure," he said.

His voice startled the woman and she turned. The state of her bloodied and horrified face threw him for a moment. But then he pulled himself together, remembered where he was.

"My name's Jareth Hicks," he told her, with calm assurance. "I'm a soldier in the US military. What's your name?"

"Cyn... Cynthia," she sobbed, still hyperventilating. "Those... Those men... They shot... They... They're getting away."

"No, they're not," he told her. "We'll catch them."

"Jareth."

He spun around, more hyper alert than jumpy (but tell that to his damn heart rate). Vince was standing beside him. The poor bastard was covered in his friend's blood.

"Ah, man," Jareth started, before realising he had nothing useful to say other than, "I'm sorry."

Vince nodded, a nasty sneer creasing his handsome features. "Those motherfucking scumbags. They won't get away with this."

"No, they won't," he said. "Not if I can help it. Acid, you stay with Cynthia, and Vince and me will— Huh? Ah, hell no."

He swung his focus around the area. Acid was nowhere in sight.

"Where'd she go?"

"She whispered for me to stay here," Cynthia said, and sniffed. "She said she was going to finish this. Her way. Then she ran off after Glick and Chief Hunger. She disappeared into the forest at the end of the track over there."

Jareth followed where Cynth was pointing.

Finish this. Her way.

Of course she was.

"We need to help her," Vince said. "Hunger and Glick might be oily sons of bitches, but they're dangerous. She's going to get herself killed going in alone."

"Maybe, maybe not." He turned to Cynthia, laying a hand gently on her shoulder. "You reckon you can make it back up there on your own? Spook's still there, looking after your old man. Help is coming. Medics."

Cynthia nodded. "I think so."

"Good, go there now," he said, straightening up and addressing Vince. "You come with me. Acid can handle herself, but it won't hurt to have backup. Besides, I want to be there when Glick gets what's coming to him. It's time to make those fuckers pay."

Chapter Thirty-Six

Fighting sharp branches and spiked fronds, Acid zig-zagged through the trees. Her eyes darted left and right, shifting focus from micro to macro as she raised the Glock, ready to fire. The air here, under the cover of the leafy canopy, was moist and smelt like snakes and chaos. A thousand bat voices chimed across her psyche, each of them delivering their unique shrieking message but all with the same theme.

Kill them.

Kill them all.

Along with the screeching bat chorus, she had the *thuck-thuck-frick* to deal with as branches whipped across her face and ears. It meant she couldn't hear any suggestion of Glick and Hunger on the path ahead, but really they only had one way to go. Down. In more ways than one.

She saw a gap in the trees, but the light was bad so she had trouble deciphering what she was looking at. Once through into the next clearing, however, she saw the instantly recognizable figures of Glick (tall, broad, bounding in long strides) and Hunger (short, skinny, bumbling and uncoordinated) before they vanished behind a large mound of rocks across the path.

"There you are, my pretties," she whispered. The ground beneath her feet was firmer here and she quickened her pace, skidding down the path as it sloped around the rocks. She was still some distance behind them. Feeling the weight of the Glock, she surmised she only had five or six rounds left to play with. Enough for what she needed to do, but it would be tight.

The pressure in her head and chest were now reaching critical levels and she had but one outlet. With her muscles burning, though spurred on by beatific vengeance, she continued her pursuit.

"There's nowhere for you to go," she screamed. "Nowhere to hide."

Her voice echoed through the trees, causing Glick to turn back. She saw now he was carrying his own revolver, which he pointed her way, firing off two stray shots that thudded into bark a few yards away but didn't trouble her. It was what she'd hoped for. It had slowed the bastard.

Close enough now to take a shot.

She grabbed the thin trunk of a nearby fir, steadying herself as she aimed at Glick. He was a wily one, she'd give him that. Weaving from left to right to evade her aim. But he was also a big man. A decent-sized target. She pulled the trigger, heard the crack, saw the bastard reel to one side and crash into a large pine tree.

She was over to him in less than three seconds, her vision focused only on his gun, which she kicked from his hand as she got close. Now, unarmed and with a gunshot wound in his right shoulder seeping out deep crimson, he was far from the arrogant figure he'd presented on the mountain top. He grimaced through the pain, considering Acid with bitter eyes as she stood over him.

"It's over," she said. "You've failed."

"I never fail," he hissed, shifting onto his left side and using his good arm to right himself.

She stepped astride him, kicking the support away and raising the Glock at his head. Keeping him in her peripheral vision she scoped out the area, eyes narrow and alert for danger. Hunger would have heard the shot, but he was nowhere to be seen. The coward. No doubt he was scurrying through the trees at the foot of the mountain, heading for his escape vehicle. But they'd get him. And right now she had Glick where she wanted him. After swiping her gaze once more around her, she leant down and hooked the Stetson off his head with the barrel of the Glock.

"Screw you," he wheezed.

"Nah. I don't think so." She pressed the gun muzzle against his forehead. "You know, it's funny you say you don't fail. Because right now you look like a total bloody failure, *Mr Glick*."

He looked up and sighed, like all the vitality had been sucked out of him. "I will not beg for my life."

"I don't want you to beg," she told him, grinding her teeth. "Horrible pricks like you, they think they can do what they like. Take from people. Destroy lives. And for what? Money? Power? Ego? You make me sick."

She screwed the end of the Glock into his skull, her entire body shivering with a heightened rush of expectation and desire. One more word from him and he was a dead man. One more word and...

Shit.

She twisted, swinging the gun around as a twig snapped behind her. It was too late. A dark figure lunged forward, knocking her off balance. Hunger. The bastard. She lashed out with the heel of her fist, manoeuvring her weapon as best she could. She heard a deep grunt, felt something whip past her vision. Then a sharp pain shot up her arm, making her release her grip on the gun.

"Dumb fucking bitch."

Another blow slammed into her ribs. It felt like an iron bar. Was probably a thick branch. It knocked all the air out of her and knocked her off her feet as well. She flayed with her fists and feet, her boot colliding with something soft and fleshy before something hard and flat smashed into the side of her head. The forest floor rushed up to meet her. She flipped herself over, ready to pounce, when she came face to muzzle with her own gun.

"What was it you were saying, bitch?" Hunger's lascivious sneer was more pronounced than ever. "*We* make *you* sick? How do you think we feel? Raymond and I were only trying to do something good for the people of Blackfell Ridge, trying to drag this backward town into the twenty-first century. But no. We get blocked at every turn. First by those damn bikers who were too stupid to sell up, and then by that pathetic do-goody mayor. Well, it's too late. We win. We always win."

He waved the gun in her face. His bony finger quivered on the trigger. Next to her, she sensed Glick clambering to his feet, heard him grumbling as he scooped up his stupid bloody cowboy hat. She didn't take her eyes from Hunger's finger.

"My friends are right behind me," she told him. "You won't get far."

"Oh, for Christ's sake, Aldous," Glick growled. "Shoot the damn woman and let's get out of here."

Acid shifted her weight onto her elbows. "Go on," she whispered. "Do it."

Hunger tightened his grip and tensed, readying to take the shot. Acid closed her eyes. The bats had chewed her nerves raw. Here she was, looking down the barrel of another gun, staring death in the face once more. She held her breath, waited.

"Jesus, Hunger," Glick yelled. "Pull the damn trigger."

A loud bang split the air in half and something warm splattered across her face. Acid froze, scanning her body for pain, for signs of life. Through the muted throb buzzing in her ears, she heard distant shouts. Then a weight on top of her, pressing her down. She opened her eyes to see Hunger's weasel face leering over her. His bloodshot eyes were wide and lifeless, and he had a large exit wound in the middle of his forehead. With a grunt of effort, she heaved him off her and rolled onto her front as another gunshot permeated the muted white noise, filling her ears. Confusion battled with chaos in her consciousness, but instinct was her driver. She lifted herself up onto all fours. Except before she could stand a dark figure barged into her.

Glick.

"Stop right there," a voice called out. "Police."

Acid jerked her head up to see the cop with the bad moustache striding towards them. He held an old police-issue revolver and as he got closer he fired again, shooting over her head at the escaping Glick.

"You okay, miss?" he asked, grabbing her arm and placing it over his shoulder, helping her up.

"I'll live," she told him, shrugging his arm away and adjusting her jacket. "Thank you. That was close."

"I'll say." He forced out a weak smile, but he was shaking. Poor bastard.

"Brooke. You did it!"

They both looked up the track to see Jareth and Vince running towards them.

"You beautiful bastard!" Jareth yelled, slowing his pace when he saw there was no threat. "I knew you had it in you. Acid, you okay?"

She offered him a rudimentary salute but, despite feeling better for seeing him, she wasn't letting herself relax. Not yet. She rolled her shoulders back. Except for a dull pain in her side, she felt good. She glanced from Jareth to the track.

"Let him go," he told her. "Everyone's safe and the Feds will be on their way. They'll get him."

Except Acid couldn't let him go. Whether it was for Spook or the mayor or her own chaotic semblance of justice, she wasn't sure, but the bats weren't letting it go. They needed blood. They needed retribution. They needed justice.

Before Jareth and Vince had caught up with them, she grabbed the pistol out of Brooke's hand.

"Hey," he cried. "You can't do that."

She was already speeding down the track in pursuit of Raymond Glick. Her legs burned and her heart and lungs felt like they might implode any second, but this was her mission. This was her calling. A deep clarity washed over her as she skidded and almost fell forward down the mountain, running as fast as she had ever run. For the first time since she'd left Caesar, she felt connected to her future like never before.

This *was* her mission.

This *was* her calling.

This *was* her future.

Spook had been right all along, and if she survived she'd

let her know. It didn't matter if she called herself Alice Vandella or any of the hundreds of aliases she'd used over the years. Whether in name or character alone, she was Acid Vanilla and always would be. And that person was now a force for good. An avenging angel. And Raymond Glick was going to rue the day he ever messed with her and her friends.

Chapter Thirty-Seven

Acid got the bastard in her sights as she scrambled over a small rock formation and dropped the short distance onto the stony terrain below. Down in front of her, the steep incline levelled and the dry, sharp grass of the mountain turned into the softer, greener variety of firmer ground. She took aim and fired. A sharp rush of annoyance pierced her heart as the Glock's action snapped back. Out of ammo.

Shitting hell.

With the needle pushed all the way into the red, and little regard for her own safety or pain barrier, she flung the pistol away and leapt down the final few rocks. At the bottom of the mountain she saw a black Jeep, and Glick making a beeline for it.

No.

Not today, boss man.

Raymond Glick might have struck an ominous figure in the boardroom, but out in the wild his colossal frame was his downfall. Every second that ticked by she decreased the distance between them. He'd almost reached the Jeep and was struggling to pull the key fob out of his pocket when she caught up with him. A sharp diving elbow in the middle of the back knocked the wind out of him and sent him stumbling into the vehicle's fender.

"Get to hell." He swung back wildly with his fist, catching her with a large meat hook around her head that knocked her sideways. He came again, slashing wildly at her, his keys protruding through his fingers like metal claws. Acid yelled out as an intense pain ripped across her throat. Glick stepped back, baring his teeth at the sight, his eyes wide with lustful rage. He held up his fist, the sharp metal keys covered in blood. Her blood. She felt at her neck, fingertips brushing against swollen, torn flesh as an icy wave of emotion flooded her system. It wasn't fear exactly, but it wasn't far off. Shit. There were too many thoughts in her head. She had too much to lose.

As Glick readied himself for another attack, she let out a shrieking battle cry that mimicked the bats in her head. At the same time, she sprang towards him, seeing in his smug face every man, woman and beast who'd ever wronged her.

Glick thought he had the upper hand.

Not a chance.

Acid shifted her weight onto her left foot, dodging under the swing of his fist and kneeing him on the top of his thigh. She'd been aiming for his groin and the resulting blow did little to stop him, but she went again, spinning around and smashing her elbow into his chest. He let out a strange guttural groan and staggered back, a look of shock whitening his face. She went again. This time he shifted to one side, and on the turn of the spin grabbed her by the back of the head. His sharp fingers spanned her entire cranium, digging in deep as he controlled her like a puppet, running her face-first into the side of the Jeep. She put her hands up to cushion the impact but it wasn't enough. Hard metal slammed into her forehead sending shockwaves deep into her skull. As pink fog clouded her vision she fell back, unsure where the sky ended and hell began. She hit the ground with a thud, unable to catch her breath before a heavy presence pressed down on her.

The thought exploded in her mind that she was having a heart attack, or that her lungs had collapsed. She couldn't breathe, couldn't expand her ribs at all. She felt hands around her throat and her entire body went into spasm as Glick shoved his fat finger into the deep wound in her neck. The pain was intense but she couldn't scream. The fog across her vision grew darker as he squeezed tighter.

"This is what happens to meddling females who try to put one over on Raymond Glick," he hissed in her ear. "This is what happens to those people who get in my way. Everyone pays in the end. You stupid fucking c—"

Through the murky realms of near-oblivion it seemed that Glick's head had turned all the way around, like an owl. A figure stood behind him, a thick branch held aloft. As Acid fought to stay conscious, they struck out with their makeshift club for a second time, smashing it around the back of Glick's skull. Acid heard a dull thump, saw the lights go out in his eyes. Before hers closed too, she saw him slump over to one side and fall from view.

"Acid. Stay with me. Please."

"Spook…?"

She struggled to open her eyes as the kid dropped the club and knelt beside her, pressing a cool hand over the wound on her neck, stroking at her forehead with the other.

"It's all right," she whispered. "Everyone's here. The medics are on their way. Hang in there."

Acid tried to sit up but she couldn't. It felt like her body wasn't her own. "I'm sorry," she whispered. It hurt to speak. "I should have listened to you."

"No, I'm sorry." Spook's voice quivered with emotion. "I'm a total dick sometimes. Running off like that, thinking I could save everyone. I'm no hero. Not like you."

Acid swallowed. "No. Not true. You did good. You saved me."

She wanted to say more, so much more, but every nerve ending, every cell, muscle and neuron in her body had other ideas. The last words that crossed her mind as oblivion took hold were, *That's my girl, Spook.*

That's my girl.

Chapter Thirty-Eight

Spook's usual pattern of panic and detachment had only lasted until Acid and the three men disappeared over the side of the mountain. Once alone, something else had kicked in, something that was rare for Spook but not disagreeable. It felt a lot like courage. But coupled with a calm focus that at first she didn't know what to do with. For the first time in forever her mind was working for her, rather than playing sick games.

After calling 911 and explaining what had transpired – insisting they inform the FBI as well as sending out every emergency service going – she'd raced to the intimidating wooden structure that hung out over the sheer cliff face. Mr Donovan was still clinging onto the plank when she got there. And still alive, as far as she could tell. But all the courage and cool-headedness she'd been experiencing dropped away as she teetered onto the plank, taking in the rocks below. One hell of a long way down.

You can do this, kid.

Acid's voice in her head had spurred her on as she'd

lowered herself onto all fours and edged along the first few inches, her arm outstretched for Mr Donovan to grab.

You've got this.

You've damn well got this…

But standing here now, with Search and Rescue helicopters hovering overhead and medics attending to Mr Donovan and Acid, Spook realised it hadn't been Acid's voice at all up there on the plank. That voice in her head was all hers. She was the one urging herself on. Spook Horowitz. When it mattered most, her thinking had been strategic and brave. She'd pushed through her fears so she could do what was needed.

And maybe Acid was right. Maybe she was more of a hero than she realised.

"Does it hurt?" she asked, as the medic finished the sutures on Acid's neck and placed a large swab over the wound.

"I've had worse," came the pithy reply. Acid back to her cynical old self. Spook wouldn't want it any other way.

"That's some swing you got there, shorty."

She looked up to see the long-haired biker walking towards them.

"The big man and I saw you swinging for the bleachers as we made our way down. You almost knocked that motherfucker's head clean off. I'm Vince, by the way. Vince Elway."

He held out his hand and she shook it. "Pleased to meet you. I'm Spook."

"Cool name."

Spook laughed but resisted the urge to look away. "Thank you."

Vince stepped past her to take in Acid. "And how are you doing, Ms Vanilla?"

"It'll take more than a swaggering piece of shit in a cowboy hat to take me down," she told him. "But we couldn't have done it without you. Thank you. And I'm so sorry about Guitar."

The biker's throat tightened. "He was a good guy," he said. "One of the best. But he was a soldier. He knew what was out there for him. Every Cheetah makes peace with the fact this lifestyle could kill him. One way or another."

Acid closed one eye as she considered the statement. "Yeah. I know all about that."

"Is that right?" Vince said, head tilting to one side as he tried to get a read on her. "Hell, I don't think I've ever met a woman quite like you, Acid Vanilla."

"She gets that a lot," Spook said, risking a hard stare from Acid, which she countered with a wink.

"I bet she does." Vince's eyes danced between the two of them, then settled again on Acid. "You know, I reckon you'd make a first-class old lady if you wanted to stick around. I mean, we'd start slow, of course. See how things go, but—"

"I'm no one's old lady," Acid said, cutting him off. "But I appreciate the offer."

Spook looked at her hands, finding a minor bruise on her wrist incredibly interesting. Renewed confidence aside, she still struggled with butt-clenching awkwardness. Thankfully, when she looked up, Deputy Brooke was striding over to them.

"I'm going to need to take statements from all of you before you leave town," he said, as he got closer. "So don't be heading off anywhere in a hurry."

"No problem," Acid said. "How's the mayor?"

Brooke looked back over his shoulder. "Better than we

first thought, although he's going to lose his eye unfortunately."

"Ah shit." Vince sucked air over his teeth. "But then Doug always looked a little wet behind the ear. I reckon an eye patch will give him a certain… gravitas. Don't ya think?"

"I think it's a little soon to be making jokes, Elway. This is a total shitshow, you know that? I've already got my superiors breathing down my neck, demanding answers. Not to mention the Feds have just rolled up. I don't know what the hell to tell them."

"We'll think of something," Vince told him, resting a hand on the nervous deputy's shoulder. "We just need to provide them a decent timeline and enough evidence so they can put Glick away. We can put the rest of the shit on Hunger and Crawford. Both of which are obligingly dead."

Brooke sniffed. "You think we'll come up with something will satisfy them?"

"Clever guys like you and me? Sure," Vince replied. "Then, soon as Donovan is out of hospital, what's say you, me and him have a sit-down? Work out how we're going to get this town back on its feet."

"Really?"

"Why not? We can work together. The Cheetahs, the mayor's office, and the…" he patted Brooke on the chest, "new chief of police. Hell, we'll have Blackfell Ridge back to its former glory in no time at all. What d'ya say?"

"Chief of police. Shit." Brooke forced a smile. "But yeah, I'm in. I guess.

"Don't look so worried," Spook piped up. "You saved my friend's life. You helped stopped Hunger and Glick from ruining the town. I reckon your superiors will be calling you in Monday morning to commend you on a job well done."

Brooke gave her a withering look. "I wish I had your confidence."

Spook glanced at Acid and they shared a secret smile. It felt good.

"I never did get your first name," Brooke said, turning to Acid. "Did I hear someone say it was—"

"My name's Alice," she told him, keeping her eyes on Spook as she said it. "Alice Vandella."

"Well, I don't know what in the name of hell happened since you rolled into town, but I guess it all worked out for the best in the end. So, thank you, I think." The down-turned eyebrows may have stated a different emotion but there was humour behind his words.

"You're very welcome."

"And about that sit-down," Brooke said, turning to Vince. "Do you have a few minutes right now? I could do with running over a few aspects of the timeline. Before the Feds get involved."

"No problem," Vince replied, narrowing his eyes at Acid. "I meant what I said, about you sticking around. Think about it."

Acid smiled as he and Brooke walked away to talk in private. Spook watched them go before turning back to her friend.

"Still fighting them off, I see?"

"I don't encourage them."

"Sure you don't."

"Anyway, Spooky," Acid said, with a flick of her chin. "You seem to be doing okay for yourself."

"How do you mean?"

Acid gestured over to where Cynthia was standing beside her father's gurney, holding his hand as they wheeled him into the back of a waiting ambulance. She looked pale and tired, but Spook could see the tears running down her face were happy tears.

"We're just friends," she said. "I'm starting to think I'm not cut out for relationships. I've got bigger things I want to do with my time."

"Yes, about that," Acid told her, before glancing at something over Spook's shoulder. "Oh. Hold that thought, will you?"

"What is it?" Spook turned, following her friend's gaze over to where the big American guy was leaning against Glick's Jeep, his arms folded as he looked their way with an unreadable expression clouding his features, like he was deep in thought.

"Give me five minutes," Acid said, getting to her feet. "There's something I need to say to someone."

Chapter Thirty-Nine

Acid felt Jareth's eyes on her as she approached, but didn't look right at him. In fact, she looked anywhere but at him. At the helicopters circling above. At the medic vehicles as they trundled down the road towards the nearest hospital (they'd wanted to take her, but she'd refused). Then over to Vince and Brooke where they wandered near the foot of the mountain, engaged in animated discussion.

"That's one hell of a hickey you've got there, Slick." He eyed her bandaged neck as she got close.

"Yeah, but he couldn't handle me," she replied. "And we call them love bites. *Actually*."

He cast the comment away with that lopsided grin of his. "Well, you did it, Acid. Unorthodox perhaps, but you saved the day. Got your friend back safe and well."

"*We* did it," she said. "Team effort."

"That is very noble of you."

"You don't know the half of it." She toed the earth with her boot. "So what now, soldier boy?"

"Geez, will you give it a rest? Boy? Seriously? You know

I'm almost forty-three?" He squinted into the afternoon sun. "But plans-wise, I'm thinking I'll head back to LA for a while, then maybe Europe, or South America. Keep on moving."

"*Keep on moving.* I see."

"Well, ya know, if you ain't moving forward, you're standing still."

Acid frowned. He laughed.

"Yeah. Not one of my better ones."

"It might need some workshopping."

A silence fell between them. It wasn't awkward, but it was heavy with subtext all the same. Neither of them seemed to want to do anything to change it as they gazed into each other's eyes.

"I don't suppose you fancy some company?" she asked, blurting it out before she could stop herself. "On your travels, I mean. It could be fun."

Jareth smiled. "Oh, it'd be fun. I don't doubt that. But no. I need to be alone for a while. Maybe forever. Don't ask me why. I'm not sure I even have the answer to that. Only that I know it's the right thing for me."

"Oh yeah, sure. I get it," she said, with a shrug of her shoulder. "I feel the same, to be honest. I don't even know why I said that, and I—"

He reached out to gently grip her chin between his thumb and index finger. And when he leaned in, she parted her lips.

"If I did want company, Acid, then I can't think of anyone I'd rather spend my time with than you."

She flicked her head away and he lowered his hand. "Sure, whatever. It was just an idea off the top of my head. It wouldn't work anyway. You're way too macho for me. And too clean-cut."

"Clean-cut? Really?"

"Absolutely. Ex-soldier? Ex-military? Eugh. Not sure what the hell I was even thinking, to be honest with you."

"Damn it, Acid. You know you're the most infuriating woman I've ever met?"

"Really? Why don't you tell me something I haven't heard a thousand times before?"

"All right. You are fucking infuriating, but you're also the most beautiful, engaging, perplexing and astonishing woman I've ever known."

"Jesus." She dug her boot into the ground some more. "Calm it down, will you?"

"You're brave, strong, clever as hell, with a biting wit. Not to mention those amazing eyes."

She looked away. Her cheeks were burning. They never did that. "I assumed you hadn't noticed my eyes," she mumbled.

"Of course I have. But I also figured every dude who ever tries talking to you mentions them, so I chose not to. I don't want to be just another sleazy guy to you."

"And what do you want to be?"

He stuck out his bottom lip, play-acting like he was thinking hard. "The one that got away? The most stupid bastard in the entire world?"

She jutted out her chin. "Yes, I'd say both of those are accurate."

He bowed his head and clicked his boots together, as if standing to attention. "I'll see you around, Alice."

She looked away, widening her eyes lest a tear escape. But it was too late. She wiped it with the heel of her thumb and sniffed back a lifetime of regret.

"So long, Jareth Hicks."

He went to kiss her but she moved away, pressing her hand onto his chest.

"Don't."

He got the message. Instead, he patted her gently on the shoulder, before moving past her and heading for the road into town. There was nothing more to be said. Nothing more to be done. She watched him for a few seconds, then turned away.

"How you doing?" Spook was standing where Jareth had been a moment earlier. She'd probably been watching the whole exchange.

Acid sniffed again. "I'm fine. Thanks to you."

"Don't mention it."

"Yes, well, I won't ever again." She rubbed at her eyes. *Get it to-bloody-gether.* "What did the Feds say?"

"Not much. I told them what had happened. Left you out of it, of course. *Alice.*"

The urge welled up in her to say something, but she let it go. "Well, we should think about getting back to the cabin and then on to the UK, don't you think?"

"Sounds like a good plan," Spook said. "But can we wait a day or so? Just so I can properly say goodbye to Cynthia once her dad is stable."

Acid glanced back down the track after Jareth, but he was nowhere in sight. "Yes, of course."

"And then…" Spook began, and then stopped.

"What?"

"Well, you seem – I don't know – a little down for one reason or another. I was thinking it might be good to have something else to focus on. And I was wondering if, when we get back to London, you might want to reconsider my idea."

"The agency?"

"Yep. The agency. Helping people who the authorities can't, or won't. People like Cynthia, people like me when you found me. I've no idea how it will work or what it'll look like, but that isn't important right now, is it? We'll learn on the job."

Acid smiled to herself. Glanced at her friend. "You know what, Spook? That sounds great."

And for the first time since Spook had floated the idea two years ago, she meant it. The motivation was there. The drive to help others who couldn't help themselves. It might even go some way to helping her atone for all the horrible shit she'd done in her life. Plus it would keep her on her toes, keep life interesting. Even if it did mean her days would never be easy or comfortable.

Because she now understood. This was the bed she'd made for herself and there was no going back. Whether she called herself Alice Vandella or Acid Vanilla, it didn't matter.

She was who she was. And who she would continue to be.

As the bats screeched their chaotic agreement, she placed an arm around Spook's shoulders and pulled her close.

Well, shit.

Life was never meant to be an easy ride.

Where was the fun in that?

Next in the Acid Vanilla series

vinci-books.com/iamakiller

She made peace with her bloodstained past. Now someone wants to take her future.

Get your FREE ebook

We'll send you a free Acid Vanilla prequel.

Discover how Acid Vanilla transformed from a London teenager into the world's deadliest female assassin.

vinci-books.com/making-a-killer

About the Author

Over the last twenty years Matthew Hattersley has toured Europe in rock n roll bands, trained as a professional actor and founded a theatre and media company. He's also had a lot of dead end jobs…

Now he writes high-octane pulp action thrillers and crime fiction.

He lives with his wife and daughter in Derbyshire, UK and doesn't feel that comfortable writing about himself in the third person.